CW00665010

TERMINAL MEMORY

A Sam Raven Thriller

Brian Drake

WOLFPACK
PUBLISHING
— EST 2013 —

WOLFPACK
PUBLISHING
— EST 2013 —

Terminal Memory
Paperback Edition
Copyright © 2021 Brian Drake

Wolfpack Publishing
5130 S. Fort Apache Road 215-380
Las Vegas, NV 89148

Paperback ISBN 978-1-64734-528-0
Ebook ISBN 978-1-64734-525-9

TERMINAL MEMORY

PROLOGUE

Two minutes.

No more.

Two minutes to rescue Wendy Tannen from her kidnappers. Hit fast, get out, get Wendy home. Sam Raven faced not getting the young woman out alive if he took longer. He wasn't going to tell her parents he'd failed. He needed to avoid a protracted firefight.

The two-story cabin sat nestled in a nook surrounded by trees, foothills, and dry brush. It appeared tranquil enough; inside, a different story. Wendy Tannen was held against her will, at the mercy of cutthroats willing to kill. They wanted money in exchange for her life.

A rail of logs protected the front porch. Larger posts held up the roof's extended overhang, a chimney sticking up from the second level. Dirt driveway.

Raven took in the details from 50 yards away. He wore combat black, combat cosmetics smeared across his face, black cap over his head.

Wendy Tannen was 23-years-old, daughter of Andrew Tannen, millionaire media mogul. The cabin served as the Tannen's vacation home; now, it was a prison. Wendy's prison.

Andrew Tannen had told Raven the kidnappers grabbed his daughter off a street in New York City. The ransom demand followed after 24 hours. No police. No FBI. Only Tannen, alone, with the money. "Bring it to the cabin or she dies." The only indication of Wendy's well-being was over the phone. She shouted in the background, screaming as the kidnappers pulled her away.

"Delivering ransom isn't usually what I do," Raven explained. He sat with Mr. and Mrs. Tannen in their opulent New York City penthouse.

"I'm not paying a cent," the older man said, trying to remain dignified despite the worry etched on his face. His wife, sitting near him on the living room couch, appeared worse. She didn't talk during the meeting.

"Breaking her out is dangerous," Raven said. "I'm not going to sugar coat this. The only advantage is them using your property."

"I can tell you every detail of the cabin. Plenty of pictures beginning from the first day of construction."

"How many am I facing?"

"No idea. I've only spoken with one person."

"Who hates you enough to take your daughter, Mr. Tannen?"

"It doesn't have anything to do with hate. I run radio and television stations; the only enemies I have are my poker buddies, and only then if I take their money."

"You're simply the target they picked."

"If not me, somebody else, yeah."

"They did their homework if they knew about the cabin."

Tannen nodded. His wife remained mute and on the verge of tears.

"How long ago was she taken?"

"Two days."

Raven nodded. "All right. You want her out and—"

"Whatever happens to the people who took her, we don't need to know about."

"It will become a police matter when I'm done."

Tannen's face blanched. "What do you suggest?"

"You'll have a lot of explaining to do. And you probably won't want the cabin any longer."

"I'll burn it to the ground," Tannen said.

"Fair enough. Have your lawyer on stand-by. You'll need him."

"Money's no object."

"I'm not worried about money right now," Raven said. "If I bring Wendy back, pay me what you think I'm worth. If I fail, you don't owe me anything."

Tannen's wife's face paled. She clutched at her husband. He said, "What? Fail?"

"If I fail, Mr. Tannen, I won't be around to argue over the results."

Two minutes.

From his observation, Raven counted only three kidnappers in the cabin. One was a smoker who ventured onto the front porch every half hour. Two others joined him for a few minutes at a time before going back inside. Nobody patrolled the perimeter of the cabin. They felt secure enough not to check for surveillance.

Having studied the layout of the cabin, he knew the front room had the living area, television, kitchen and dining table. Bedrooms lined a short hallway. Out back, a hot tub. Wendy would be in one of the bedrooms, but he'd have to check each one.

He had a lot to do in two minutes.

Lights glowed within but they'd left the porch light off. Only the flaring tip of the smoker's cigarette marked his position.

Raven was prepared to meet the kidnappers with force.

A Nighthawk Custom Talon .45 autoloader rode on a shoulder harness under his left arm. Spare 10-round magazines secured in a pouch under his right. Across his back, a Colt M-4 Commando, 30-round magazine attached. Infrared optic in place of iron sights. The M-4 Commando was a shorter version of the US M-4 carbine, with an eleven-and-a-half-inch barrel. A suppressor attached to the barrel guaranteed quiet shots.

Raven removed the M-4 Commando from his back and started forward at a low crawl, head down. Brush and rocks covered his approach. The rough ground grated against his body, smaller rocks digging through his clothes. He ignored the discomfort. He angled his body toward the edge of the dirt road leading to the clear patch in front of the house. Two compact SUVs sat in the circle.

Raven reached the edge of the dirt road and stopped. The brush extended over his head. Gaps in the brush allowed a look at the porch, but vehicles partially blocked the view.

The smoker finished his cigarette and turned for the door.

Raven sighted on his back.

He pulled the trigger twice, the *phuts* from the M-4 Commando echoing. The smoker's clipped yell signaled both bullets hit home. His body pitched forward through the doorway.

Shouting inside.

Raven bounded for one of the SUVs, stopping by the rear spare tire. He checked behind him, pivoted back to the porch. Somebody grabbed the smoker's body and began to drag him into the house. Raven moved quick, bounding up the porch steps, firing rapidly. The kidnapper trying to get his comrade inside only had time to gasp in fright. The M-4 Commando's 5.56mm slugs ripped through his chest.

Raven stepped over the bodies, moving left across the front room. He swung his muzzle toward the couches and kitchen.

No targets. The TV glared.

"Wendy!" he shouted.

A woman screamed from somewhere along the hall.

Raven pressed against a wall. The hallway appeared clear. There was still one kidnapper to take care of. Where had he gone?

Raven tried the first bedroom, kicking the door open, advancing with the M-4 Commando in the lead. Empty. Second bedroom, paydirt. He found Wendy with her hands tied behind her back, ankles taped together. They'd let her keep her tennis shoes; dirt stained her jeans and frilly pink top. She wore her dark hair in a short bob. Wendy Tannen's big eyes widened in fright as Raven knelt beside her, positioned so he faced the door. With a knife he cut the tie behind her back, then slashed the tape at her wrists.

"Your father sent me," he said.

Tears in her eyes, she tried to talk, he shushed her. "Where's the third?"

"He ruh...ruh...*ran*. Down the hall. I think!"

Time running out.

"Can you shoot a gun?"

"What? No!"

"Okay, I need you to stay put."

"You're going to leave me?"

"I have to find the other guy otherwise this is a lousy rescue."

She let out a cry of protest as he rose and paused in the doorway to peek around the edge of the doorway. The hall was in partial darkness. He spotted a light switch on the wall.

"Are they armed?" he said.

"Yeah they have guns."

"Pistols? Rifles?"

"Handguns."

"Stay," he said. He looked back at her. She was trying to crawl under the bed.

Raven pressed the M-4 Commando to his shoulder and side-stepped through the doorway. He triggered two random shots down the hall and dropped to one knee, bracing his arms against the wall. No return fire.

The hallway ended at a 90-degree corner leading to the master bedroom. A sliding glass door in the bedroom led to the rear deck and hot tub.

If Raven had been running, he'd go out the back and into the forest. Plenty of cover. If the kidnappers had established an escape route, he'd be well on his way.

Not much longer...

But Raven couldn't leave a loose end. He had to make sure the last kidnapper wasn't waiting in ambush. If he'd run, Raven hoped he was still running. If he wasn't, Wendy's life would be at greater risk than she'd already faced.

He advanced along the hall, senses alert, his right index finger taking up the trigger slack. All he'd have to do is twitch and the carbine would fire.

He reached the corner and began a side-step left, the doorway to the bedroom wide open, and a cold draft flowing.

Raven entered the master bedroom, swinging his weapon left, right, checking the bathroom. Nobody hiding. The patio door was wide open, hence the draft, and he lowered the carbine. The third man had taken off.

But had he run far?

Raven's mental alarm clock chimed. *No more time.* He raced back to Wendy, who was half under the bed, grabbing an arm with his free hand and helping her to her feet. She had wiped her eyes, but still looked a mess.

"Stay behind me. Keep one hand on my back. We're going out. Don't look at the floor."

He turned. She put a hand on his right shoulder. He led her out of the bedroom, through the living room, where she screamed at the sight of the dead bodies on the floor.

"Told you not to look."

"They're blocking the door!"

"Step over them, like this."

Raven showed her, and she followed. When they touched the wooden porch, he thrust her forward. "Stay in the tree cover!"

Her long legs carried her away. Raven hustled to keep up while reversing every few steps to check their backside.

Two shots cracked from the rear of the house, Raven spotting the muzzle flash. The third man was shooting from the back corner. Raven fired twice in return, yelling for Wendy to run faster. He pivoted and ran after her, catching up. She stumbled on the rough ground but didn't fall. She tried to look back, but Raven told her not to. "Black Chevy, end of the driveway," he said.

Raven didn't tell her the third man was in pursuit. He could hear the man's pounding footsteps behind him.

They reached the road at the end of the driveway, and Raven's Tahoe sat where he said it would be. He clicked the remote to open the door and secured Wendy inside. "Stay low."

Raven didn't go to the driver's side. He dropped into brush at the side of the road.

The third man broke out of the shadows, aiming his pistol as he ran. Amateur. Raven fired twice and stood. There was no reason for a third shot. The third kidnapper tumbled as he hit the ground, spinning several times, coming to a stop on his back. Raven walked over to him. The kidnapper's dead eye stared at the night sky. Raven's shots had punched neat holes in his upper chest.

He was a young man, Caucasian, shaggy dark hair. Raven wondered who he and his partners thought they were kidding.

They didn't look old enough to pull a proper bank robbery, let alone a kidnapping.

He'd leave identification to the cops. His job was done.

Raven joined Wendy in the Tahoe and started the car. She finally sat up, locking her seat belt in place. She said, "Who are you?"

"My name is Sam."

"I'm Wendy."

He smiled at her. "I know." He handed her a cell phone he'd placed in a cup holder. "Call home."

She dialed, yelling to whoever answered she was okay, and Raven tuned out the chatter. Mission accomplished. Wendy Tannen was going home to her family. Many victims like Wendy didn't have the option. Raven renewed his vow to make sure he helped as many victims survive as possible. If they didn't, he'd avenge them.

The mountain road went straight for a while, then began a series of turns as they neared the city.

Wendy handed Raven the phone. "My father."

Raven took the phone. "Yes, Mr. Tannen."

"I can't thank you enough."

"I'll bring her back as soon as I can."

"The plane is ready," Tannen said.

"It better be," Raven said, "considering I left your pilots at the airport."

"Of course. You're the expert at this. Thank you, Mr. Raven."

"Sure." He hung up and put the phone back in the cup holder.

"What now?" Wendy said.

"Your father has a plane waiting for us, and you go home to New York City."

"Are you, um—"

"What?"

"Going to wear *that*?" She pointed at his clothes.

He laughed. "We'll stop long enough for me to wipe this crap off my face and pack my weapons so they won't be found. We'll be fine."

She sat without speaking the rest of the ride.

Raven remained quiet as well, but all was not calm in his soul. He lived a dichotomy. He could save others, but he hadn't been able to save those closest to him. His crusade against predators in all forms was his way at atonement. The massive debt was too large to ever repay.

He'd be fighting till the end.

But tonight, there was victory. He could rest for a while.

CHAPTER ONE

"You don't know how much I appreciate you coming."

"How could I refuse?" Sam Raven said.

Raven faced Victor Matson across the table in a restaurant in downtown Madrid. Matson had called with an SOS a day earlier and looked rough. Dark circles under his eyes, puffy cheeks, as if he hadn't been sleeping, and drinking a lot of alcohol. Stress made even the strongest man reach for the bottle from time to time. Victor Matson was a man who had a lot on his mind, and it was causing terrific stress.

"Tell me what's bothering you," Raven said.

"You sound like a shrink."

"That's not a bad thing."

"I hope you believe me," Matson said.

"We won't know until you tell me." Raven smiled, trying to reassure his old friend, but Matson's expression did not change.

Victor Matson sipped his coffee. Like Raven, a former CIA officer. Unlike Raven, he'd found a notch in civilian life, moving to Madrid to marry a woman who divorced him a few years later. He'd opened an architecture firm and did well designing homes and office buildings.

Raven squeezed juice from a lemon wedge into his green

tea as Matson assembled his thoughts. He tapped his fingertips together, staring past Raven's left arm at the carpet.

"I think somebody's trying to kill me."

Raven looked up sharply. "I wasn't expecting to hear those words, Vic."

Matson stopped fidgeting and leaned forward. "Why? Because I'm a civilian now? Got the architecture business?"

"Exactly. Of the two of us, I'm the only one—"

"You may be next. You and Mara."

Raven sipped his tea, watching Matson over the rim of the mug. "You better fill me in."

"A week ago, I caught three men following me."

"As a group? Did they trade off?"

"No, they worked a triangular pattern like the shop taught us. The only reason I spotted them was because—"

"We used to do the same thing."

"Right."

Raven had led a team of five agents, including Vic and Mara Cole, as part of the CIA's counterterrorism efforts. Classified missions were their bread-and-butter.

They'd often tagged along with Marine Recon units performing similar tasks in the "sand box" of Iraq and Afghanistan. The Marines looked the other way when they broke off to complete their true missions. Raven and his crew had been referred to as ghost soldiers. They came and went, leaving destruction in their wake. As long as it was the enemy in ruins, nobody complained.

"Did these three men," Raven said, "attempt to murder you?"

"I think they wanted to try the other day."

"What happened?"

"I saw a car following me. At first it didn't seem like much, because we were going in the same direction. But then the car moved ahead of me, and we came to an intersection. The car would have been right in front of me while we waited for the light, but I got suspicious and made a right turn instead. The driver of the other car cut somebody off trying to stay with me."

"And then?"

"I turned into another neighborhood, backtracked to the road again, and went on my way. I'd lost them."

"You think they were going to track you, from behind or in front, and wait for an ambush point?"

"Or try to force me off the road. You know, make it look like an accident. It sure seemed like they wanted to."

"Vic, that could have been a coincidence."

"The shop tried to say the same thing."

"You called—"

"I did! I wanted to see if they'd heard anything about ex-officers being, you know, targeted. Dammit, Sam, none of the people we knew are there anymore. It's all these young bucks who have no idea what we did."

"Or of our existence," Raven said. "I hear you." He sipped some more tea but noticed Victor hadn't touched his coffee. "Clark Wilson is still there," he added.

"I couldn't reach him. Can you believe I forgot my security code? No way they'd let me through without using the code, and I'm in no position to watch him leave the building." Matson paused, then: "I started asking around some other, unofficial channels." He dug out his cell phone, continuing. "Those inquiries didn't go anywhere. But then I found these." He made two selections on the screen and passed the phone across the table.

Raven read the screen shot of a news article. Neighbors had found a man dead in his apartment in Seattle, Washington. Three weeks earlier. Police said somebody killed him in his home during a robbery. Police also suspected he surprised the burglars by being home instead of out. In their escape, they shot the man twice.

Raven read midway down the page until he saw the name of the victim.

"Oh, no."

"Right?" Matson said.

Carlos Vega, 38, who ran a chain of craft supply stores.

Explosives expert. Loved reading joke books and sharing the crudest with his teammates. Vega had been on the same squad as Raven and Matson.

Raven handed back the phone. "I didn't know. This is awful news."

Matson didn't take the offered cell. "He's not the only one. They got Billy too. Scroll left."

Raven let out a curse and did as Matson said. Another screen shot, another man dead.

Billy Anzell, 37, US Army veteran. Built detailed model planes in his spare time. Former diplomatic assistant at the State Department. The victim of a carjacking on the streets of Detroit, Michigan.

Billy would have liked knowing his cover story had remained in place even at his death. Raven wanted to laugh, but the heaviness in his chest prevented him from doing so.

Raven hurt deep down. His friends had made it out, but peace eluded them. They weren't supposed to die by violence after leaving the shadow world for peaceful civilian life.

Raven had enjoyed his brief slice of a normal life, before fate took it away. The locket he wore around his neck, hidden under his shirt, was the only reminder he carried of his old life. It motivated his "second life", currently in progress. The life where he killed the kind of people who murdered his friends.

Raven handed back the phone.

"What's happening, Sam?"

"Somebody's killing off our crew. You were right to get away from that car, Vic."

"Well you-know-who are no help. I know you're still, you know—"

"Yes, I keep busy using my old skill set."

"Sam, we are being targeted, and it's no joke. We need to find out why."

Raven swallowed more tea and tried to think. He had to separate the emotion of learning two friends had died from strategic thoughts. He thought back on his activity in recent weeks. He hadn't noticed anybody following him. No attempts made on his life outside the course of a job. No stealthy assassin had attempted to murder him on his houseboat.

"First thing we do," Raven said, "is get out of Madrid. Do you know how to reach Mara?"

"Not at all. After Afghanistan, she dropped off the face of the planet."

"Who could blame her."

"She might be in London. I vaguely remember—"

"I have no idea, Vic."

"I thought you two—"

"It ended after Afghanistan. I haven't seen her since. I mean, we tried, but what happened in that cave really messed her up. I don't think she'll ever fully recover."

"I still have nightmares."

"Me too," Raven said.

"Even you?"

"Afghanistan nightmares compete with other nightmares in sort of a satanic rotation, yes. Even 'Old Solid' has a touch of PTSD from the ordeal."

Matson shook his head. "With everything they trained us for—"

"I know. Hey. Were you followed here?"

Matson shook his head. "I drove in circles, grabbed a backup car I'd parked elsewhere. My backside was clear all the way."

"Let's take my car. Can somebody from the company collect yours?"

"Yeah, it's fine. I need to get something from inside."

Raven rose from the table. He put enough money down to cover the cost of the coffee and tea and a decent tip for the waitress.

They exited the restaurant. It was hot outside, but the sky was clear. On the way out, Sam Raven unzipped his jacket halfway. He wanted quick access to the .45-caliber autoloader holstered under his left arm. The Nighthawk Custom Talon was his constant companion.

He noted Victor Matson grabbed a plastic shopping bag from the passenger seat of his car.

The bag contained something heavy.

From the trunk Matson collected a very full backpack and followed Raven to his car.

CHAPTER TWO

Matson let Raven see inside the bag once they were on the road.

"Looks impressive," Raven said.

"Korth three-fifty-seven Magnum. It's called the Mongoose."

The gleaming stainless-steel revolver looked like it could slay a dragon or two.

"You still hate semi-automatics?"

"Revolvers don't jam." Matson put the bag on the floor between his feet.

"That's the rumor, anyway," Raven said. "Are you fit for travel?"

"Everything's in my pack. Some extra clothes, passport, cash."

"Bug out bag like the old days?"

"What do they say about old habits?"

"Too true."

Raven glanced in the rearview mirror. Plenty of traffic surrounded them, but a particular car had his attention. He changed lanes to make the next left.

"Where are you going?" Matson said.

"We may have picked up a tail after all, Vic."

"What?" Matson twisted around in his seat to look out the back window. He said, "I swear, Sam, I checked and doubled checked!"

"I know you did."

Matson learned forward. He pulled his Korth Mongoose revolver out of the plastic shopping bag. "Then how did they—"

"You've been out of the game a few years. They had you tag-teamed and you only shook one set."

"Insanity." Matson hid the revolver under the flap of his jacket but kept his hand on the checkered wooden grips.

Raven changed lanes again and made a right turn. The car he watched for, a blue sedan, made the turn as well. There were enough cars on the road Raven shouldn't have picked him out so fast. The driver was lousy at using traffic for cover.

Matson shifted in the seat, breathing hard, wiping nervous sweat from his face.

"Steady," Raven said.

"It's been a long time since I was in a gun fight, Sam."

"Who says we're going to have a gun fight?"

Raven lived by two rules. The first was not getting involved in a shooting while in public. Too many innocents might get hurt, and he detested collateral damage. The goal of his crusade was to protect and avenge victims, not create more. He'd avoid a fight if he could or lead the enemy to a location where a shootout wouldn't pose a risk to civilians.

But sometimes, despite his best efforts, a public fight was inevitable. In those cases, he had to make sure his aim was sure, and the fight didn't last long.

"How many teams do you think they have on us?" Matson said.

"So far only the blue car seems to be sticking with us."

Raven made another turn, stopping for a light. He wasn't

able to clear the yellow before it turned red, so he stopped.

"With all these turns," Matson said, "they have to know we're onto them."

Raven's eyes didn't leave the rearview. The blue sedan was one lane over and three cars back. "I don't think they're bothered if we are."

He couldn't see the driver or passenger or any other shooters in the back seat was impossible. He knew they faced at least two. But Raven wasn't counting on such a gift.

He looked around. Storefronts and restaurants lined the street. Plenty of pedestrians went about their business. It was a lousy place for a fight. The enemy had to realize the same thing. They wouldn't want collateral damage any more than he did. Nobody wanted the cops showing up. The enemy had worked hard to make Carlos and Billy's deaths look like random acts of violence. They weren't going to get sloppy unless Raven forced their hand.

"We can still buy some time," Raven said.

"Right," Matson said.

"We'll be okay."

The light changed and traffic rolled forward.

"Any suggestions?" Raven said.

"There's a fork coming up. Stay left. The roadway splits in half and goes around a building. On the other side is a plaza. It's closed for renovations right now."

Raven nodded. "Might be a good spot to make a stand."

He knew the Plaza del Parterre well. A tranquil spot. Full of bright flowers and creatively sculpted trees. Concrete pathways cut cross-sections through squares of grass. A museum housed historical artifacts of Madrid's storied past. In the old days, Raven had taken great pleasure in such places.

Raven took the fork and followed the road as it made a gentle curve to the left, then straightened. The plaza lay two blocks ahead.

Matson turned in his seat again, straining against his seatbelt. "They're still with us. The passenger is talking into a walkie-talkie."

"Great," Raven said, "calling the second team."

So much for even odds.

Matson sat forward and cursed.

"Steady," Raven said again.

Raven's nerves were calm. This was another day for him. He'd tried to exit a life of violence, but fate had called him back. He knew he could handle the situation. Had he been alone, he wouldn't have worried.

But he did worry about Victor Matson. Victor had been an excellent operative once, but civilian life had softened him. Would he be able to perform when the bullets started flying? Would his panic cause a mistake?

Raven started to sweat. He was too focused on doubt. He needed to focus on the problem and solve the problem. Part of his solution was Victor Matson, faithful ally. He knew Vic would rise to the occasion. He needed a bit of motivation, so Raven said, "Remember, they killed two of our friends. This is a chance to settle the score a little."

Matson said, "Yeah," and took what Raven hoped was a calming deep breath.

"Front sight, squeeze," Raven advised.

"I remember."

"You better. It's both our necks if you flinch."

Raven observed the plaza as they approached. Signs of heavy equipment, partially planted trees, but no workers. Lunch hour. Raven turned right, cutting across the opposing lane. He drove a little too fast into the empty parking lot. The rental jolted as the wheels hit the lip of the driveway.

"Out," Raven said, "and run like hell."

Raven and Matson exited the car in a hurry. A coupe screeched into the driveway, two men inside. The passenger spoke into a walkie-talkie. Raven and Matson raced along a straight path to the center of the plaza.

The bright flower beds and sculpted trees didn't register in Raven's mind as he focused on the fountain. A fence surrounded it, but there were hedgerows on the opposite side. Raven would have preferred a stone wall. They stopped bullets better. What he needed most was an area free of civilians, and at least he had that.

They raced around the deactivated fountain and leaped over a hedge to drop onto soft grass. Raven, on his belly, moved to the edge, and peeked around.

He had a view of the parking lot. The back-up team in a red coupe joined the blue sedan. Two men climbed out of each vehicle. The driver of the blue sedan gave orders. The two-man teams split to approach from separate directions. They employed three-second rushes, moving from tree to tree with a short pause in between.

"Incoming," Raven said.

"I'm ready!"

Raven reached under his left arm for the Nighthawk Custom Talon .45 autoloader. Eight rounds in the magazine, one in the chamber, and two spare 10-round mags under his left arm. He hoped he had enough ammo. The approaching enemy toted submachine guns. Perhaps thirty rounds each, with spares, and full-auto capability. Raven didn't often feel outgunned, but he did now.

Raven looked behind him. The plaza garden continued, but on the far side sat a large building, the museum. A good fallback position.

"We shoot and we move," Raven said.

"Okay!"

The gunners from the red coupe neared. Raven gripped the .45 in both hands, resting his arms on the ground. When the two gunners made their next advance, he fired. His round caught one of them in the open, slamming into the man's chest, stopping his forward movement as if he'd hit a wall. The gunner dropped.

His partner stopped, taking a knee and scrunching his shoulders to create a small target. He shouldered his SMG and returned fire, the salvo of nine-millimeter hornets flashing from the muzzle. The slugs chewed up the ground around Raven, clipping the hedge. Raven fired again as the man rose but missed. The shooter reached a tree but dropped and rolled. Raven fired twice more. One of the shots scored, stopping the man's rolling movement and leaving his body face down in the grass.

More submachine gun fire racked the hedge, Matson screaming. He returned fire from over the top of the hedge, his .357 booming once, twice.

"Fall back!" Raven shouted. Matson ran, staying low. Raven fired twice to cover the retreat and let a third round go as he started running backwards. He turned to run forward, slapping a 10-round mag into the Talon. He dashed around a bench, then dropped low underneath, the concrete warmed by the sun. He felt the heat through his clothes, and the coarse roughness of the pavement on his left hand. He scanned for the last two shooters.

"Got 'em!" Matson shouted. The .357 boomed again. Raven shifted right, the shooters visible on the other side of the fountain. Approximately 25-yards away.

Another revolver blast. Neither of the shooters dropped. Matson yelled as he took off. Raven caught the sprint in his peripheral vision. One of the shooters aimed at Matson, and Raven fired, scoring a head shot. The falling gunner tripped his companion as the last shooter ran in pursuit of Matson.

Raven left the bench, tracking the gunner. He fired once, missed. Raven charged ahead. Matson found a cluster of sculpted trees to hide behind.

The shooter took aim as he broke for his own cover, but he didn't look behind him. Raven's double-tap opened two holes in his back, the shooter pitching forward. He landed half on grass, half on concrete. Raven ran to Matson.

"Too close," Raven said.

Matson stood, breathing hard, his sweat-stained shirt clinging to his chest, managed to nod.

"Come on."

The pair ran back toward the parking lot. They passed the fountain a second time, and Raven stopped short. He yelled for Matson to get down.

The second gunman, the one he thought was dead, was back on his feet, holding his SMG with one hand.

Raven's shots had torn up his left side, and blood covered the front of his clothes, but he was on his feet with a weapon.

The gunner fired.

Matson, who didn't drop at Raven's command, stopped mid-stride as the salvo cut through his chest. The bullets punched out his back, spraying Raven with blood and pieces of flesh. Raven didn't flinch. The Talon, steady in his two-hand grip, roared twice more. Part of the gunner's face vanished as the .45 ACP hollow-points split it in half.

The gunner and Matson hit the ground at the same time.

Raven ran to his friend, whose eyes remained open, but life had left them.

Raven dropped his head and let out a curse. He looked around for further threats, wanting to lash out one final time, but there were no targets.

He let out a breath, looked down at Matson one last time.

Vic Matson the civilian, who'd handled the fight like the former pro he was.

"I'm sorry, Vic," Raven said. He thumbed Matson's eyes closed and stood up.

He had no time to mourn. He had to get out of there before police showed up.

Raven ran to the dead gunner, stopping long enough to grab his walkie-talkie. It was still on, and Raven held onto it and his .45 as he ran toward the parking lot. He stopped long enough to examine the first man he'd shot, who was quite dead, and examined his face.

Middle Eastern, no doubt. Dark hair, narrow face, bony jaw, dark eyes, currently locked in a death stare.

Jihadists?

Why?

The rental's engine rumbled to life as he pressed the starter. He pulled into traffic too fast, cutting off another car, ignoring the indignant horn blast.

Three of his friends were dead.

Killed by a hit team of Middle Eastern origin intent on wiping them out.

Only he and Mara Cole remained.

And Raven had no idea where Mara was, no way to reach her to shout a warning.

She might be in London.

Raven hoped Matson was right. It was the only lead he had, but how do you find one person in a city of millions? Especially one who wouldn't want to be found?

The walkie-talkie crackled to life in Raven's lap.

"Red and Blue Team, report."

A woman's voice. Deep, commanding.

How cute, Raven thought. Their team colors matched their respective cars.

He picked up the radio.

"Hello?"

"Who is this?"

"This is Sam Raven, love. Check your list, I might be on it."

"I know who you are."

"Good. We can forget the pleasantries. Your men are dead. I'm alive."

"Not for long, Mr. Raven."

"You've killed several of my friends. I promise, when I find you, I'm going to rip off your head and shit down your neck."

The woman's laugh sounded rich even through the small radio speaker. "I can't wait," she said.

Raven spat out a curse and tossed the walkie-talkie out the window. He threw the radio with enough force it broke into pieces on impact with the street.

Rage burned throughout his body, Raven gripping the wheel tight as he drove, weaving in and out of lanes. *Steady.* He slowed down, controlled his breathing. Time to focus on the goal he'd set for him and Matson when they'd left the restaurant.

Get out of Madrid.

That was the easy part. Raven had chartered a flight into the city, and the pilot was standing by for a return flight to Sweden. Raven had other plans now. He was going to London. He had to find Mara before the enemy did.

Somehow.

CHAPTER THREE

Raven sat in the rear forward-facing passenger cabin of the Beechcraft C90 King Air. The other three seats were empty. The sense of loneliness felt heavy. Raven had expected company on the flight. He'd expected Vic Matson to be with him.

Insulation in the body of the turbo-prop plane kept the drone of the engines to a minimum. The wood paneling in the passenger section was a nice touch. If Raven wanted, a table folded out from the fuselage on his left. Instead he sat with his legs crossed and slouched in the soft leather seat.

The seating area in the back had been converted into a galley. A small refrigerator containing drinks and cold pre-packaged sandwiches. A microwave sat on top of a small cabinet to heat water for coffee and tea. But Raven didn't partake in any refreshments. Other matters occupied his mind.

Raven spent the flight sending emails on his cell phone. He repeated the same message to informants and other contacts in Europe. He told them he was going to London. He asked them to talk about him being there, to make it casual, but spread the word.

He wanted the as-yet unknown enemy to know exactly

where he was. He wanted them to come to him. After his exchange with the woman, whoever she was, they'd know he expected an attack. Raven wanted a showdown.

Who wanted them dead?

One way or another, he'd solve the mystery and avenge his friends.

And hopefully reach Mara in time to keep her alive. With everything she'd been through on their final mission, she deserved whatever slice of peace she'd carved out.

Finished with his task, Raven put away his phone. He looked out the very wide and circular Plexiglass window on his left. The land below was indistinguishable at their altitude; he stared out at the blue sky instead.

He wanted to make himself easy to find but wondered how the enemy would approach. He knew they were coming; they knew he was expecting them. An ambush of some sort seemed likely, but Raven bet they'd be a little more creative. Part of the fun in getting even would be watching exactly how creative they tried to be.

He wanted the woman on the other end of the walkie-talkie to participate. He'd made a promise to her he intended to keep.

Raven loved London. It was one of those cities, even in the worst of winter, where he could melt into the huge crowds and disappear.

His favorite pub was Cahoots, a throwback to the '40s in its décor and attitude. He chose the Underground Cahoots where sitting areas resembled old train cars. Tables on either side with a narrow walkway between. The polished wood surrounding him, with assorted vintage decorations on display. It was a nice change to the gaudiness of contemporary night clubs where he no longer fit. He was a dinosaur compared to the rest of the clientele. Cahoots catered to a different sort. Even the younger people behaved in a more reserved fashion.

He sat at a corner table, a pint of the house pale ale and a roast beef sandwich piled with meat in front of him. The sandwich had plenty of mustard, the requisite lettuce, tomato, and sliced pickles. The toasted wheat bun had more flavor than the rest of the sandwich combined.

He'd been visiting Cahoots every night for the last three days. He'd booked a room at the Strand Palace, another older building in the city. For some reason, Raven found comfort in old stuff. He was quite aware he lived on borrowed time. Old things suggested one might live beyond a natural expiration date and still have value. It was a fantasy, but the thought gave him confidence he existed for more than what lurked on life's bare surface.

He wasn't alone in the train car. Couples and groups of four, the limit for each table, sat around him. They enjoyed their conversations combined with quick glimpses at smart phones. They took pictures of each other, which Raven appreciated. Life should be lived, and enjoyed, and documented for rough days where a reminder of good times soothed frustration. There was always a pub to help forget the day's difficulties and attack the following day with renewed vigor.

He hadn't noticed any surveillance since his arrival. If the enemy knew he was here, they were either biding their time, or hadn't reached the city yet. Raven didn't mind. He was quite patient and spent the down time on constant watch. They'd come. When they did, he'd be ready.

When the woman entered, carrying her own full pint, Raven wasn't the only one who noticed.

She had the dark skin and features of a Persian, dark hair tied back with stray strands falling around her ears. She was still dressed in work clothes, simple white blouse, skirt and blazer. The blouse's upper button had been undone, showing she was ready for a night out and wasn't afraid of showing off a little.

She had a lot of show off. The woman filled the suit quite well, curves swelling in the appropriate places. Raven wondered how many male eyes had followed her as she entered and searched for a seat.

Raven ate his sandwich as the hairs on the back of his neck stood up. He didn't react, but he did acknowledge the sixth sense. It had kept him alive for so many years.

He wanted to hear the woman talk and, specifically, laugh.

When she saw him and approached his table with a smile, he knew he'd get the opportunity for both.

"May I join you, Mr. Raven?"

He set down his sandwich and laughed. "Please."

She was the woman on the walkie-talkie; the same rich, commanding voice.

Raven moved the seat opposite him out from the table with a foot, and the woman set her glass down.

She sat and cracked half a smile.

Raven looked into her dark eyes and saw death waiting for him within.

He said, "Shall we talk before we kill each other?"

"Talk away. I love hearing last words."

She smiled.

CHAPTER FOUR

"I suppose," Raven said, pushing his unfinished plate of food aside, "you followed the breadcrumbs I left?"

"It was so obvious," the woman said. "You want a showdown. We're going to give you one."

"How many with you?"

"Oh, it's only me," she said. "The rest of my crew is... elsewhere."

"I thought Vic and I wiped them out."

Had they already found Mara?

"You wish."

"I try to be sporting," he said, "but I'm afraid I'm working from a disadvantage. You know me, but I don't know you. I'm allowed to know the name of my executioner."

"I am Fatima Najjar," she said. "Perhaps you've heard of me?"

Raven let out a low laugh. "Fatima the Undertaker. Prized assassin of the jihad. For hire, and not cheap."

"No, I'm not."

"You also don't fail."

"No," she said again, "I don't. Tell me how many confirmed kills."

"Oh, I'd be guessing."

"Tell me."

"You also have a tremendous ego."

She laughed. "We're two of a kind. We have to be to survive as long as we have, no?"

"Drink your beer, love," he said. "Cahoots works hard on that stuff."

She took a long drink. Her eyes never left Raven's face. She set the glass down again on the wood table.

"We can't do it here," Raven said.

"I have no intention of spoiling anybody's night."

"Your place or mine?"

She laughed, the rich bellow coming from deep down, her mouth open. Her lips were wet with lipstick, dark red to match her skin tone.

"It depends," Fatima said. "I'm not the kind of girl who lowers herself to shoddy domiciles."

"You probably know where I'm staying."

"The Strand. Good choice. I wouldn't mind sleeping there. In your bed. While your body decomposes on the carpet."

Raven laughed again. "What if I shoot you where you sit?"

"We both know you won't. You'd be too afraid your bullet would pass through me and hit somebody else."

Raven only smiled.

"No," she said, "we'll do it the right way."

"Then you'll collect your pay."

"Part of the deal," she said. "I'm only paid when I deliver a body."

"So to speak," Raven said. "You've so far left the bodies of my friends where they fell."

"Professional courtesy. They're lucky I don't collect ears to make into a necklace."

"Who hired you?"

"I can't tell you."

"Humor me, as the minutes of my life tick to zero."

"Sorry, Mr. Raven. You'll go to your grave not knowing the answer, but you won't care once you fade into the dark."

"We're all going there, aren't we? One way or another."

"Save a seat for me," she said. She drank some more beer. "You're right. This is good beer."

"It's my favorite pub."

"Finish your sandwich, Mr. Raven. The condemned always get a last meal."

"Does the condemned in this case," he said, "also get a final request?"

"Maybe."

"Then let's go back to my hotel and answer the carnal question currently in the back of both our minds. Are you game, Fatima?"

"I'm game for anything, Mr. Raven."

Before the door to his room had shut all the way, he pinned Fatima Najjar to the wall.

She didn't resist as he put his mouth on hers, feeling the heat of her body through her clothes. Wild passion awakened as she responded. Her hands snaked under his jacket, feeling his body, bypassing the shoulder harness containing his .45 pistol.

They breathed heavily, Raven moving from her lips to her very slender and very warm neck. Fatima moaned. She removed her jacket, let it fall. Raven let his hands roam over the soft curves of her hips, then went for the buttons on her blouse. He didn't hurry, and when the blouse was open, she helped him pull it from the waistband of her skirt. It joined the jacket on the floor.

Raven picked her up and dropped her on the bed. She unzipped her skirt as he shed the rest of his clothes. He tossed his locket on the pile, climbing on top of her.

Soon their bodies melted together in a lustful embrace. When he slipped inside her, she arched her back, let out another moan. They climbed a mountain together, reached the peak, and held a moment before the downward decent began and they remained still.

He lifted his face to hers. "Did we answer the question?"

"Yes, we did."

She punched him.

There was a lot of power behind the otherwise small feminine fist, and the jolt of the blow took Raven by surprise. As Raven recoiled, she struck again, an elbow to his jaw this time, and he rolled off her. They were close to the edge of the bed, so Raven fell to the floor, the carpet rough against his skin. He was on his belly, his head spinning. Fatima leaped off the bed as he pushed to hands and knees.

Then she straddled his back, and he couldn't breathe.

He grabbed at the constriction around his throat, and almost laughed. She was trying to strangle him with her bra, the band between the cups stretching, but not breaking. Steel wire lined the band. It doubled as a garrote. The cups were around his ears, and the sight would have been hilarious if taken as part of a rowdy bachelor party. Raven visualized the picture. Yeah, he looked ridiculous.

She said, "The great Sam Raven, humiliated at the hands of a woman who's never missed a kill."

She pulled harder, almost jerking him upright. Raven made horrendous gurgling noises, his arms flailing in search of a counterattack. Fatima Najjar laughed.

"When I'm done with you, I'm *keeping* your locket! The whole world will know what Sam Raven has been hiding!"

Raven's hands finally found her ankles.

CHAPTER FIVE

Raven yanked as hard as his strength allowed, her feet slipping on the carpet. Fatima let out a shriek as she fell back. The garrote tightened a moment before one of her hands slipped from the trick weapon. The bra stung his left cheek as it whipped across his face. Raven sucked in as much air as his deprived lungs allowed. Her body landed behind him with a solid thud.

He rose, pivoting. The room tilted. He stood with his legs spread and his arms out for balance. Fatima moaned and started to sit up.

Raven dived on top of her once again, but this time his hands were around her throat, fire in his eyes, rage in his belly. Fatima's eyes widened as she beat against him, the blows ineffectual. Raven tightened his grip on her neck. He pressed harder, digging his thumbs into her throat, her eyes tearing as she continued to try and fight. He kept her legs pinned, putting all his weight on her neck. Finally, the return hits faded, her arms dropping to either side. When her eyes finally rolled back into her head and her body went limp, Raven rolled off, rose to his feet. His neck hurt; his face hurt; he felt dizzy.

A monstrous noise croaked from Fatima's mouth as she tried to breathe again, her face twisted in pain.

Raven stepped over her, trying not to fall over, and went to his leather shoulder harness where it lay on the floor. He bent down to retrieve the harness and his vision spun a little. He grabbed the edge of the dresser against the wall. Fatima croaked again, her body shifting on the carpet.

Raven's vision cleared. He pulled the Nighthawk Custom from the holster. He'd changed the barrel to one with a threaded extension. Twisted onto the threads was his custom-made suppressor.

Fatima Najjar rolled onto on her belly, face in the carpet, trying to push herself off the floor. Her muscles strained with the effort. The gagging sounds continued as she tried to suck air.

Raven's face showed no emotion. He raised the .45. Her head turned. Her eyes looked dull, but a spark of life remained. But not for long.

Raven's voice sounded scratchy as he said, "You'll reach the dark before me, Fatima." He didn't know if she heard him. Her face showed no sign of comprehension. It didn't matter. His finger eased back on the trigger. The sharp phut of the suppressed .45 ACP sounded loud in the confines of the hotel room. Her head popped like a vase dropped from a shelf.

Raven spent no time studying the kill. He tossed the smoking gun on the rumpled bedspread, then dressed, taking his time. He slipped his head through the chain of the locket last, the locket dangling halfway down his chest. He never opened the locket, but it contained the fuel for his crusade. It was his only link to his past life, a link only for him, and damn Fatima for trying to exploit it.

He remained in a great deal of pain, but he had to push through. Raven tightened the shoulder harness across his back and returned the .45 to its snug confines. The suppressor extended through the opening in the bottom.

He glanced at her as he pulled on his jacket. Fatima the Undertaker would kill no more.

One more for Vic, Billy, and Carlos.

He still needed the big fish. The commanding general behind the murders. The one who knew why a bunch of retired CIA officers were marked for death.

And he needed to find Mara before it was too late.

Raven dumped the contents of her purse onto the bed and rifled through the items, setting aside a cell phone. There wasn't anything else of value, but the cell phone required a thumb print to unlock. He knelt down, grabbed her right thumb. He pressed it to the phone, then turned off the security feature. He dropped the cell phone into the inside pocket of his jacket.

Using a wet washcloth from the bathroom, he wiped down everything he had touched. He pocketed the spent shell casing last. He'd registered under an assumed name with the proper identification to make it stick. The cover identity was now burned, no longer of use, and the London police would have a DNA sample to go with the name.

London police might look for him, but the government would take over. MI5 and MI6 would whisper a thank you to whoever had removed a cancer from the world.

Raven shut the door quietly as he exited. He could breathe easier, but his face and neck still hurt.

He'd booked another room, under his real name, at the Park Plaza Westminster Bridge. He drove there in his rental.

Closing himself within the room, he hung his jacket and shoulder harness in the closet. Room service delivered a pot of hot water and a selection of tea. Raven over tipped for the waiter's effort at such a late hour. He then retrieved the dead woman's cell phone.

Dizziness continued to come and go. Raven stretched on out the bed, shoes off, feet crossed at the ankles, his head sinking into the soft pillows. A night's rest would work wonders. Muted street sounds reached through the window glass. It was only 7:30, the night young for most people.

He hoped Mara was out there somewhere.

He searched the cell phone for clues.

CHAPTER SIX

Raven cursed and bolted upright. All aches and pains vanished as he stared at the display on the late Fatima Najjar's phone.

Mara.

Two pictures sent to Fatima as part of a text message showed Mara Cole behind the counter at a flower shop. One of her working the register, another showing her organizing a batch of red roses.

She was older, same as he was, but it was her. The long curly black hair, sharp jaw, small nose; it was her. He scrolled to read the text message.

Target: Mara Cole.

Place: Flowers by the Bridge.

Deadline: Thursday night when the shop closes at 8pm. Preferably a robbery.

It was almost a quarter to eight.

Raven searched for Flower by the Bridge. The flower shop was near the Westminster Bridge. About a block away. He pressed the phone icon to dial the listed number.

Three rings...

"Good evening, Flowers by the Bridge."

Raven tried to talk but the words choked in his throat. He'd never expected to hear Mara's voice again and listening to her talk again sent his pulse racing.

"Hello?"

Raven pulled himself together. "Hello. May I speak with Mara please."

"Um...who is this?"

She recognized his voice too.

"Mara. It's Sam."

"What? How did you——"

Raven jumped off the bed. "Mara, listen to me very carefully. Vic and Billy and Carlos are dead. Somebody is coming after us, and you and I are the only ones left."

"I'm hanging up, do *not* contact me again."

"Mara! I'm coming over. Stay inside until I get there."

"Sam, you stay away from me!"

"Mara——"

"Go to hell!"

She hung up.

Raven's pulse pounded as he dropped Fatima Najjar's phone. He raced to pull on his shoes, shoulder harness, and jacket, blessing the impulse to hire a car for his stay in London.

7:50.

He took the stairs to the lobby, another set of stairs to the garage, and found his car. The BMW's engine fired when he pressed the starter.

If the killers expected her to lock up at 8pm sharp, they'd be waiting when she stepped outside. They'd brace her with weapons, force her back into the shop, get any cash out the safe, and leave her dead.

He wasn't surprised by her reaction to his call. They had a past, and not a good one. He had to go to her anyway. They may have ended badly, but he was going to keep her alive if he could. And maybe they could work together long enough to find out what was behind the murders.

By the time Raven drove by the shop, it was 7:58. The bridge spanned the River Thames to his right. The brightly lighted Elizabeth Tower, on the opposite side, stood like a sentinel over the water. Raven had confused the tower for Big Ben on his first trip to London, which seemed like a lifetime ago now. Lights remained on behind the shop windows, but the sign in the door read CLOSED.

He pulled the BMW into a small parking lot beside the store, where only one other car sat, a Nissan. Had to be Mara's. He locked the car and approached the shop. The exterior had no side entrance. Behind the wide front window, a bright display of flowers of various colors teased the merchandise inside.

He pulled on the door handle. The lock held sure. He tapped on the glass, yelling, "Mara!"

Nobody behind the counter. Nobody near the refrigerated display cases.

He pulled on the door harder.

Mara Cole sat in her tiny office with her face in her hands.

She had several hours' worth of paperwork in her desk. Bills to pay. Order forms to fill out. The things she needed to do to keep her shop open.

But Sam Raven had called, and now she couldn't think straight, her mind a flurry of emotions refusing to settle.

He'd come crashing into her life in typical Sam Raven style, expecting her to listen to his ramblings about dead friends and the need to...what? Hide? Run? Fight?

She'd left the CIA behind long ago. After what happened in Afghanistan, all she wanted was to put the horror behind her and find a rhythm to life again. But now the past was calling.

Finally moving her hands away, she reached for the phone on the corner of her desk. She dialed a number from memory she'd never expected to dial again.

A woman answered curtly. "Yes?"

"Clark Wilson please."

"Security code."

Mara closed her eyes. As much as she wanted to slice the CIA out of her life for good, she'd found it impossible. Same as she'd found it impossible to get on with her life and live like a normal person. She lived like a hermit, kept her drapes closed, and never went anywhere except home and work.

"Delta two-seven, Whiskey, Zebra nine."

"One moment."

The line clicked, but she hadn't been disconnected.

A moment later a man spoke.

"Mara?"

"Hello, Clark."

Clark Wilson, a Senior Staff Operations Officer for the CIA's Special Activities Center, forced a laugh.

"Well, um, hello," he said. "Are you in the States?"

"I'm in London," she said.

"What are you doing—"

"Clark, I heard from Sam Raven a few minutes ago. Why is he calling me?"

"I don't understand."

She explained the call, adding: "He was ranting about Billy and Carlos and Vic being dead, and he and I are the only two left. Do you know what's going on?"

Wilson let out a sigh. "Mara, I have some really bad news."

"You mean—"

"He's telling the truth. Billy, Carlos, and Vic are dead. Vic was killed four days ago in Madrid. Four other men, all carrying submachine guns, were found with his body."

"Four other—"

"Sam flew into Madrid on a chartered flight."

"Did he—"

"We think he was there to meet with Vic."

Mara tried to control rising panic and stuttered as she tried to ask another question.

Wilson cut her off. "Mara, we have no idea what's going on. We're trying to find out, but our sources have no information."

She sank in her chair. She sounded tiny as she said, "What do I do, Clark?"

"Talk to Raven. Get him in touch with me as soon as you can. We'll figure things out."

"Oh my God—"

"Mara, we need your help. Please."

"Clark, I can't—"

She jolted with a gasp as somebody pulled on the front door. When she heard her name, when she heard Sam shouting her name, she froze in her chair.

"I gotta go, Clark."

She heard him yelling for her to stay on the line as she slammed the phone down.

CHAPTER SEVEN

She moved almost like a zombie, pushing back her chair, the wheels squeaking, pausing in the doorway. The short hallway led to the front of the store on the right, and the rear door on the left. She could easily turn left, run out the back, and get away from Sam before he ever saw her.

"Mara!"

He wasn't going to go away. She went back for her purse, and as she stepped through the door, determined to go left, she looked right.

And there he was.

Framed in the doorway, his eyes pleading, they made eye contact and he yelled for her to open the door.

She shook her head and turned left.

Mara walked slowly at first, then picked up speed, nearing the rear exit as fast as she could.

She stopped short as something hard bashed into the lock. She blinked, mesmerized, and then the doorframe exploded as a shotgun blast tore into the frame, shattering the steel lock, a spray of wood debris flying at her. She screamed as she turned away, bringing up a hand to protect her face.

The rear door opened on whiny hinges and two men in

facemasks, each carrying a shotgun, stepped toward her.

She screamed, her feet slipping as she turned to run, the shoes finally digging in, and she bolted for the front.

The two gunmen yelled behind her, and she knew one was raising his weapon to fire into her back. She saw him moving in slow motion, in her mind's eyes, as she neared the counter. The counter would not protect her from the blast. It was made of wood, painted white, and not strong enough to stop a load of buckshot and especially not strong enough to stop a bullet.

And what she thought she'd left behind so many years ago came flooding back to her in a rush. She reached out with both hands, grasping the top of the counter, pumping her legs to jump, flinging her body over the top of the counter to land hard on the tiled floor. Breath left her, and she scrambled forward on hands and knees as the shotgun blast roared in the narrow hallway, a section of the counter disintegrating behind her, the pellets brushing her back.

She kept sliding across the floor, her movement finally halted by one of the large refrigerators storing her flowers. She rolled onto her back, screaming again.

Sam Raven, at the door, smashed through the glass with a gun. He reached in, turned the lock, and shoved through the door. The extended snout at the muzzle of his gun, a suppressor, spit lead in rapid succession.

The gunners reached the counter as Raven fired, his first two rounds stabbing through one shotgunner's chest, the other bringing up his weapon. Raven fired again, and the second shotgunner dropped out of sight.

Mara sat up, inching back to bump into the refrigerator, feeling the cold glass door at her neck.

Sam Raven approached her, a gun in one hand, his other extended to help her up.

"We have to go!"

"Get away from me!"

"Mara, now! There's no time for this!"

He reached down with his free hand and grabbed an arm, pulling. She had no choice but to rise. She matched him in height, his eyes boring into hers. He put his gun away and put both hands on her, pushing her forward, her legs responding, finally getting her wits back. She ran with him out the door, glancing back as they turned into the parking lot beside the shop.

She'd worked hard to get the business up and running, and a knowing sensation in her gut suggested she'd never see it again.

Raven was pushing her toward a black BMW. He helped her into the passenger seat and shut the door. Then he was beside her, the car running, backing out quickly and spinning the wheel to point the car at the street. He accelerated away, the rush of forward movement pushing her back in the seat.

"Buckle up," he said.

"Huh?"

"Seatbelt."

She reached robotically for the seat strap and locked it in place across her lap and chest.

"What's happening, Sam?"

"I don't know."

"What do you *mean* you *don't* know?"

He said nothing as he drove, weaving through traffic.

"Where are we going?"

"Back to my hotel. Not far from here."

"How long have you been in London?"

"Three days, looking for you."

"*Looking?*"

"I had to find the killers first."

"There are two of them back there!"

"I found their boss. She tried to kill me a couple hours ago."

"Oh my God, what is happening!"

He had no answer for her.

They couldn't stay at the hotel for long, but Raven had to get Mara calmed down enough to talk.

She wouldn't sit. She paced the floor, back and forth between the bed and dresser, as he stood helplessly, watching her.

"Please sit," he said.

She did not.

"I'm surprised you're still alive," she said.

"Isn't life full of surprises?"

"Tonight is a surprise I don't need!"

He took the chair in front of the desk, near the wall. She stopped and stared at him, her arms folded, her purse still over her shoulder. Finally, she set the purse on the dresser and dropped into the bigger chair near the bed.

"Happy? Why are you holding your phone?"

"It's not mine," he said. He tapped the screen and made a selection, opening the text message on Fatima Najjar's phone to prove the killers had her location and pictures. He went over and showed her, explaining, without too much detail, how he'd acquired the phone.

She sank in the chair and stared at the carpet.

"I don't believe this."

"It's true." Raven returned to his chair. "And I don't know how to explain it any more than you do."

"Clark wants to talk to you."

"Wilson?"

"He's at headquarters. *God* did I say that?"

He tossed her the phone. She snapped up her hands and caught it.

"You better dial. Then I'll talk to him."

"Forget your security code?"

"I've tried to forget a lot of things," he said. "Same as you."

"But you can't."

"No," he said. He looked sad. "Not at all."

She dialed the number.

CHAPTER EIGHT

"Are you two safe?" Clark Wilson said.

"For the moment," Raven told him.

"All right. Stay put as long as you can. I'll start working from this end."

"You've heard nothing? No chatter?"

"Not a word, I swear. It took Billy and Carlos dying before we picked up a possible pattern. Vic confirmed it. Were you there when he died?"

"I was," Raven said.

"Do you have anything to give us a clue?"

"Fatima Najjar."

"The Undertaker?" Wilson said. "She's involved?"

"No longer. Her body will be discovered at the Strand, if it hasn't already."

"Wow. Good kill, Sam. All right. I'll be in touch."

Wilson ended the call.

Raven sighed and set the phone on the dresser. He looked at it a moment. He'd have to destroy the phone. The enemy might try and track it. He wasn't ready for them to come at him again until he had some answers.

"What are we going to do?"

"Have you eaten?"

"You expect me to eat after this?"

"We need to eat, and then we need some sleep."

"I am *not* staying in this room with you!"

"Stop yelling." He kept his voice calm. "We don't need the front desk calling."

She crossed her arms and didn't look at him.

"You can have the bed. I'll have a rollaway sent up for me."

"Such a gentleman."

Raven watched her. He felt as helpless as he had during their captivity and, later, after their escape, when she quit the Agency. And shut everybody close to her out of her life. He didn't think she hated him; what had he done? He'd loved her once, and then everything went off the rails, and she wanted him gone.

But his protective instincts didn't care about the past. He felt guilty about not being able to shield her while tied up in a cave. It wasn't his fault he couldn't prevent what happened or take the torture instead. They'd all been tortured, on a rotating schedule.

She'd come around once the full impact on the attempt on her life broke through the haze in her mind. The woman he'd known was still there, hiding in a shell. Once the shell cracked, she'd be ready for a fight.

He sat on the bed.

"A flower shop?" he said.

"When I left, I came here, yeah. Started working there as a clerk and took over when the owner retired. I got a loan and bought him out."

"Any friends around here?"

"What do you think?" Her accusing look stabbed him through the chest. "No, Sam. I go to work, I go home. Every few hours I eat something. I don't even have a cat."

She drew her knees up to her chest, wrapped her arms around them, and pulled herself into a ball. She put her head between her knees.

He used the hotel phone to call the front desk for a rollaway bed. It arrived ten minutes later, and Raven set it near the window, as far from the bed as possible. Mara remained in her ball, not watching.

"Looks a little small for me," he said, "but I'll manage."

She grunted. Then she looked up sharply. "I need clothes."

"I'll go to your place and get what you need."

"No! You are *not* going through my things."

"And if they're waiting for you at your home? What then?"

"If they're waiting, they'll kill *you* this time."

"And then where will you be?"

She moved her mouth to reply, but no words came out.

"Give me your keys and your address and a list of what you want."

She stared at him.

"I'm not asking again, Mara."

"Keys are in my purse."

He collected the purse from the dresser and was about to open it but stopped. He handed her the purse. She opened it and took out her keys, told him her address, and he repeated it back to memorize the location.

"I'll be back as soon as I can."

"Hurry," she said. "I can't be alone here."

"I'll be fast. What do you need?" He pulled on his jacket to cover the shoulder harness. She gave him her list and told him where to find things.

"Lock the door behind me," he said.

He grabbed Fatima's cell phone and went out.

Mara jumped from the chair and hurried to the door, turning the bolt, slamming the security lock in place. She turned and leaned against the door a moment, then went into the bathroom to splash water on her face. She kept the washcloth pressed close, enjoying the feeling of the cold water. She let out a painful moan. Jumping over the counter left her body achy. Leaving the washcloth on the counter, she exited the bathroom and avoided her reflection. She didn't want to look at herself. She was sure she looked frightful.

She stretched out on the bed and rolled onto her side, curling up with her arms close to her head.

She didn't want him around. She didn't want to be around him. He did nothing but stir memories she'd tried hard to bury. But he was there, he'd saved her life, and he was the only person she could trust for now. She had to put her fears aside.

Then she realized she was shaking. Adrenaline wearing off. She kept her head on the pillow. The scene at the flower shop played through her mind. She watched herself absently, as if it were a movie. The gunmen. The counter. Raven's pistol spitting death in return.

She shut her eyes tight and started crying, her body rocking with the heavy sobs. Her tears staining the pillow and creating a cold wet spot. She shifted her head.

What was happening?

Why was it happening?

And why was it happening to *her?*

Mara Cole had never hurt anybody; done anything to deserve what she'd been forced to endure.

Life was a joke without a punch line.

She had joined the CIA with the best of intentions. She wanted to serve her country. The army had been a godsend, letting her escape from a broken home with an unstable single mother. The thought of leaving the military after six years to try and make her way as a civilian had not appealed to her one bit. Continuing to serve her country did. At least it kept her from returning to a home no longer in existence, and one she didn't want to revisit anyway. Hell with her mother. She could rot away in an alcoholic haze for all Mara cared. And she probably had. Mara had no idea if the woman was still alive.

She'd applied for a job at CIA and they hired her. Her experience with Army Intelligence and the Criminal Investigations Division paved her way. She had the skills the CIA needed, and they put her to work with Sam Raven. And the others whose names she couldn't verbalize without an ache filling her gut.

The tears stopped and she lay quietly. Other sounds in the hallway broke the room's silence. She found the sounds oddly comforting.

CHAPTER NINE

The assassin fired from the kitchen.

Raven shined his cell phone light on the door before entering Mara's apartment. The locks were old, and any pick scratches weren't obvious.

The deadbolt snapped back with a twist of his wrist and he put the other key in the bottom lock. He eased the door open with the suppressor-fitted Nighthawk Talon in his right hand.

He opened the door enough to squeeze through, closing the door silently.

The interior was dark except for the clock on the kitchen microwave, on his left. The green glow of the clock highlighted sudden movement near the stove.

The killer moved his right arm. Raven hit the floor as the gun blast shook the room and the slug chunked into the wall. Raven fired once. The killer let out a short cry as the bullet took him down. His body landed in a sprawl, his pistol sliding across the tile.

Raven crawled to the body, using the light from his cell to examine the man's face. Another Middle Easterner with hard features. The .45 hollow-point had punched a nice hole in his chest, and Raven felt the pool of blood from the man's back touch his hand. He moved back to the door and waited, pistol at the ready.

Movement. Ahead was the T point of a short hall, living room to the left, bedroom and bathroom right. Mara had described the layout, so Raven knew where to go quickly.

A voice. A man whispering another's name. Raven followed the wall, moving slowly. The second killer spoke no more.

He reached the corner. "You guys don't know when to quit," Raven said.

He shifted the gun to his left hand and swung his arm around the corner. He caught the second assassin in the bedroom doorway a few feet away. The man didn't get a chance to use his weapon. The .45 spoke twice. The killer fell against the bedroom closet, crashing into the sliding doors. Raven stepped over to the body and fired twice more.

He found a light switch and lit the bedroom. He needed to move the body to get into the closet. Returning the gun to its holster, he grabbed the dead killer under his arms and pulled him away from the sliding doors.

Inside the closet, on the top shelf, he found the empty suitcase Mara had said would be there. He moved fast between bedroom and bathroom, filling the case. He added her phone charger, passport, and stopped long enough to grab a bottle of Jack Daniels and Russian Standard from her liquor rack. He forced them into the suitcase and only managed to move the zipper halfway. No matter. He needed a solid drink and figured Mara wouldn't refuse one either.

Securing both locks, he hurried back to his car.

The killers worked in pairs.

Their failure at the flower shop required two more to wait at Mara's apartment.

With Fatima Najjar gone, who was giving the orders? Who was her number two?

Too many questions.

And they were both living on borrowed time until they learned the answers.

Raven no longer worried about Fatima Najjar's cell phone. He'd tossed it out onto the roadway during his drive to Mara's apartment. If the enemy didn't know she was dead yet, they wouldn't have had time to ping the location.

He hoped.

Raven called Mara's cell using his own phone, and she answered with a sleepy voice.

"Did I wake you?"

"No."

"I'm on my way. Any trouble?"

"No."

"Are you hungry?"

"Yes."

"Order some food up if you feel safe answering the door. I'll be back shortly."

"Okay."

Raven hung up. He was glad he'd grabbed the booze. If nothing else Mara could drink herself to sleep.

He shut the door. Mara sat cross-legged on the bed, a towel over her lap, eating a hamburger. She'd tied her hair back.

The TV was on, though Raven made no note of the show right away. He set down her suitcase.

"You got everything?" she said.

"And two bottles of booze."

"I got you a burger," she said, pointing at the dresser. His plate was still covered by the silver room service lid. Luckily, the room had a microwave in a nook close to the bathroom. Raven zapped the burger and fries to warm things up, then sat at the desk. Away from her.

She muted the TV. "Everything all right?"

"No." Raven chewed a French fry. "There were two more killers waiting for you there."

"You shot them?"

"They're quite dead." Raven took a big bite of his burger. He thanked her for having it sent up.

"It's your money," she said.

"Yes, but it was thoughtful of you not to forget about me."

"You're saying I'm selfish?" she said.

"Mara, are you going to fight all the time?"

"I only asked you a question!"

"No, you're accusing me of—" He stopped. She glared at him; he shook his head. "What are you doing?"

"This a huge shock, all right?"

"Having killers come after you usually is. But I'm here to help. I didn't have to bother with you, Mara."

"You're still pissed at me leaving?"

"Let's say maybe things would be different if you'd stayed."

"What do you mean?"

He'd said far too much. *If he and Mara had stayed together, maybe he wouldn't have—*

He bit off a curse. He turned his attention back to his burger and ate some more. He felt her staring at him. He ignored her. He would not bring up the topic again. He didn't want her to get the idea he blamed her for the turn in his life.

She interrupted his thought. "Seeing you—"

"I know," he said.

"You're right, I'm surprised you bothered."

"You don't stop caring for the people you once loved."

She nodded and unmuted the television. She had a sitcom

on. Raven didn't know the name of the show. Television wasn't his thing.

The microwave hadn't reheated Raven's burger all the way. Some bites were a little colder than others, but he wolfed it down, and the bottle of water she'd included.

They finished their meals and Mara turned off the television after Raven said he had no use for it. She thanked him for the suitcase, removing the Jack Daniels and Russian Standard. She took the case into the bathroom. Shortly the shower started running, and Raven paced a little as he tried to figure out what to do next.

It was a shock for her; it was a shock for him, too.

"Afghanistan nightmares compete with other nightmares in sort of a satanic rotation, yes. Even 'Old Solid' has a touch of PTSD from the ordeal."

He'd been too focused during the ride to and from Mara's apartment to let his mind wander. Now he was alone, she was in the shower, and his pulse quickened. His mind filled with flashbacks to their last mission. Afghanistan. The failed raid. The capture. The endless torture. The escape.

A race for their lives followed; the enemy at their heels the entire way. As Raven stood in the middle of the hotel room, he couldn't help but feel the confines of the cave once again. The cave where he was sure he'd die, his body never to be found, where he, Vic, Billy and Carlos had been tortured, and Mara raped.

Survival had seemed like a miracle.

CHAPTER TEN

Mara Cole lay awake thinking some things never changed.

Raven still snored.

She'd taken to using earplugs to keep from being kept awake by the saw-wielding lumberjack in bed next to her. None were available now. She didn't think she had even owned a pair of earplugs since dumping him.

And there was no sugarcoating their end. She'd dropped him like a hot potato, like a radioactive rock, and with prejudice. After Afghanistan, she couldn't bear to be with any man, one she loved or not. Whoever had attacked her in the cave had taken more from her than was possible to account for. She still saw part of her rapist's face in her dreams, imagined his breath on her, from time to time.

The alarm clock on the nightstand showed 4:30am. Dressed in a long shirt and underwear, she slipped out of the bed. Raven lay on his side on the rollaway, his bare back to her, but in the dark, there was no way to see any detail of his body. She wondered how many of his scars from the whippings had healed, or if they'd healed at all.

She pulled on a pair of jeans and slipped into her tennis shoes, grabbing her suitcase. She'd kept her personal items in the case; nothing remained in the bathroom. She'd learned long ago to travel light and be ready to move at a moment's notice.

Mara Cole wasn't going to stay.

She'd run before, from home at age 18, jumping into a friend's car and heading for the nearest bus station. She had not left a note for her mother.

She'd run again when the nightmares became too much. The only way to save herself, she thought, had been to cut all ties with those she'd once held dear and find a place to hide.

Now it was time to run again.

She had money. She had her passport. She could fly to another country, change her name, and start again. A new identity actually might work wonders for her psyche. Unfortunately, changing her face wasn't in the cards, as the cost of the operation would wipe out her nest egg.

Mara Cole did not want to deal with her old life anymore. Sam Raven represented the past more than anybody or anything. She was sad her former friends were dead. It had been a long time since she'd seen them, and she'd worked hard to forget. Their deaths were afterthoughts considering everything else she now faced.

Mara slipped out of the room and into the hall.

She tried not to tiptoe down the hall, but found she was forcing herself to walk lightly. The elevator took a few moments to reach her. When the doors rumbled shut, she started to panic.

What waited for her outside?

Two killers at the flower shop. Backup crew at her apartment. Was there now a crew of assassins looking at faces on the street, like prospectors panning for gold? Had they drawn the city into quadrants for teams to search? Had they staked out the airports and railways?

Sam Raven had his big gun to protect him from such measures.

Mara Cole hadn't fired a gun since...

The elevator opened into the lobby, and she wasn't alone. Hotel workers and a few guests milled about. Tourists suffering jet lag.

Some turned to look at her as she headed for the exit, but she ignored them. Surely her demeanor made anybody looking at her wonder about her state of mind.

She wondered too.

Mara stopped halfway to the exit. The electronic sliding glass doors would allow her access to the street. There was still traffic, not a lot, but enough, and eventually she could find a cab or the Underground.

It will be easy; *do it!*

She pivoted right and marched past the lobby restaurant and ran for the ladies' room.

She checked to make sure the stalls were empty, then ran to the sink. Setting her suitcase on the counter, she splashed water over her face, dried with a paper towel, and leaned both hands on the counter.

She didn't want to look at herself, but she had to. With great difficulty, she raised her head, and looked into her own eyes. She looked worn out, her eyes resembling a sad dog's. She stared at her reflection and tried to slow her breathing, slow her pulse.

Tell me honestly you can do this again.
I don't think I can.
Why?
I'm not who I used to be.
Who are you?
I don't know anymore.
How come?
Too much... I can't!
Why have you failed?

Because I don't know who I am anymore!
What if Raven can help?
How?
I don't know.
What good is asking then?
Doesn't he deserve a chance?

Mara took a deep breath and turned to lean against the counter, folding her arms, bowing her head. The tile on the floor was spotless. She'd expect nothing less in such a fancy hotel; then again, it had probably been cleaned only an hour or two ago.

Raven had risked his life for her. She owed him the chance to help her face her demons. Maybe this was her opportunity. Maybe surviving once again might help her bury the past once and for all.

If she survived. If she didn't make it, she'd find a solution of a different kind, in the next life, if there was such a thing. Or she'd finally find peace.

Mara grabbed her suitcase and rode the elevator back to the room. She realized as she stood in front of the door, she had no way to get into the room.

She knocked. She knocked again. Finally, the door opened a crack. Shirtless Raven opened the door, wearing sweatpants, and the silver locket. His pistol was in his right hand, held against his leg. He blinked at her.

"Um—"

"Come back to bed," he said. He opened the door.

She went back inside.

CHAPTER ELEVEN

"Hurry up and eat," Raven said. "We need to get out of here."

He placed the breakfast dishes around the room's table, pulling the silver lids off. Since he was in London, he'd wanted a full English breakfast; what had been served on the plates was nothing of the sort. Scrambled eggs, toast, sausage links. Mara was a tea drinker same as him, so no coffee, but two pots of hot water instead and a selection of teas and lemon wedges. They started eating.

"How did you sleep?" he said. He didn't want to bring up her attempt at running away until she was ready to talk about it. She'd be ready when she mentioned it, he figured.

"Off and on."

"You still look tired."

"I still *feel* tired."

Their silverware made clinks and scrapes on the plates as they ate, Raven trying to hurry. He'd placed the order, packed, and all they needed to do was scoot. Mara was still packed. She never used anything from her suitcase without putting something back. The only change Raven had made was moving the still-unopened liquor to his larger bag.

"Where are you living now?" she said.

"I travel a lot. But I have a place in Stockholm. A houseboat. It's at the Navishamn marina."

"Wow, really? A houseboat was never on your top ten list in the past."

"Things change." He swallowed some tea.

She mumbled an agreement and went back to her breakfast.

"Where are we heading?" she said.

"Somewhere. By now Fatima the Undertaker's body, the carnage at the flower shop and at your apartment has been found. I'm sure we're both wanted for questioning."

"Clark can sort it out. When they identify the bodies—"

"MI5 will take over, and they'll want to know what we know."

"We don't *know* anything!"

"Exactly."

"Maybe MI5 can protect us."

"The killings didn't begin in London, and they won't end here, either. The British won't be interested any longer than they have to be."

"Then Clark is our only option. Get him to step in and get their attention off of us."

"We can ask," he said, "but I'm not expecting any favors."

"Because you're on your own now?"

He nodded. "It's the choice I made, yeah. I've done a few favors for our former employer, but they were strictly by contract. Once the job was done, I was done."

"What happened to you, Sam?"

"Never mind." He went back to eating.

"What's in the locket?"

"What did I tell you?"

"All right," she said.

They ate without speaking for a few minutes. Finally, Mara finished, poured more tea, and held her mug in front of her face, like a shield, as she said, "I tried to run."

"You did," he said. "What else could you do?"

"I didn't get past the lobby, Sam."

"Why?"

"I'm not who I used to be."

"I wasn't aware you thought you were."

"What do you mean?"

"You still have some instincts. Like leaping over the counter at the flower shop without a second thought. It's natural not everything would stick with you."

"I hoped it'd all come back. You know, like in the movies."

"You might need a bit more time."

"You aren't mad?"

"I'm not your keeper, Mara. I'm not holding you prisoner."

"What if I hadn't come back?"

He shrugged. "I'd have found you. One way or another."

"You mean alive or dead?"

"Pretty much. We're dealing with a very determined enemy."

"But it makes no sense!"

"It makes sense to somebody. We know something; we saw something; we're suddenly a liability, where we weren't before."

"It's been *years* since we worked for the Agency."

"Yup."

"How could we threaten anyone now?"

"Every assassin we've encountered has been Middle Eastern. Could be revenge for an old job. Grudges can last a long time."

"Why aren't you more upset about this?"

"I'm used to it."

"Why?"

He said, "It's a long story."

Mara took a deep breath. "Sam, I need your help."

"You don't have to ask."

She drank some of her tea.

"Should we," he said, "talk about a few other things too?"

"No."

"Mara—"

"Remember what you said about your contract jobs?" She set her mug down. "Once the job was done, you were done. Same applies here, too. When this is over, I want you out of my life. I haven't worked as hard as I have to have my past thrown back in my face. When we solve this problem, I'm going back to—"

"To what?"

"Whatever life I can salvage."

"All right. Whatever you say."

She dropped her eyes.

Raven wiped his mouth and set about clearing the table. He returned the dishes and cutlery to the room service cart and pushing it into the hallway.

She'd laid down the terms, didn't pull any punches, and let him know exactly where they stood. Fine. He hoped she'd come around. He wasn't her enemy. Their enemy was whoever was trying to kill them.

And what really angered him was the old enemy who had turned the formerly bright and happy Mara Cole into a shadow of her former self.

Basheer el-Dowd. One enemy who still lived.

He went back into the room with a frown. Could there be a connection? They'd failed to kill el-Dowd. He'd gone into hiding after their assassination attempt. Had he emerged to get revenge?

It made sense.

Still, damage done. No going back. If he was still capable of loving somebody without the fear of losing them, and if she hadn't been so traumatized, their forced togetherness would be different. But it wasn't.

The door closed behind him and he stood in the doorway looking into the room. Looking at Mara as she sat at the table. She looked at him. Neither had anything more to say.

CHAPTER TWELVE

Mara watched Raven in the doorway and wondered if she should tell him about the dreams.

The dreams where she was back in the cave. The voices. The faces. Something about those faces created an urge to identify them. They were white faces, out of place with the others, with American accents. They spoke of an arrangement with Basheer el-Dowd. And they weren't happy he'd taken the CIA agents hostage and demanded their execution.

She wondered if she should tell him about seeing a psychologist to sort out the dreams. Her subconscious kept those faces concealed. She hoped therapy might help her identify them.

The psychologist, recommended by Clark Wilson, knew more about her CIA work than her colleagues.

It was all too much to deal with.

And now somebody was trying very hard to kill her.

Was there a connection? Had she set this horrible turn of events in motion because she'd reached out for help?

She couldn't continue to wallow in self-pity. She didn't need to remember how to fight or shoot a weapon. What she needed to remember was how to reach down deep, find the courage and strength to survive, and focus on winning the battle. No more freaking out. She'd come back to Raven because she knew she needed him. And he needed her as much as she needed him.

Finally, he spoke. "Are you ready?"

"Yes," she said.

Clark Wilson poured another cup of coffee. The caffeine was no longer working as much as he would have liked.

The sun was up in London. The sun was down in Langley, Virginia, where Wilson worked with an analyst within CIA headquarters. They were in "the Pit" of the Special Activities Center, a cluster of empty desks encircled by the offices of the staff operations officers.

Wilson stood behind Paul Heinrich, a new hire. He was in his mid-20s, with a short haircut and sharp jaw, and wore the standard issue CIA suit-and-tie like a pro. Wilson was a little more unkempt, his shirt wrinkled after too many hours, his tie loose. Wilson had been around long enough to know he could break the rules after hours.

Wilson and Heinrich watched, on Heinrich's flat screen monitor, CCTV camera footage. The camera had caught the incident at the flower shop, but no details of what took place inside. What the CIA men watched was Raven and Mara escaping and running for a car.

"Who is this guy?"

"Former operative," Wilson said. "They both are."

They watched Raven's car flash out of the frame, and the video remained focused on the flower shop.

Heinrich stopped the video.

Wilson set his coffee on Heinrich's desk, put his hands on his hips, and paced a few steps.

"I figure they were involved," Heinrich said, "in classified stuff?"

"Yeah. Before your time," Wilson added. He didn't want a lot of questions from the newbie. Heinrich was a good analyst who had recently uncovered a money trail leading to several jihadist groups. Wilson wanted his sharp eyes and mind on the Raven / Cole problem. But he didn't want to have to give him a history on the pair because his clearance didn't extend him the privilege.

"The cops have found the bodies," Wilson said, "at the Strand hotel, the flower shop, and Mara's apartment."

"Right. No IDs yet."

"And when they are IDed, MI5 will take over."

"Correct," Heinrich said. "Will they pass any information to us?"

"We'd have to ask nicely, and they'll want something in return, like what it's all about. And we don't have anything to give them."

Heinrich cleared his computer screen and switched to another file. "I pulled the files on the dead agents as well as Raven and Cole, but—"

"I've already read them, Paul."

Heinrich tapped another key and cleared the files from his screen.

Wilson said, "I don't know what I was looking for in those files, but the answers aren't there."

"What is there?"

"Reports on past missions, ones they completed, ones they didn't."

Heinrich turned in his chair to look up at Wilson. "Could this be related to a mission they didn't complete?"

"It could be related to a mission they did complete."

"So you're thinking it's a revenge hit."

"Whoever it is has waited a long time."

"That means somebody had to tell them—"

"Exactly. Somebody told them where to find Raven, Mara, and the others. And somebody has gone to a lot of trouble to get rid of them."

Wilson stopped pacing and sat on the edge of a neighboring desk with his arms folded.

"We have to narrow down a few suspects. Let's separate the completed missions from the incomplete."

Wilson took Heinrich's seat. He used his passwords to unlock the classified operation files. They printed reports one by one, starting with the incomplete missions.

There hadn't been many jobs Raven's team didn't finish. Supplemental reports stated other teams completed the tasks.

The completed mission files were much greater in number. They read through several before Heinrich began looking at the first pages of other files. He compared them with others, rechecking the incomplete files.

"What did you find?"

"I think I have the answer, Clark."

"Tell me."

Heinrich held out the file on Basheer el-Dowd. "Billy Anzell and Carlos Vega were the first two killed. Neither participated in any other missions with Raven's team. They transferred to his to replace two others who changed assignments. The only assignment all of them worked together was the strike against el-Dowd."

Wilson, bleary-eyed and exhausted, needed a moment to process the information. "I think el-Dowd is our man."

"Who was he?"

"Kingpin of Afghanistan," Wilson said. He sat on another desk. "He controlled it then, and probably still does, the opium trade in the southern region. The mission failed when Raven and his team were captured. They escaped, and then el-Dowd vanished. His organization operated in his absence."

"Was he wounded? I mean, was there a reason for him to disappear? Maybe to recover from injuries?"

"We don't know."

"He'd have the money to hire the Undertaker."

"He would."

"But after so many years—"

"Yeah," Wilson said, "why take the risk of whacking a bunch of agents when it would only piss us off and cause retaliation? We came close to nailing him once. He wouldn't want to take that risk again."

"Nobody ever said drug dealers were smart."

"But el-Dowd," Wilson said, "was smarter than average."

"Is somebody sponsoring him?"

"What do you mean?" Wilson said.

"Is there now somebody behind el-Dowd with enough power and influence he feels safe carrying out these murders? In other words, he knows we won't be able to get to him."

Wilson stared into space, zoning out, tired to the point where he couldn't function any longer. If el-Dowd had plugged in with another organization, expanding his reach in the drug trade, he was a volcano waiting to explode. He perked up as another idea entered his mind.

"How about this," he said.

Heinrich paid attention.

"Mara called me a year ago, and said she wanted the name of a psychologist. She wanted to talk to about the el-Dowd mission and what she went through. I gave her the name of our man in London."

"Remember who he is?"

Wilson gave Heinrich the name, and Heinrich did a search.

"Still in London, keeping regular hours from eight to five."

"That might be a lead."

"You think he's selling information?"

"If he has been, he's managed to stay off the radar until now. I think we should give him a closer look. Later. I don't know about you, but I'm about to pass out."

Heinrich agreed.

"It's glamorous work, isn't it?"

Heinrich smiled. "I didn't sign up for a boring job."

Wilson laughed and crossed the room to his office. "You wait, kid."

Wilson gathered his jacket and briefcase. Heinrich closed down his machine, and they left the office.

CHAPTER THIRTEEN

Clark Wilson parked his SUV in the garage next to his wife's car. Their home wasn't extravagant, but it was better than all their overseas residences combined. He'd spent many years working overseas, always a staff operations officer. His job was to coordinate projects between field personnel and headquarters. Now he did it at home. Clark and Monica Wilson were happy to finally be back in the United States.

Being in Virginia meant living closer to Monica's parents (his lived in Idaho). It meant their two teenagers could finish their junior and senior years at an American high school. The promotion to Senior Staff Operations Officer came with a bump in pay, but Wilson always complained CIA pay, no matter the level, was insulting considering the nature of the job. He had thought about taking a cushy security consulting position in the private sector but nixed the idea. The pay might not be great, but the job came with rewards no other offered.

The automatic garage door slid closed. Wilson stood in the doorway to the house watching the door lower every last inch. He had a good security system in the house, complete with overhead monitors in the kitchen and his den. His work in counterterrorism efforts had made him security-conscious beyond repair. He wasn't going to leave his safety to a camera lens. It was something he tried to teach his kids too. They didn't know who he really worked for. He had business cards in his wallet stating he worked for the State Department. Diplomatic Assistant. A pencil pusher for policy. It was a tough balancing act.

The garage door closed, and he went into the house. The only illumination came from the hallway nightlights. He quietly stepped into the master bedroom where his wife already slept. She was on her stomach, an arm flung out onto his side of the bed. She joked she didn't mind when he worked late because she had the whole bed to herself, and sometimes he believed her. But he noted she'd only begun making the joke since their return to the US. Overseas, she'd stayed up late worrying about him.

Wilson cleaned his teeth, undressed, and slid under the covers beside his wife, who didn't stir. He rolled onto his side and looked at the clock. He'd be well past nine a.m. getting back to the office but didn't want to be too late. Once he had a handle on the situation, he'd have to work nights to keep up with Sam Raven's waking hours on the other side of the world.

He wished he and his old friend could talk the way they used to. They'd been close. Once. But then Raven left the CIA for civilian life, and then left civilian life for the shadows once again. Wilson could rationalize the break between them any way he wanted, but there were truly only three reasons.

One slept beside Wilson.

The other two slept in their own beds down the hall.

Clark Wilson had what Sam Raven had lost.

Mara Cole didn't recognize the twisty country road Raven drove along. With her window cracked, she enjoyed the fresh air and clear sky. At least it wasn't overcast and rainy right now. Huge plus. The lush green hills and trees and flowers were a nice distraction from the horror of the previous night.

"Where are we going?" she said.

"I have a country cottage," Raven said.

"A what?"

"A place here. I use it every once in a great while, so it might be dusty. But it should be safe."

"Why stay in the city if you had this place?"

"How long have we been driving?"

"Fair enough," she said. They had been on the road for at least two hours, she realized. Certainly not a fast hop to and from London.

He finally turned the rented BMW off the road and onto a dirt driveway. The car jostled as he eased along the rutted path. He finally stopped at what was indeed a small cottage with overgrown landscape. The remains of dead flowers covered the front.

"Sorry about the mess," Raven said. "But the roof doesn't leak."

"Do you have hot water at least?"

"Yes. Water is pumped in from the creek about a quarter-mile away, it runs through a heater, I don't live like a bum when I'm here."

"What's a quarter mile?" she said, grinning.

It was nice to see her smile. He hoped the ice would further thaw. He wanted the old Mara back, but feared she might be gone forever.

"Very funny," he said.

They exited the car and carried their luggage inside along with two sacks of groceries.

The furniture was covered with tarps. After fifteen minutes of removing and folding the tarps to place them on the back porch, Raven opened the windows. The fresh air circulated the smell of dust and out of the cottage. Mara wondered if they shouldn't give the place a good cleaning before doing anything else.

Raven agreed and produced the necessary equipment from a hall closet. They divided up the chores and swept, dusted, and mopped.

An hour later, both tired from the effort, Raven turned on the stove. He cooked steak and vegetables while Mara stood with him in the kitchen.

"We should call Clark," Mara said.

Raven checked his watch. "If I know my old pal, he's been up late working on our problem, and is probably still in bed. Let's eat first and then we'll call him."

"But—"

"Mara, there's nothing we can do right now."

She sighed. "All right. Fine."

Raven used dry seasonings on the meat, and a little salt on the asparagus, and they ate at his now dust-free dining table. Mara had left her suitcase in the guest bedroom. Raven would use the master, where he'd shown her not only his Nighthawk Custom, but his M-4 Commando carbine too.

She had taken particular interest in the handgun. "A raven and his talon?" she said. The word *TALON* was carved on the left side of the pistol.

He'd snatched it back without comment. From a compartment concealed beneath a cut-away section of carpet, also in the master bedroom, Raven showed her three handguns of various makes. There was plenty of firepower available should the need arise.

She'd looked at the guns with a look of discomfort. He

didn't ask her why, but figured she was so out of practice he'd have to go through the basics with her. He didn't want her to shoot her eye out. The cottage was isolated so they could fire into the creek without being disturbed. Or receive attention from the local constable. Raven had not been hasty in selecting the location for his UK hideaway.

Lunch finished, the dishes cleaned, they sat on the living room couch. Raven called Clark Wilson on his cell. He turned on the speaker phone so they could both hear what the CIA man had to say.

"Wilson," the CIA man answered.

"It's me," Raven told him.

"You and Mara ready for some ideas?"

"Go," Raven said.

CHAPTER FOURTEEN

"Our best guess is a revenge hit," Clark Wilson said.

"Who wants revenge? The list has to be—"

"My main suspect is Basheer el-Dowd."

Mara Cole gasped. Raven glanced at her. Color had drained from her face. He didn't blame her. A sense of dread fell over him as well.

"Why?" Raven said.

"Billy and Carlos. They weren't with you, Mara, or Vic on other missions. El-Dowd is the only mission on which all of you worked together."

"What happened to el-Dowd after we escaped?"

"Got away clean, went underground, and left his business to others. We suspect he kept giving the orders."

"He's still in charge of the opium crop in the southern regions?" Raven said.

"He's grown. He made take-over bids on the other regions, clashed with most of them, and kept the spoils."

"How much does he control now?"

"Southern and northern regions. The rest he keeps taking pot shots at to keep them from getting too big."

"Did anybody else try for him?" Raven said.

"Doesn't appear so. There are token reports of possible sightings, but nothing anybody acted on."

"We were told he was a primary target. Why was he then ignored?"

"I don't know."

"What you're saying is nothing we attempted mattered, and el-Dowd only grew in power."

"Yes," Wilson said. "He'd also have the money to hire Fatima Najjar."

"Have you spoken with MI-Five or -Six about us yet?"

"I'm calling them next, Sam. Mara?"

"I'm here, Clark."

"I have something I need to ask you. A year ago, you wanted a referral to a psychiatrist—"

Her eyes widened. She glanced at Raven, who only shrugged. He couldn't talk about a subject of which he had no knowledge.

"Mara?"

"Yes."

"What did you tell him?"

"We talked about the el-Dowd mission. The caves."

Raven jumped in. "Do you think he leaked the information, Clark?"

"It's all we have right now, and we can make a connection. Mara talks to the shrink, then somebody starts killing off your team. How else would he know to *specifically* target all of you?"

Mara sat back against the couch cushion, frightened. Raven reached out to squeeze her hand in support, but she flinched and pulled away.

"Clark," Raven said, "give me and Mara some time. We'll talk about this and get back to you. Meanwhile, see what you can do with the Brits. I'd like to be able to fly out of here without getting stopped at the airport. Or anywhere else."

"Will do."

Raven ended the call without a goodbye. He stowed the phone in his shirt pocket.

He said to Mara, "Well?"

"This is *all* my fault!"

"Mara!" He grabbed her shoulders and turned her to face him. "Get hold of yourself. Now, who is this psychiatrist, and what did you tell him about el-Dowd?"

She whispered. "Everything."

"All of it?"

"*Everything*," she repeated. "I couldn't help it, Sam. I keep having nightmares. I still hear them talking before—" She inhaled sharply. "I *see* their faces! Or parts of their faces. One in particular. He's a blur, half in shadow, but dammit I think he means something, and I need to find out who he is!"

Raven let go of her and she turned away.

"I had hoped the psychiatrist might be able to help me visualize the face better. Maybe if I could ID the man—"

"The one you thought was American?"

"There was more than one!"

"I remember."

"He's the only one I saw up close." She looked back at him. "You think Dr. Harrison betrayed us?"

"We're going to find out. Very soon."

"I don't know if I'm up for anything rough. You should go alone."

"No," Raven said. "We go together."

"Sam—"

"Only you and he know precisely what you talked about," Sam said. "If he sees a potential victim face-to-face, and he's been talking out of school, it might help to break him down."

It was a flimsy excuse, he knew. If this Dr. Harrison had

betrayed them, Raven would make the man so miserable he'd confess to stealing candy as a teenager. He didn't need Mara there. But he didn't want to leave her alone.

The truth was he wanted Mara with him because he needed her support. He didn't want to get caught in a weak moment, either, and miss an important detail. Mara may have suffered the worst of them, but every member of the team had been closer to death than ever before. One simply doesn't bring up those memories without consequences.

"This doctor is in London?" he said.

"Yes. Frank Harrison. Private practice."

"Clark recommended him?"

"He sees a lot of the local CIA people and MI-Five and -Six people too. High clearance. Clark said I could talk freely."

"Clark had no idea exactly what you were going to tell him?"

"No, Sam."

"Okay." He took out his cell phone. "Let's plot our way to Dr. Frank Harrison's office, and make a plan."

"Are we going right now?"

"Yes."

The more time they wasted, a greater chance of failure arose.

Because if Dr. Frank Harrison had sold information to Basheer el-Dowd, he was a loose end.

And there were determined assassins in operation with orders to kill off loose ends.

CHAPTER FIFTEEN

Heading back into the city from the cottage made the trip longer. He'd shown Mara how to use one of his spare pistols, a Glock-19 semi-auto, and it was stowed in the glove box in case of emergency. Mara was at least familiar with the pistol from her days as an active operator, and it was simple to use. She only had to remember how to aim.

Doctor Frank Harrison kept an office on 2 Victoria Avenue. Traffic was at least light, and they reached the office in good time. Victoria Avenue was a dead-end cul-de-sac. Raven parked the car on the street a few blocks away, and they returned on foot.

It was 4:30. Mara said Dr. Harrison left his office at five o'clock every day to meet pals at his favorite pub.

"Does he see regular patients or only spies?"

"Both," she said.

The drab office building in which Harrison worked matched other drab buildings nearby. All displayed shades of brown and gray, and if the sun hadn't been out, the location might seem dreary indeed.

They entered the lobby, which was nothing more than an elevator. An OUT OF ORDER sign was on the elevator doors.

Raven followed Mara up the steps. She knew the way, and they climbed three flights. At the third floor, Mara was breathing hard, but not Raven. Another sign she wasn't in fighting shape.

They walked down a brown-carpeted hall, plain white walls on either side. Brown doors marking the offices. Raven counted several therapist offices. Mara finally stopped at a door marked #357. Dr. Harrison's name was on the name plate stuck in the center.

He followed Mara into the waiting room.

The receptionist, a middle-aged blonde with hair going gray, smiled.

"Did you have an appointment today, Mara?" the receptionist said.

Mara stood before the woman's desk. "No, but we need to see Dr. Harrison. Tell him it's a direct request from Clark Wilson in the US."

"He's busy right now, I don't—"

"Please tell him, Tammy, it's important."

"Very well." She told them to have a seat while she lifted the handset of her telephone, a sour look on her face. The doctor had his routine, and as the gatekeeper it was her job to make sure he kept to routine. Keep your boss happy and you're happy. Mara sat down on a couch across from the desk. Raven remained standing. He looked at a coffee table with magazines stacked in a staggered pattern. A glance at the covers on top showed current dates, so at least Harrison didn't keep too many old ones around.

The waiting room was spare but not without decoration. Pictures of calming nature scenes, and advisories about medications, hung on the wall. He wore the Nighthawk .45 under his jacket, minus the suppressor this time. A leather sap filled the right pocket of the jacket as well. The sap's tip, loaded with lead shot, came in handy as a persuader to those unwilling to talk. A gun wasn't always the best threat. Whack a guy a few times with the sap, and they usually turned to Jell-O and found ways to cooperate.

Raven hoped it wouldn't be necessary.

Tammy the receptionist delivered the message and said, "He'll see you right now, Mara."

Mara bounced from the couch. "We won't be long, I promise."

Raven followed her to a door marked Private. She walked into the inner office like she owned the place.

Frank Harrison was at least in his mid-60s, but had most of his hair, most of it gray, and too long for Raven's taste. The doctor reminded him of old hippies in the states who still wore their hair long despite being at an age where one should cease adherence to such a haircut. Any statements they'd made as a youth were far behind them; they only looked silly. But Raven had to admire their persistence. Nobody liked to get old, or admit they had nothing more to contribute once the kids were grown. Hanging on to an old haircut seemed to satisfy their desire for relevance in a world leaving them behind.

"What is it, Mara?" He spoke gruffly, with a light accent.

Mara Cole stood in front of the man's desk, looking down at him, as he refused to leave his seat.

Mara glanced over her shoulder. "Sam?"

Raven moved fast, startling Harrison with his speed. He grabbed two fistfuls of Harrison's tweet coat, hauled the doctor to his feet, and slammed him against the wall. Harrison's breath left him, his eyes startled, as Raven held him in place.

"What's the meaning of this? Mara, please! Get this oaf away from me!"

"Doctor, somebody is sharing secrets, and I want to know who you've talked to about our sessions."

"What? No! I'm not going to risk my clearance and I don't need money."

TERMINAL MEMORY | 89

"Three agents are dead, and they all have something in common," she said. "They were on the same mission I've talked to you about. Care to explain?"

"It wasn't me! Mara, I swear. I work with you people because I'm a patriot and I want to help."

Raven glared at the man despite the doctor keeping his attention on Mara.

Raven said, "That's cute."

"Who are you? I'm devoted to doing my part. You people take tremendous risks under extreme pressure. You sometimes need help. I'm here to provide help. Mara, this is crazy. If there's a leak, it didn't come from me!"

"You can tell us," Mara said, "or we send you to the ministry, and they don't be nice."

"What can I tell you?" The doctor started to sweat. "You can't make me lie!"

Raven watched the man's eyes. He didn't see any deception there. Truly, he didn't. Harrison wasn't lying. He was a civilian, not a trained operator. No way he'd be able to stand up against the force Raven represented.

"Sam?"

"I think he's right."

"Then let me go! My goodness, look at your face. Maybe I should be seeing *you*, too, whoever you are. You're obviously in need of somebody to talk to."

Raven let go of the tweed coat and took two steps back. Harrison adjusted his jacket, wiped his face, and gave them both a defeated look.

"Clark sent you?" he said.

"This was Clark's idea."

"The man has gone insane. I should set up an office in the

US. Clearly, I'm needed there."

On shaky legs, Harrison returned to his desk chair and dropped. He wiped his face again, rubbing his hands on his slacks. "This is a lousy way to end the day," he said.

"I think he's a dead end."

"Good heavens, man, find another word!"

Mara stared at the doctor with her arms folded, her face stern, eyes focused on the doctor's reaction.

Raven wondered what she saw and what she might be thinking.

"You can bet I'll be on the phone to Clark later tonight," Harrison said. "This is outrageous."

"If you're lying," Mara said, "you'll be dropped into a hole so deep you'll never see the sun again."

"I live in London, dear," Harrison said. "We don't see the sun most of the year. It won't make any difference."

Raven said, "Let's go." He headed for the door and Mara followed. Tammy the receptionist, looking worried enough to be on the verge of calling the police, said nothing as they exited.

CHAPTER SIXTEEN

"Guess I need a new therapist."

Raven laughed.

"I'm glad you find this funny, Sam."

"I don't," he said, "not really."

They walked the two blocks to where Raven had left the rented BMW and climbed inside. They had a long drive back, and nothing to show for the effort.

Raven joined the flow of traffic.

"You believe him?" she said.

"I do, but I'm curious about what you're thinking."

"How could I think back there," she said, "while pretending to be tough again?"

"You handled it like a pro."

"I was shaking inside."

"Understandable."

"But I don't think anybody not properly trained could react like he did."

"My thoughts exactly."

"What do we tell Clark?"

"The leak is from somewhere else, or, worse, Basheer el-Dowd has nothing to do with this."

"What does your gut tell you?"

"We're on the right track, but without any leads to follow."

"It will change soon," she said.

"You're sure?"

"Positive."

Raven headed out of the city.

By the time they were on the road heading through the country, Raven said, "Get the Glock out, Mara."

Her face flushed with concern. She opened the glove box and took out the polymer-framed pistol.

"Why?"

"We have a friend who stayed with us all the way from London, and now he's exposed. We're the only two cars out here."

"Does that mean—"

"It means the last time we made this trip, I watched other cars turn off the road. This one isn't."

"But it doesn't mean they're after us."

"We aren't in a position to take any chances, are we?"

She snapped back the Glock's slide to chamber a round. "No, we aren't."

The nice thing about the country, Raven decided, is it was the perfect place for a gun fight.

There was no way to leave the road turning right; the edge of the road gave way to open field. On the left, trees, now and then a driveway. The car behind refused to turn into any of them.

He didn't think the BMW sedan would go well off-road. He pressed the accelerator, letting the engine growl. The extra speed took them further away from the pursuit car. Raven watched in the mirror. The other driver sped up too, his headlamps growing larger.

"I'm going to turn off," Raven said. "Get out of the car, and we'll set up a crossfire."

Mara was already nervous, sweat coating her forehead. Her wide eyes took in the scenery around them. The instincts were still there, buried deep, bubbling to the surface, albeit slowly. She'd look around to find cover, concealment, a place to fight.

"Can you do it?" he said.

"If not, we get killed," she said, "and I have no intention of getting killed."

"Good."

Raven spotted a break in the trees ahead, slowed the BMW, and made the turn, the car jolting as it left the paved road. The ground was dry and uneven. Shifting into Park, he bolted from the driver's seat. Mara followed. Raven shouted for her to get to cover while he knelt in front of the bonnet with the .45 filling his right hand. The residual heat of the engine bay made the car hot, but it was better to be singed than shot.

The other car, another sedan, cut across the opposing lane and stopped on the shoulder. The passenger climbed out, the driver sliding across the seat to exit as well. The passenger sprayed fire from a submachine gun over the roof of the car, giving his partner time to get out. Once again, they faced a pair of killers.

Raven hit the dirt as the bullets flew around him, snapping twigs, chunking into tree trunks. Debris landed around him, and he shook his head as a piece of tree bark landed in his hair. The gunner was firing for effect, not aiming. Raven made himself a smaller target by moving to the center of the hood. He aimed around the front tire.

The .45 kicked in his hand, the shooter ducking and moving to the boot of his car, the driver shooting over the bonnet. The BMW blocked Raven's view of the bonnet and he hoped Mara had a sight picture.

Mara's Glock cracked in quick succession, a burst of four or five rounds, and the driver let out a yell.

"One down!" she shouted.

That left only the passenger, who sprayed a burst Raven's way. He was a small target like Raven, hunkered down, but he'd left a knee partially exposed below the bumper. Raven took careful aim. His shot popped the knee like a balloon, and the shooter cried out as he tumbled onto the road.

Raven leaped up and charged over the uneven dirt. He reached the road as the shooter raised his weapon to fire while on his back. Raven had hoped to question him, but there was nothing to do but fire the Nighthawk again and turn the man's face into mush. The bullet carried through the man's head, blasting out the back. The gunner flopped once, arms falling to his sides, his legs spread.

Raven lowered his gun and ran around to the front of the car to examine the driver. Mara's burst had stitched a ragged pattern through his chest, one round through his throat.

Mara ran up beside him. "You okay?"

"No holes I wasn't born with." Raven brushed dirt off his clothes.

"How did they find us?"

"Maybe we should ask your doctor friend."

"Or Clark."

"It had better not be Clark."

"Somebody else in the office?"

"We can't discuss this here."

Raven started for the BMW and she hurried to join him. Raven backed the car onto the road, and drove forward again, kicking up a cloud of dust behind them.

"Good shooting," he told her.

"It's like riding a bike. You put a lighter trigger in this

gun, too."

"See?"

She put the Glock back into the glove box, wiping her hands on her jeans.

He glanced at her. She seemed calm; nervousness gone. Maybe she felt better for having taken a measure of control.

"Promise me something," she said.

"Anything."

"You won't run away on me."

"Never."

"I can't do this alone, Sam."

"Hey." He patted her leg. She didn't flinch this time. "We're a team. All the way to the end. And then you'll never see me again."

She didn't say anything more.

Her lack of reply made Raven feel sad. Perhaps the ice between them was thawing, but not enough. Not yet.

But he wasn't going to run. She needed him. And, deep down, he needed her. He'd lost too much already. He didn't want to lose anything more, even if she forced him from her life at the end.

He hoped she didn't.

CHAPTER SEVENTEEN

It felt good shooting the bastard.

Mara had followed instructions and found cover straight away. She dropped behind a tree with its narrow trunks split into a V, and in the V she braced her pistol. Her instructors had always said a spot to rest a gun gave better control than free hand. She'd remembered.

The driver of the car hadn't seen her, exposing himself as he sought to hide from Raven's gun. Her sights had found him, and she pulled the trigger without a second thought. One is none, her instructor had said, about bullet placement. Two is one, three is better. She'd fired more than three because of the lightweight trigger. The light nine-millimeter with its low bore axis was easy to control in rapid fire. The killer pitched over on the ground and stopped moving.

Mara felt very satisfied with the kill. One more for Billy, Carlos, and Vic.

And then you'll never see me again.

She wasn't sure what to respond with and was afraid her silence only emphasized her earlier point to Raven. She didn't want to hurt him, but also didn't want to be hurt *by* him. Something terrible had happened to make Raven step back into a life of constant violence. He was too good with his gun. It meant he used it often.

But like her, he had secrets he'd never tell.

Maybe it might help if she told some of her own.

There was only one way to find out.

Another late night.

Wilson sat at his desk. Classified reports on operations around the globe formed a pile in one corner. Not everything came on a tablet. He had to sign the reports and pass them up the chain to the eventual archivist who filed all the paperwork.

But he wasn't doing paperwork. The stack only provided a visual distraction to his phone conversation. The voice on his speaker phone had a British accent and the conversation wasn't cordial.

"We don't like," said Virgil Stout of MI6, "Americans running around London shooting people."

"Virgil, I've explained the problem. And why are you more concerned with my people than all the dead bodies they're leaving you to clean up?"

"The clean-up has created a headache for us."

"Have you identified any of the bodies?"

"The first batch is still being processed, and we found some new ones today on a country road."

"We'd appreciate any help you're willing to give us, Virgil. We have nothing."

"Hard to believe."

"There's only a theory, and it's not proven. Meanwhile I have three former agents dead, and two on the run."

"If you are in contact with them, we want them out of the country. They will not be flagged or accosted at any airport or train station. Tell them to get out."

"In exchange for identities on the dead killers, yes?"

"I will call you personally," Stout said. "Give me another twenty-four hours."

"Sixteen."

"As soon as possible."

"Thank you, Virgil."

Wilson pressed a button to hang up the call and inhaled deep, exhaling with frustration. The Brits were mad, and he didn't blame them, but they didn't understand the problem. The incidents weren't related to a current CIA mission. Langley couldn't pull the plug. They faced a delicate problem, and each passing hour brought more unanswered questions. And more bodies like the two found on the country road. Raven and Mara might end up dead before any question received an answer.

Somebody knocked on the door frame of Wilson's office. Wilson looked up. Paul Heinrich stood there holding a file folder.

"You have answers, Paul?"

"Probably," Heinrich said.

Wilson gestured to the seat in front of his desk. Heinrich took the seat, set the folder on crossed legs, and gave Wilson the rundown, referencing notes in the file.

"I checked the accounts we know Basheer el-Dowd uses, and there's been some transfers."

"Large amounts?"

"Yes."

"To where?"

"A company in Turkey with a disconnected phone and the given address is an empty lot."

"We still don't know if the money was used to hire Fatima Najjar."

"I also made a query about any recent sightings of her."

"Was she in Turkey?"

"Yes. Until two weeks ago."

"Billy Anzell was killed two weeks ago."

"And Carlos Vega two days after Anzell, and Victor Matson a week later."

"All right."

Heinrich rose and left the office.

Wilson grabbed a pen and absently tapped it on the desktop. He needed more than a coincidence. Fatima Najjar leaving Turkey after a bunch of money was sent to a Turkish shell company wasn't enough to hang a case on.

Wilson reconsidered. It wasn't a coincidence; it was a thread to add to the one they had. Billy Anzell and Carlos Vega were new to Raven's team when they hit el-Dowd. And if they pulled on the thread hard enough, maybe the pattern would unravel and give them answers. He wanted a connection between el-Dowd and Fatima Najjar. The bosses on seventh floor wouldn't authorize a second termination protocol without hard data.

But it was late. He needed to get home and actually see his family. The pit had cleared out hours earlier; only he and Heinrich remained. Wilson grabbed his coat, locked his office, and told Heinrich to turn off his computer and go home for the night.

Heinrich didn't need to be told twice.

Mara Cole said, "You're a good cook."

"It's something to do," Raven said. "I watch the cooking shows and try things."

They'd finished dinner ten minutes earlier, and sat in the living room, on separate ends of the couch. They held steaming cups of tea. Raven had no radio or television in the cottage, telling her he liked the quiet. She told him she always had the TV on to fill silence, otherwise her thoughts ran away on her.

"I'm sorry I hurt you," she said.

Raven raised his eyebrows. "Apology accepted."

"I wouldn't blame you if you hated me."

"How could I? We had a good relationship until—"

"Afghanistan. Say it."

"Afghanistan," he repeated. "We all lost something in those caves, Mara."

She looked into her cup, finally taking a sip. "I let everybody down."

"How?"

"By not being stronger."

"What happened wasn't your fault."

"You try telling *yourself* sometime."

"How do you know I don't tell myself every day?"

"For the same reason?"

"Other reasons," he said.

"And maybe you wouldn't have those other reasons if I hadn't—"

"Don't start."

"There was no way I could continue with you, Sam." She kept her head down. "I told you I don't have any friends. I tried, but I can't trust anybody."

"Mara—"

She set her tea on the coffee table and left the couch. "I'm taking a shower and going to bed."

Raven watched her leave the room. He didn't say anything.

By the time Raven finished his tea, Mara left the bathroom and shut the door to her bedroom. Raven decided he might as well turn in himself. He'd call Clark Wilson later. They needed to get out of London, and he wanted to know if Wilson had cleared the way with the British government.

He lay in bed a long time, thinking about what Mara said. Maybe things would have turned out differently had he and

Mara stayed together. Maybe it would be her picture in the locket instead of who resided there now.

He had nothing but *what ifs* and *maybes*.

He felt himself dozing off when Mara entered the room. She shed her bathrobe, only her birthday suit underneath, and climbed into bed beside him. Raven moved over to give her room. She clung to him.

"Hold me please. I can't be alone."

He felt her naked body against his, her body heat enveloping him, and he put both arms around her. She felt light; almost fragile. Her soft breasts pressed against his chest and it was hard not to respond to the stimulation. Then her mouth found his, her kisses hesitant at first, probing for permission, then stronger as he responded. They melted together, each taking solace in the other's presence. They quickly hopped a wave of pleasure as she let him roll on top and guided him inside her. Mara dug her nails into his back and kept her legs tight around him as if hanging on for fear of drowning. Finally, they settled on calm seas, wrapped in a mutual embrace neither needed to acknowledge.

CHAPTER EIGHTEEN

Mara awoke with a scream.

She jolted Raven awake, who pulled her to him as she tried to get out of bed. She was shaking.

"What's wrong?"

She whispered. "Nightmare."

He lay back and pulled her to him. She buried her head in his chest hair.

"I saw his face again."

He rubbed her back.

"I was saying something to him."

"What?"

"It was gibberish. Meant nothing." She squeezed him. "I'm glad you're here."

"Is this the first time you've talked in this nightmare?"

"No. I'd hoped...Dr. Harrison...might help me find an answer."

Fat chance now.

Raven said nothing more. A glance out the window showed the early signs of dawn.

The only goal in his mind was getting out of London and striking back. The solution to the mystery might only be found in action. Raven started thinking of options. Wilson had convinced him el-Dowd was the man responsible, but how do you find a man the CIA had lost track of? He was a needle in a global haystack.

There had to be a way.

Mara dozed off again and snored quietly while Raven remained awake. She shifted, but her head remained on his chest. He stroked her hair and wondered what it might take to free Mara from her continued captivity.

Basheer el-Dowd felt good in the tailored Savile Row suit.

He cut a striking figure, lean and muscular, the sharp features of his face catching many a woman's eye. He wasn't in Brussels to meet women. He was there to meet a contact, and the sooner the two men spoke, the sooner he could return to Afghanistan.

He sat in a suite in The Brussels Hotel, on a beige couch with a window behind him overlooking the sprawling city. He stared at the blue sky.

Whoever designed the room color scheme at the hotel went heavy on beige. The couch, bedspread, and the paint on the wall matched; the carpet was light tan. It all looked...bland. The paintings hung on one wall were generic illustrations of city life, stick figures and cars with swirly lines for exhaust fumes. Not the art el-Dowd preferred. He admired the old masters and the new generation carrying on their work. His penthouse condo in Bahrain contained a terrific facsimile collection of rare pieces. One didn't need originals to admire when a copy sufficed.

Great art brought calm to his busy mind. Detailed paintings were the best. Whenever he looked at any section, he discovered something not seen before.

He'd learned to appreciate art from his father, who'd had a tremendous collection. What he didn't have, he collected photographs of. He wanted to admire the great works whether he had the real thing, a copy, or a computer printout. His father's work with the Mujahedeen rebels during the Soviet occupation kept him from following his passion as much as he wanted.

The "family business" for the el-Dowds was opium cultivation. El-Dowd the Elder's firm control of production in the Helmand Province eventually passed to his son, Basheer. The son quickly became the biggest narco trafficker in the region. He'd supported the fight against the Taliban during the US invasion via drug money. His cash purchased weapons and support for militias engaged by the United States. The reputation his father established made the Americans comfortable using his resources. They, in turn, ignored his drug business. The fact his opium, refined into heroin, made its way to the US didn't bother the American administrations. His competitors? They didn't like it and tried to take him out.

But he struck back. Hard.

Raid after raid broke the backs of el-Dowds's fellow narco kings, leaving him to scoop up the remains. He'd grown his empire from the south, to the western provinces, and areas of the northern regions. The northern cartels provided the biggest challenge. But el-Dowd felt confident he'd wipe them out and enjoy the spoils any day now. Stragglers who stuck around to fight would meet the might of his private army.

The CIA, always interested in sources of money for black ops programs, aided el-Dowd for a cut of the proceeds. Some of it lined the pockets of the Agency representatives, and US leadership.

And now his American allies were proposing a new plan. They would increase the amount of stateside Afghan heroin traffic using mafia connections eager for a cut of the profits.

There was one problem, though.

Well, *five* problems, each to be solved individually. While three of those problems had been removed from circulation, two remained, and needed to be killed before el-Dowd, the Americans, and their new mob friends lost *billions* of dollars.

El-Dowd checked his watch. His contact was five minutes late. He reached for the glass of white wine on the table in front of him and swallowed another mouthful.

The guard near the door, in a black suit opposite el-Dowd's navy blue, stood against the wall with his hands clasped in front of him. The young guard's suit wasn't as tailored as el-Dowd's. The gun in the guard's shoulder holster bulged under his left arm. El-Dowd examined the young man, his stoic expression. The kid was probably glad to be out of the desert for a change.

El-Dowd set his glass down. He frowned at his watch. Seven minutes.

A coded knock on the door broke him from his thoughts. After a pause, the person on the other side repeated the code. El-Dowd nodded to the guard, who took out his Beretta hand-gun before approaching the door.

The guard pulled the door open, keeping it between him and the arrival. The man in the hallway stood alone.

El-Dowd said, "Welcome, James." He stood.

James Duran ignored the guard as he entered the room. The guard closed the door and resumed his position.

James Duran loomed over the shorter el-Dowd. Both were trim, their power suits establishing both were of means. They shook hands.

"Glass of wine?"

"I'll take one."

Duran sat on the couch as El-Dowd filled the second glass on the table. Duran took the offered glass.

"Forgive me," el-Dowd said, "if I don't make a toast."

He sat.

"This meeting was supposed to celebrate a victory," Duran said.

"Sam Raven and Mara Cole are still alive, Fatima Najjar is dead, and humiliated as well. They found her naked in a hotel room with part of her face gone."

"I'm aware."

"We've lost many soldiers. Yes, this is no time to celebrate."

James Duran drank some wine. He held the glass in his left hand, and the cuffs of his jacket and shirt shifted to reveal a silver Rolex Sea Dweller.

"Where are they?" el-Dowd said.

"Last contact, driving out of London."

"Where?"

"We don't know. The team was killed before Raven and Cole reached their destination."

"We should have handled Raven first."

"He's tough to find sometimes."

"What matters is we find him now. What are you people proposing next?"

"He's in touch with Clark Wilson at CIA," Duran said, "like we thought he'd be. All we have to do is stay close to Wilson."

"Will it be difficult?"

Duran shook his head. "I'm Wilson's boss, remember? My clearance is higher than his. I can monitor what he's looking at."

"I'd like to know what he's looking at."

"So far," Duran said, "they've checked into your accounts, so they know about the money transfer to Turkey. They've pulled all the reports on missions Raven and his team participated in. I'm not sure your name has appeared yet, or if they've discovered how the murders link to you."

"In other words—"

"He may not know you're responsible. Yet. Best case, Raven

goes on a wild goose chase looking for a bad guy and gets killed in the process. Problem solved."

"They can't have identified me if searching old reports for clues is their only step so far."

"We'll tap into Wilson's phone calls and clone his cell phone if I can get close enough. I need to get him away from headquarters to do that, though. Cell phones aren't allowed in the building."

El-Dowd swallowed more wine and set his glass on the table. "I'm holding back sending more men into the field until we know where Raven and Cole are."

"I'd suggest not sending more at all."

"Why?" el-Dowd said.

"If any of them are captured, they might talk. They'll be a direct connection to you."

"Who do you suggest instead?"

"We have our own people. They'll carry out orders without asking questions. We've used them before."

"But *you*, Mr. Duran, can be connected to me as well, if you ever find yourself in custody."

The American shook his head. "No. We pay them through a cutout. They've never seen me."

"And the go-between who will handle this deal?"

"She's not aware I'm the one giving the orders. She receives a coded message, confirms with a scrambled call. My voice is disguised when I speak with her. It's how we do it, Basheer. No comebacks."

"These people are agency?"

"Good heavens, no. Mercenaries. We pay them, they do the work."

"Very well. *You* are in charge of killing Raven now."

Duran drank some more wine.

"And the rest?" el-Dowd said.

"We're moving ahead as planned. We've solidified an arrangement with local talent to process the raw material you send to us."

"The gangsters?"

"Yes."

"They know nothing of my involvement?"

"None," Duran said. "All they know is we represent a collective with access to raw opium they can process into heroin. They will process and sell in exchange for the cut we offered."

"They won't make trouble?"

"Oh, you bet they will," Duran said, "when they think the time is right. We'll handle it."

El-Dowd closed his eyes, let out a breath. He looked out the window.

"Such a beautiful city," he said.

Duran gave the view a quick glance. "It's not New York City, but it's nice."

"You New Yorkers. So loyal."

Duran smiled. "It's a sickness."

"I'm leaving tomorrow morning. I'm going to have a nice dinner tonight, visit a gallery, and then it's back to work."

Duran finished the wine and set the empty glass on the table. He rose, straightening his jacket. "Work never ends."

El-Dowd did not get up. "But it is rewarding."

"Be seeing you." Duran walked to the door. The guard, already standing by, opened the door, and Duran exited into the hallway. The guard shut the door again.

El-Dowd refilled his glass.

James Duran crossed the busy lobby to a lounge where he dropped onto another couch. Hotel guests sat around him, caught up in their own conversations. The adjacent restaurant was half-full of patrons. He dialed a phone number on his cell and reached a man in Washington, DC.

"It's about time," the DC man said. He had a gravelly voice, the attitude of a man tired of waiting.

"Meeting successful," Duran said. "Solving the problem is our responsibility now."

"Inform the appropriate parties once we get a location."

"Of course. We'll be in the clear soon."

"Soon," the DC man said, "isn't fast enough."

Duran remained silent. He wasn't going to argue with the boss.

"Report to me when you get home," the DC man said.

Duran checked his Rolex. "My flight leaves in two hours, Senator. See you soon."

CHAPTER NINETEEN

Senator Aiden Welles hung up the phone with relief. The stress of the last two weeks had made sleeping tough. He didn't mind the early morning hour, and the activity invigorated his old bones. The cash windfall from the el-Dowd arrangement would be his "retirement score". Soon he'd exit public life and spend the rest of his days living it up.

Aiden Welles, white-haired, war vet, career Senator from Arizona. Defense hawk, media darling. He'd never eyed higher office than his senate seat. There was no reason to be president when he had access to more graft than he could grab. Kick-backs fueled his fire, from lobby groups to the not-so-lowest bidders on defense contracts. Anybody who wanted to deal with Welles had to answer one question. *"What's it worth to you, and how much are you giving me up front?"*

He ran a hand through his white hair as he walked down a hallway to his bedroom. The woman waiting in bed, half his age, sat up reading.

"Finish your call?"

Welles smiled. Lucy Hunt, his assistant, dead wife replacement, and all-around Girl Friday. She wore a thin negligee. The garment drooped in front, providing an unrestricted view of the finest rack in Washington, DC.

"Business is done for the night."

She laughed. "It's three a.m."

"Whatever."

He undid the belt around his robe as she put her book on the nightstand.

She said, "It is time to legislate?" She bit her lower lip, still slick with glistening red lipstick. Her face was lightly made up. Enough to look good, but still retain the natural flair Welles preferred.

Welles dropped the robe. His rotund naked body showed his age as much as the lines on his face, but Lucy Hunt didn't seem to mind. She dropped the shoulder strap of the negligee some more. There was no delay on the effect on Welles.

"Oh, it's time to legislate," Welles said. The only thing now on his mind was plunging into her amazingly supple body. "We're going to legislate till the sun comes up."

She laughed as he yanked the covers away, grabbed her slender ankles, and pulled her to the center of the bed. He climbed on top of her, and their legislating began in earnest.

For Welles, there was no better stress relief.

Leading a double life certainly had its share of stress.

Aiden Welles hadn't always engaged in duplicity. His career started with wins in his home state. The senate followed. He established himself as a firm patriot, but one willing to negotiate with the other side when policy conflicts required compromise. He'd become a golden boy for the effort, the one each side could talk to with no fear of partisan bickering.

There were areas where Welles didn't budge, defense spending being one of them. And attacking America's enemies before they struck. After his selection to the Senate Intelligence Committee, he found a new forum to push his "defense first" agenda.

His dedication caught the attention of certain elements in the Central Intelligence Agency. They wanted a congressional ally to smooth the rails on matters never discussed in the open. They showed him the benefits of certain alliances with other players in the shadow world. Those alliances not only assured funding for defense projects, i.e. covert operations, but funneled cash into his own pockets as a reward for his dedication.

Enter Basheer el-Dowd.

The Afghanistan opium had played a major role in helping the United States oust the Taliban, and *his* reward was protection. He'd outlived many of the other proxies the CIA had used; he'd become a valuable asset. He'd be allowed to remain in business as long as he made the agreed to payoffs. Now and then, he supplied information the CIA used to show success in the so-called War on Terror.

When he brought up the subject of expanding into the US market during one of his visits to el-Dowd, the Afghan opium king wondered how it might work.

Welles proposed a deal with the DC mafia clan, who dearly wanted a larger slice of the world drug business.

El-Dowd agreed.

Secretly, the deal was closed.

And then the problems began. Some dolt decided el-Dowd need to be taken out. Another dolt approved the plan. The CIA sent out a team to do the job. Welles ordered Duran to make sure the mission failed.

Which lead to *more* problems.

With, hopefully, solutions in progress.

Paul Heinrich appeared in Clark Wilson's office doorway.

"Mr. Duran is here to see you, Clark."

Duran stood behind Heinrich, a head taller than the young

CIA analyst. Wilson set his pen down and waved Duran into the office. Heinrich departed, pulling the office door shut.

Duran sat on front of Wilson's desk without being offered the chair.

Wilson scratched his nose. Duran was the Assistant Director of Operations, overseeing Special Activities, and the man Wilson reported to. He crossed his legs and said, "What's the latest?"

Wilson provided a detailed update and mentioned his chat with the British.

"Have they IDed any of the bodies yet?" Duran asked.

"Virgil called to say information is pending."

"How many names?"

"They've matched two of the assassins to el-Dowd's organization."

"He used his own guys?"

"He hired Fatima Najjar too, we think. Money transfer to a shell company might be hers, we aren't sure. Her autopsy was...interesting."

"How?"

Wilson waved it off. "They found some DNA. In her...you know. Traced to a man name David Owen."

"Who?"

"Exactly. Total cipher. He's reportedly a sales rep for a medical device company, but the company in question has never heard of him."

"Raven?"

"Probably. He left out a few details of how he got her under his gun."

Duran shook his head. "Same old Sam."

"He's the only chance we might have of unraveling what's going on, Jim. We need to work with him."

"I didn't say no. By all means. What about Mara?"

"She's in rough shape."

"Of course."

"But she'll be of use too."

"How?"

"She's been seeing one of our psychiatrists in London. Harrison. She wanted him to help her sort out what happened in Afghanistan."

"Why would she do that?"

"Therapy, Jim. Some people need it. You all right? You look like you've seen a ghost."

"Something I ate last night. Been bothering me all morning. What did she talk to Harrison about?"

Wilson shrugged. "Your guess is as good as mine. She won't tell me."

"Uh-huh."

"PTSD stuff, most likely. Being captured on the el-Dowd mission wrecked all of them."

"If she's repressed a memory, think a good shrink might help her dig it up?"

"Do you think a repressed memory might give us a clue? Maybe she saw something she shouldn't have? We have no idea why they've been targeted, or why it's taken so long. If she saw something she shouldn't have, why worry about it now? What has changed to make them a threat now?"

"That doctor is *Harrison*, you said?"

"Yeah. Raven and Cole already confronted him about leaking information, but he claims he didn't."

"You believe him?"

"I had Heinrich check his financials," Wilson said, "and he appears clean. No sudden influx of cash, no increased spending habits."

"Keep an eye on him."

"MI5 is on it. They'll let us know."

"I want our people there."

"The Brits won't agree."

"Who says we tell the Brits?"

Wilson shrugged again. "Okay. I'll call the embassy and have them put a team on him."

Duran rose from the chair. "I want to know what he's doing every minute of the day. With three of our people dead, former agents or not, I don't trust anybody."

"I'll call them now."

Duran muttered goodbye and let himself out of the office.

Wilson reached for his desk phone.

CHAPTER TWENTY

Cell phones are prohibited inside CIA headquarters. The Agency believes cell phones pose a security risk if hacked. Microphones or cameras could be activated to monitor classified meetings. Anybody caught with a cell phone on campus faced termination. The internal security department ran a constant electronic scan to monitor for cell frequencies.

The cell phone issue posed a problem for James Duran, but a solution wasn't hard. If he wanted to clone Wilson's phone to hear conversations with Sam Raven, he needed to get close to Wilson when he had his phone on him. But Duran was in no rush. He'd find the right time, once he had the proper software installed on a cell phone of his own.

He drove off the campus and into downtown Langley, where he parked at a Starbucks. After paying for a coffee, he returned to his car and dug his cell out of the glove box.

He dialed el-Dowd.

"What is it?"

"They've figured out it was you." Duran updated el-Dowd on his conversation with Wilson.

"Any good news?"

"Raven and Cole have left London, but there's a lead we

need to check out."

"Which is?"

"A shrink named Harrison. We need to find out what he knows. It may help. He was Mara Cole's therapist. She talked to him about what happened in Afghanistan. I'm afraid she has a detail locked in her memory somewhere. Her memories will hurt us more than the website."

"How could Mara Cole remember anything in her state at the time? She was starving, dehydrated, injured."

"The mind is complex, Basheer. She *might* recall something. A face. Anything."

"And testify? With no proof but hazy recollections?"

"That's where you're wrong. She won't need to testify. All she'll need to do is tell Sam Raven. He doesn't bother with proof, Basheer. He'll come for us no matter what, and then Mara will go to that damn website and tell her story. It will explode from there."

"It will be forty-eight hours before I can get anybody there."

"Don't worry. I'll call the people I told you about and get them operational. We'll handle it," Duran said.

"You sound nervous, James."

"The stakes have risen a little higher than we expected."

"Yes, they have. Handle the doctor."

Duran ended the call, put the cell phone back, and returned to the CIA campus.

He sat and drank coffee in his car while listening to sports updates on WJFK.

The entire crisis started over a somebody claiming to be a former special ops soldier calling himself "Conspiracy Man". He put up a web site accusing the CIA of human rights abuses, foreign election interference, unlawful assassination, and forming alliances with Afghanistan drug kingpins for its own purposes. The accusations were nothing new. The CIA had faced similar finger-pointing for decades. Entire forests had been leveled to print books on the CIA's alleged crimes.

But "Conspiracy Man" had something other sites, and stacks of books, did not. He specifically accused Senator Aiden Welles of solidifying a protection deal with Basheer el-Dowd. He included pictures of a much younger Senator Aiden Welles meeting Basheer el-Dowd at his Afghanistan compound. The pictures showed the two men touring poppy fields, sitting in meetings, toasting each other with cups of tea. Other pictures showed Welles shaking hands with el-Dowd's second- and third-in-command, both of whom were known jihadists.

Duran, as a junior CIA paramilitary officer at the time, had been in charge of security, and stayed close to Welles during the visit. He recognized the people, the landmarks; the photos were not fake. A member of the security team had brought a hidden camera on the mission and documented the visit.

The photos had not yet spread to the public, but they were easy enough to debunk. Yes, Welles had met el-Dowd; no, not to strengthen the ridiculous "CIA drug connection". Instead, Welles had enlisted el-Dowd's support in classified operations against opium cartels. El-Dowd was a reformer; he hated what the drug trade was doing to his country. Details classified, no further comment.

Welles and el-Dowd decided the pictures required direct action. They wanted "Conspiracy Man" found, his website destroyed, and other potential threats wiped out.

Duran had asked Welles why he had a sudden sense of urgency on the matter.

"That visit was three years ago, Senator. If you didn't think anybody was a threat then, why now?"

"It's more than only me, the CIA, and el-Dowd now," Welles reasoned. "We're extending our reach, and our new friends are part of that. This is about protecting the triumvirate."

"The *what?*"

"The three sides of the triangle, James. Christ, do you ever read above a third-grade level?"

Duran countered that it was best to let the pictures exist and debunk when required. Killing a bunch of current and former agents would only draw unwanted attention. But Welles feared the Italians, his new friends, more than any comebacks from a series of killings.

"They're the *mafia*, get it? They'll kill us all to protect *themselves*. You want that?"

"We can control them," Duran said. "CIA and the mob go way back."

"Too much money at stake. Get it done. I want them gone."

Duran didn't like orders, but he did like his extra income. He promised to take care of the problem.

The remaining members of the security team made the death list first. Most were still active, simple to find, and killed during the course of deployment. Some met with "accidents". The only member of the team not killed had yet to be found, and Duran figured he was the website operator they wanted. Simple process of elimination.

When Welles remembered the CIA prisoners who had not only been at the el-Dowd compound at the time of the visit, but escaped shortly after, Duran looked up the mission file and added their names.

The ex-agents were supposed to meet the same fate as the rest, only Sam Raven hadn't lost his touch.

Raven, Mara, and the other three field operators never should have been captured to begin with. They certainly never should have been left alive. El-Dowd let greed get in the way of good sense. His jihadist buddies would pay good money for CIA prisoners. He'd planned to sell the agents for whatever use the jihadists dreamed up.

If they hadn't escaped, the trade would have gone through, and there'd be less of a mess to clean up.

And Welles never should have raped Mara Cole. The two men who weren't supposed to have made mistakes made the biggest ones. They put the whole plan in jeopardy whether they admitted doing so or not. The money involved kept them from backing off. It was easier to try and solve the problem than give up the money.

Duran had people looking for "Conspiracy Man". It hadn't been hard to determine his identity. He was the one member of the security team not dead—Martin Green. Discharged from the agency because of mental problems, he'd vanished without a trace. Duran's people might as well have been searching for a ghost. Dude had serious skills he used to stay hidden. Attempts to contact him via the website and lure him into a trap had not succeeded.

Duran turned off the radio and brought his coffee back into the building. He had calls to make to expert killers who wouldn't fail to kill Raven and Cole, unlike el-Dowd's brainless gorillas.

The engines of the chartered King Air droned quietly in the cabin.

Mara Cole sat across from Raven in a plush leather seat. She watched him talk on the phone, another conversation with Clark Wilson at Langley.

She thought about what had happened between them.

Mara hadn't planned on getting into Raven's bed. Being alone in a strange bedroom, her mind racing, left her disturbed and in need of security. Raven was the only other person available, and she'd long since given up on clutching childhood teddy bears for security. Making love hadn't been on her agenda either, but she hadn't resisted when nature took over. She needed close contact, and he was willing, and she'd grabbed onto him as if her life hung in the balance.

Which it did.

It was the first time she'd been with a man since the horror in the cave, and she wondered what it meant. Was she falling in love with him again, or using him as a shield? She did not need more confusion running through her mind. Dr. Harrison might have said she was reaching for anything of comfort in a time of great need.

Breakfast had been uncomfortably quiet. Neither knew how to approach the subject, or, in her case, wondered if they should bother. It had happened. She felt her inner defensive walls falling as a result. She needed to shed those walls in order to help solve their problem.

Which lead her to a bigger question. What would she do once they found resolution, and Raven was out of her life again?

She listened as he spoke, with no more answers than she'd started with.

"I'm cutting you off, Clark."

Sam Raven barked the statement after Wilson's update. Raven now knew for certain Basheer el-Dowd was responsible. Between the mission file, and connecting the London killers to the drug lord, Raven didn't need further proof.

Time to go to war.

Time to show el-Dowd the meaning of *payback*.

Wilson didn't respond happily. "You're doing *what?*"

"I have a plan, and my own people. We're going to settle this my way."

"Sam, you can't. This is as important to us as it is you."

"Anything we talk about may end up in the wrong ears. You

know *that* as well as I do."

Wilson remained silent a moment, then, quietly, said, "I understand."

"It's going to get bloody."

"Watch your back, Sam. And Mara's."

"Bet on it."

"And Sam?"

"What?"

"Officially we can't help if you're going this route, but you and I go back a way, right?"

"We do."

"Call me. When you need me."

"You got us out of London," Raven said, "and it's all we needed."

"I'd like to think our friendship means a little more."

Raven said nothing. The silence felt heavy between them. Raven had nothing in common with Clark Wilson any longer. To expect nothing had changed between them was wrong on Wilson's part.

"Take care of yourself, Sam," Wilson finally said.

Raven hung up. He looked at Mara.

"Is that necessary?" she said.

"El-Dowd has hurt us, and we need to hurt him back. If we put enough pressure on, we'll draw him out of hiding."

"How do you intend to make this happen?"

Raven smiled. "I have friends in low places. Pardon me while I make more calls. There's food and drinks in the back if you want anything."

Mara glared at him but left her seat for the rear of the plane.

Raven made another call. The first of four.

He reached Oscar Morey in Stockholm after three rings.

"Where you at?" the older man said.

"In a plane over the ocean. Wonderful view. Wish you

were here."

"Sounds nice," Morey said.

Oscar Morey, Raven's friend, intelligence chief, and personal mentor, hadn't always been a good guy. If questioned about his association with Raven and his personal crusade against the world's predators, he'd deny knowing the man. Raven often targeted the type of criminal Morey had once been. But Morey had retired to Sweden to broker information to various parties, both good and bad. He'd left his old life behind.

Morey maintained a reputation throughout Europe as somebody who kept his mouth shut. One who managed never to spend a day in jail. With eyes and ears in a variety of dark places, he could compile a terrific amount of information given enough time.

"I need a full dossier on an Afghanistan drug lord named Basheer el-Dowd. Hear of him?"

"For sure. I'm on it."

"Hold the data until I call you back."

They said goodbye, and Raven made three more calls.

To an Armenian mercenary named Zaven Darbinian, "Darbo" to his friends, of whom Raven was one.

Third call: Lia Kenisova. Sexy Russian retrieval specialist and covert ace.

Last call: Roger Justice, an American freelance black ops veteran with an appropriate surname.

Raven referred to them as his Raiders. Allies to call when in dire need of extra firepower.

Like now.

CHAPTER TWENTY-ONE

Zaven Darbinian didn't know what was crawling across his back, but he dared not move to smack it away.

He lay in the overgrown forest overlooking what remained of a road. The crumbling pavement passed through a bombed-out village, abandoned after the Serbo-Croatian-Bosnian War. Homes, buildings, schools, all destroyed. They left behind piles of rubble, building skeletons barely standing on foundations. Whoever had lived here vanished long ago; he didn't even know the village's former name.

He wasn't there to wax poetic about the past, the horrors of war he knew all too well. Darbo had been fighting most of his life. He thrived on the danger, the dance with death yet to claim him. Someday, sure. The life span of a working mercenary wasn't long, but he could defy the odds, like "Mad Mike" Hoare. Mad Mike had died at 100-years-young after a mercenary career envied by all professional soldiers. Darbo bet he could achieve such longevity as well.

The Balkan mission was simple. One group of guys, it didn't matter who, were delivering a trunk full of gold to some other guys, who also didn't matter. The gold would pay for guns. Darbo had no idea where the guns were going; he didn't care. His job was to snag the gold and bring it to Bahrain. An oil mogul needed the gold bars to pay his ex-wife's alimony. He told his less-than-savory pals he didn't want to spend his own money, somebody told him about the gold, and the mogul reached out to Darbo. Darbo wanted to point out the mogul was setting himself up for a bigger problem later. Whoever owned the gold might want to know who took it. But it wasn't his job to counsel clients when they waved a big check in front of his rough-hewn face. If the client wanted the gold, Darbo planned to deliver. He'd be long gone before the mogul realized he'd messed with the wrong people.

From his position, Darbo watched the road. The insect on his neck dropped over the side to continue on its way. Birds chirped, trees and leaves rustled with the light breeze. The road might be crumbling but remained usable. The driver would bring the gold to the destination six kilometers away. There was no other road available.

Four more men in camouflage similar to Darbo's dark-green uniform were spread out nearby. Two of his men had positioned Claymore mines on the shoulder of the road, creating the kill box. Once those detonated, the truck's tires would turn to shredded wheat. All they had to do after was take care of the two men in the cabin and the two in the truck bed. Unless their intel was wrong, and Darbo didn't think so. He'd gathered the information himself.

Darbo and his crew carried Kalashnikovs, the latest and greatest AK-104 automatic rifles. Darbo's rifle came equipped with a GP-34 40mm grenade launcher mounted under the forward grip.

Of the four men with him, two other Armenians and a Frenchman, the one Darbo didn't like was the American, John Pratt. He was sloppy with his weapons, jocular, and asked too many questions about the gold. Darbo wouldn't have hired him unless he'd needed a fifth man, and other candidates hadn't been available. He kept Pratt close by; he sat to Darbo's left, so Darbo could keep his eyes on him.

The American concealed well in the forest, not only wearing his camo uniform, but a custom-made Ghillie suit. He looked like a pile of dead leaves mixed within the real dead leaves they found all around them. The suit further masked his shape.

Even the forest had partially given up, live green mixed with dead brown. The Balkans were depressing no matter where you looked.

The road continued past Darbo's position, deeper into the forest. It passed another bombed-out village before reaching civilization once again. Darbo knew the gun sellers wouldn't be far away once the shooting started. If they raced to the scene to see what was happening, there'd be another fight for sure. Darbo and his crew had the unenviable task of getting the trunk full of gold off the truck, putting it on a sled, and dragging it twenty clicks to their own vehicle. He'd wanted to avoid blowing up the original truck, but there was no road access to their extraction point. The road went straight to the gun sellers at the other end.

No matter what, the easy part had been the plan, and the set-up of the ambush.

Once the shooting began, it would all go to hell. Darbo was certain. Yet he grinned in anticipation. Good soldiers functioned best under stress.

He was a good soldier.

The chirping birds vanished, a flock breaking skyward from a tree across the road. The rumbling motor of a heavy vehicle finally replaced the sounds of nature. Darbo clicked his tongue against the roof of his mouth three times, the signal for the crew to make ready. His AK-104 tucked into his shoulder, Darbo waited for the truck and the Claymore blast.

Pratt readied his weapon as well. Darbo saw his focused eyes peeled for the target.

The truck appeared around the corner.

A heavy-duty pick-up of undetermined make, heavily customized. Painted with a green and black camo pattern, lifted, with huge tires carving through the dirt. The exhaust pipes had been rerouted behind the cabin to belch into the air. The short bed contained side mounts for fuel cans. No spare tires. Darbo wondered the rubber they rode on wasn't bullet resistant. Or *Claymore* resistant.

The truck rumbled closer. Darbo moved his left hand to the trigger of the GP-34. He wanted to blast the cabin with a grenade before using the rifle. The grenade should make short work of the pair in the cabin, the bullets a make-sure after thought.

The truck grew larger as it neared Darbo's position on the road. He'd mentally marked the middle of the kill zone where the Claymores had been set. He aimed to blast the truck front, middle, and back. The truck entered the zone. The driver and passenger, visible through the clear windscreen glass, were none the wiser.

The Frenchman, Martineau, detonated the trio of Claymores. The one-two-three blast rocked the ground. Darbo felt the vibrations through his body. The 3.2mm steel balls within the C-4-packed mine blasted out at nearly 4000 feet-per-second.

Every action has a reaction. As the steel balls shredded the exterior body panels, they popped the tires. The two huge tires returned their own volley, shards of hot rubber and pieces of steel belt. Debris hissed over Darbo's back.

The truck, tilted sharply on the passenger side, didn't move. The two gunners in the bed leaped over the opposite side. Martineau, Pratt, and the two Armenian mercenaries opened fire.

Their AK-104s crackled with intensity. Darbo triggered his grenade launcher. The two men in the cabin never made it out. The 40mm high-explosive cartridge shattered the windshield, exploding inside. The blast propelled a burst of hot flame, followed by black smoke, through the cabin. The explosion blew out the other two windows.

"Move in!" Darbo shouted. He broke cover, crashing through the overgrowth, running for the truck. The two survivors spread out, each taking one end. As one of them neared the mid-air front wheel, Darbo took him down with a burst from the AK. The rounds stitched the gunner stomach to chest, spinning him like a top. He crashed onto the hard-packed ground.

More AK fire, followed by a cheer from the Armenians. Second gunner down.

Darbo commanded the Armenians to get the sled. He, Pratt, and the Frenchman, Martineau, ran to the truck bed.

The tilted bed had sent the heavy trunk sliding, so it was closer to the ground. All they had to do was man-handle the trunk onto the road. Pratt maintained security while Darbo and Martineau went to work. Both men grunted with strain as they used the rope grips on the trunk to pull it off the truck bed.

It took several minutes, by which time the Armenians had returned with the sled and placed it on the ground. All five mercenaries worked as one to lift it off the ground and onto the sled.

Pratt shouted, "Incoming!"

Another truck raced toward them.

The gun buyers.

Darbo dropped to one knee and fed a fresh round into the GP-34 while shouting for his men to get to cover. They ran back into the overgrowth. Martineau and Pratt fired at the oncoming vehicle.

Darbo ran to the front of the tilting truck. The driver's side tire provided ample cover as he squatted, took aim, and fired the 40mm. The cartridge left the GP's muzzle with a thumb and detonated on the front grill of the second truck.

The blast sent the hood flying into the windshield, destroying the front tires. But five men piled out, all armed with automatic rifles, and they began returning fire. Their hot rounds punched into the truck as Darbo fired back with a full-auto burst.

He broke left, into more overgrowth. He wanted to get closer. He moved fast, breathing hard, feeding another 40mm cartridge into the GP-34. He stopped beside a wide tree trunk to snap a new magazine into the AK's magwell. Sweat coating his body underneath the camo uniform. His bandanna kept droplets from falling into his eyes. This was the life. This is what he lived for. He sprinted ahead, staying low. The natural cover concealed him until he stopped ten yards from the gun buyers.

If they couldn't sell the guns, they might as well have the gold, right? Darbo grinned and fired the 40mm. The blast took out two of the shooters. A third sprinted across the road for cover. Darbo split open his back with a salvo of 7.62x39mm soft tips.

He dropped flat, looking for another target. To run into the road himself meant risking friendly fire; he didn't want to be shot by his own guys. The final two gunners were on the other side of the truck, out of view. Darbo watched for their feet beneath the truck.

There! A boot. Darbo fired a single shot. The leather split open, spraying blood. The gunner yelled as he fell, fully visible beneath the truck now, and Darbo shot him in the head.

Another volley of gunfire from his men and the last two gunners fell. Scattered shots followed as his team slowly realized the fight was over.

Darbo rose and yelled for his crew to regroup. He ran back to the truck. Only four men waited. Pratt, Martineau, one of the Armenians. The second Armenian had been killed.

Pratt volunteered to carry the man's body.

Darbo took point. The Armenian and Martineau pulled the sled. Pratt carried their dead comrade. They made the march through the forest to their waiting vehicle. Lifting the trunk onto their own truck bed strained muscles, but they made it happen. Pratt added the dead mercenary to the load and climbed into the truck bed.

Darbo moved around to the driver's side while telling Martineau to join him.

Pratt shouted Darbo's name. Darbo spun around as an AK cracked, and Pratt raised his weapon to return fire. Another shot put a hole in the American's head front and back. Parts of him leaked out either end as he fell over the side.

Darbo ran around the front of the truck with his gun up, stopping short as he met the muzzle of Martineau's AK. Behind the Frenchman lay the other Armenian.

"It's a lot of money, Darbo."

Martineau's finger tightened on the trigger.

Darbo fired first.

Martineau's face registered shock as the bullets cut through him. His eyes remained open as he fell where he stood.

Darbo cursed. He stood alone as the gunshots faded and nature sounds took its place. He slung his weapon and climbed into the truck. There was nothing to do but complete the mission, but bloody hell he had a whale of a job ahead.

Three days later, dressed in a gray suit, Zaven Darbinian sat alone in a Bahrain bar nursing a beer. He scrolled through emails from potential clients looking for soldiers on his phone.

He'd expected trouble from Pratt, but the Frenchman had been the bad guy in the end. There had been no warning and no way to stop Martineau from killing his crew. Mission accomplished, but it left him with a sour taste on the tip of his tongue.

The phone rang. The caller ID displayed a name.

Sam Raven.

Darbo answered. "Hello."

"Darbo?"

A hum filled the background of the call. "Where are you, Sam?"

"On a plane over the ocean. I have work if you're available."

"You caught me at the right time."

"Usual spot in Stockholm. As fast as you can."

Darbo smiled. If Sam Raven was calling about a job, it would be a good one, exciting, dangerous, and well-paying. "Keep the beer cold. I'm on my way."

CHAPTER TWENTY-TWO

Lia Kenisova knew how to make an entrance.

The party was in full swing at the triple-story chalet in Blatten, Switzerland, a village nestled in the Lötschental valley.

In the dark, Lia had no way to take in the lush green of the valley or the snow-peaked Alps towering over the village. The Alps looked large enough to touch. The chalet, brightly lighted in a variety of colors, was an impressive sight too.

The middle level sported a raised deck extending from the house, packed with partygoers. They drank and danced to loud trance music thump-bumping throughout the property.

Flat grass in front of the house, with tables and chairs set out. More partygoers sitting or standing. The outside only hinted at the festivity and debauchery taking place within.

The owners of the chalet, brothers, had placed a parking zone ten yards from the house. Lia followed an attendant's direction and parked her bright red Land Rover Sport between an orange Lamborghini and a black Ferrari.

She exited the Land Rover one leg at a time, testing her heels in the soft grass. They weren't the right shoes at all, but a strip of steel lined each tip. The stilettos were key tools in tonight's arsenal.

The attendant offered a hand, and she accepted the support and stood at full height. The attendant's face, illuminated by the lamps hung on posts around them, brightened at the sight of her.

She was worth looking at. Thin, supple, graceful, taller than him. A long spaghetti-strap black party dress encased her curvy figure. Fiery red hair cascaded past her shoulders in even waves.

Lia Kenisova flashed a killer smile, backed by her sparkling blue eyes, and started for the party. The attendant was too stunned to say anything, though she figured he'd decide what to say as soon as she was gone.

The black leather purse slung across her chest bounced against her right hip as she walked. The purse was empty. By the time she departed, it wouldn't be.

She wasn't there to enjoy the festivities. Well, not entirely. She planned to have a good time, but work was her priority. To accomplish the task, she carried a .25-caliber Beretta 950 Jetfire strapped to a garter holster inside her left thigh. The gun rubbed awkwardly as she walked, but she ignored the discomfort. You don't walk into a den of tigers without a whip.

The brothers hosting the party, Adrian and Jiri Burgi, allegedly ran a software company supplying the Swiss banking industry with state-of-the-art programming. In reality, they were thieves specializing in jewelry robberies. They targeted the jet set circuit. The previous week, in London, they'd lifted a diamond necklace from a bratty royal niece during one of the wild parties she threw to mask her loneliness.

Poor little bitch. Lia had no sympathy, having worked hard for everything in her life. She'd been brought up by her janitor father and school-teacher mother. Money was always tight. They'd had four daughters to raise.

When Lia left home to join the Russian army and later GRU, the military intelligence apparatus, she'd avoided her family's financial failings. She'd filled her pockets via the graft and corruption rampant in the Russian government.

Using her nest egg to launch a freelance career, she was now in high demand as a retrieval specialist. The royal niece's family reached out to her to get the necklace back. According to them, it was a priceless family heirloom. How nice for them. To Lia, it was half-a-million US dollars, half up front.

Retrieval specialist, gun *girl*, Jill-of-all-covert-trades. Her resume included counter-terrorist efforts to protect her country from those who wanted to destroy it. She relished every kill preventing casualties to the Motherland.

The admiring glances from males and females didn't faze her as she climbed the steps alongside the chalet. She entered the second level of the house, the center of activity.

The brothers had cleared furniture to make room for dancing. Seats sat along the glass windows making up three sides of the chalet. Beyond the lights in front and in the parking area, the deep black of the secluded area was like staring into a void.

The music assaulted her hears, bass vibrating the wood floor. A DJ stood behind his sound equipment on a raised platform. He wore a large pair of headphones and danced as he adjusted his mixing console. The latest trance hits blared from big speakers.

A bar sat immediately to her right. Lia pushed between others waiting for drinks to get the bartenders attention. Her smile and red hair won again. Presently she collected a glass of champagne, to the annoyance of a fellow at her left elbow.

"What makes you so special?" the man said. French accent, arrogant eyes, dark hair and a narrow chin lined with dark stubble. She looked him up and down and found nothing desirable packed in his black suit. He might do well if he found a girl with the IQ of a radish.

Lia laughed and walked away.

She scanned the crowd. Adrian Burgi was the primary target, and she tried to pick him out of the crowd.

She'd been in the village for a week already, watching the chalet from a distance with a high-powered scope. She'd covered the front and both sides of the house. The big windows helped her gather a tremendous amount of data.

First floor. Kitchen and dining area, garage in the back.

Second floor. Open living space, television.

Third floor. Four bedrooms along a wide hallway with white carpeting. Two for the brothers, two spares. The large window in the master, used by Adrian, revealed to Lia the safe where they kept stolen goods. The safe was in the wall behind an abstract painting of purple and black slashes.

She needed to get into Adrian's bedroom. To do so, she needed to get to Adrian. If he were like every other man she'd encountered, he'd turn to Jell-O at the sight of her. And then it was only a matter of guiding him upstairs by the chin.

Or whatever other part of him she happened to grab.

She spotted him across the room, near the windows, holding court with three women shorter than him. They had to look up to meet his eyes, he looked down to meet theirs, and one of the girls swayed as the music played. She wasn't getting as much attention so the hell with him. The brunette had his focus, but as Lia weaved through the crush of bodies to reach her quarry, she smiled at anticipating his sudden shift in attention.

Find another sucker, you whores. I need new shoes.

She reached around the swaying blonde and touched Adrian Burgi's shoulder. He turned sharply, reacting with a start.

Bye, bitches.

"Oh my God, Adrian, so nice to see you! Great party!"

"Hi!" he said, turning to face her, the brunette and her friends scowling as they faded into the crowd. They recognized a lost opportunity.

Go talk to the French guy.

"It's been so long since Ibiza your invitation really surprised me."

"Right." He nodded, a flash of confusion on his face. She laughed. He'd never seen her before but wasn't about to admit the truth. "Well, I never forget a friend."

Lia downed her champagne and held up the glass by the stem. "What do I do with this?"

He took it. "Refill?"

"No, you big dummy, dance with me!"

Adrian Burgi laughed and set the glass on the floor near a seat. She grabbed him before he was ready and pulled him into the crush of moving bodies.

And the hook was firmly in Adrian Burgi's cheek. They danced, drank, laughed. He never questioned the story of their previous meeting. After three drinks it was time for the final approach, but he beat her to the question.

"Come upstairs with me."

"I don't know, Adrian."

Hands on her wrists, he pulled her toward him. "Come on, it will be like last time."

"It needs to be *better* than last time!"

My goodness you're simple.

"Trust me." He started walking backwards, still holding her wrists, and she followed.

"Don't try the swirl. It's gross."

"I've perfected the swirl!"

"*No* swirl," she said, laughing.

When he turned to head for the stairs, he had his arm around her. She leaned against him, already slipping a finger between the buttons of his silk shirt to rub his chest.

They weren't the only ones upstairs. She didn't know where Jiri was. The door to his bedroom at the end of the hall remained open. The spare bedrooms were closed. The music below didn't mask the gasps or the thumps of beds hitting walls on the other side of the doors.

"Quite a party," she said.

"We like to have a good time."

She pushed him into the wall, running a hand to his crotch. "How about right here?"

His breath was hot on her neck as he nibbled on her skin. "Somebody will see." Despite herself, Lia tingled at the touch of his lips.

She tilted her head back to give him extra room to work. "It's more fun. More *dangerous.*"

He bit her earlobe. She moaned.

"Then I get to try the swirl."

She laughed, breaking away but leaving her hand in place, and shook her head.

He gave her a gentle shove toward the open bedroom opposite Jiri's, closing the door.

Her eyes locked on the abstract painting on the wall. Not much longer now.

She began pulling the dress up, bunching it around her hips. Adrian grinned in anticipation as he stepped forward.

Lia's hand flashed to her left thigh where the garter holster held the .25 Beretta. She ripped it from the Velcro clasp, pushing the muzzle into Adrian's nose.

He hands went up. "Whoa, hey, what—"

"Strip."

"What?"

"Get your clothes off, idiot."

Lia used her free hand to put her dress back in place while Adrian followed orders. His hands shook, confusion covering his face.

"So, um, is this your version of the swirl?"

His slacks dropped, and she kicked him in the balls.

His eyes bulged as the pain filled his body. Doubling over, he hit the carpet, his pants halfway to his ankles. He squeezed his legs together and curled into a ball. His eyes pleaded with her for understanding as she kicked him again, this time in the side of the head.

The steel-toed stiletto performed as designed, and Adrian's lights went out.

Lia transferred the .25 Beretta to her left hand and knocked the ugly painting off the wall. The wall safe had a push-button combo lock. She'd watched Adrian enter the combo several times during her surveillance. He liked to gaze at the royal necklace often, holding it up to the light streaming through the bedroom window. The light had made the diamonds sparkle.

Idiot.

She punched in the combination, opened the safe, and found the necklace inside. She grabbed the necklace and put it in her purse. And since the rest of the stuff was there for the taking, she grabbed a few more as a bonus. Now the leather purse felt heavy.

Lia paused long enough to lift her dress again and refastened the Beretta. Everything back in place, she marched out of the room with a proud strut.

Mission accomplished.

The parking attendant still hadn't found his voice when she returned to collect her Land Rover. She gave him another smile before driving away.

Three days later, at a spa in Zurich where, after the luxu-rious full treatment, she sat by the pool.

Her phone rang.

Lia set aside her magazine and found the cell at the bottom

of her bag. The caller ID said Sam Raven.

"Hello, darling," she said.

"Are you busy?"

"I have a delivery to make tomorrow in London, and then I'm free. What's on your mind?"

Raven laughed. "I left London this morning. It's a little busy lately. Can you meet up at the usual place?"

"Anything for you, darling. I'll be there."

CHAPTER TWENTY-THREE

Nigeria was a horrible place to die.

Roger Justice held on for dear life as the old Jeep bounced on the rutted desert ground. Destination: a trio of beat-up silver planes in line for takeoff.

It was not an official airport, only a stretch of desert wide and flat enough to accommodate the planes. Nigerians, mostly Christians, wanted to flee the Magumeri Local Government Area in the state of Borno, part of the north-eastern region of Nigeria.

They were running from Boko Haram, jihadists intent of overthrowing the Nigerian government. And installing an Islamic State in its place.

The Nigerian army, with assistance from mercenary forces, had recently kicked Boko Haram out of all but one region of the north-east. They were holed up, controlling the state, and weren't giving up, destroying and killing everything their eyes saw.

The fierce fighting claimed thousands of lives. In a region comprised mostly of farmers, those who could had escaped via convoy, families and cattle in tow. The convoys moved slow and had little defense, so they were easy pickings for roaming BH patrols.

Others with more resources available hoped to escape to neighboring Chad or Cameroon via plane. The three planes were the only way out.

Justice, part of a mercenary army hired by Nigeria to help defeat Boko Haram, wanted out. The planes offered a way out. He didn't care if he landed in Chad or Cameroon; he had the money to travel anywhere he wanted after. The conflict was fierce, and he'd been part of the fighting for six months and saw no reason to extend his contract. Pushing BK out of most of the north-eastern states had convinced him victory might be achieved. Then the siege of Borno changed his mind.

Nigeria wasn't equipped for the fight, and Justice had no desire to fight for the losing side. He didn't want to die for nothing.

The war had raged for ten years, pure attrition, both sides killing each other in equal numbers. Boko Haram never seemed to have trouble replacing lost fighters. Nigeria? Different story. Corruption and partisan politics at the top kept the government from fighting effectively. To make up for the problems, they hired mercenaries. Cutthroats, professionals, all points in between. Their only job was to kill Boko Haram.

What had seemed to Justice like a simple mission with an attainable goal had turned into a never-ending series of battles where the enemy kept coming. They multiplied despite losses, never tired, intent on their goal of takeover and subjugation.

Two other mercs in the Jeep with him, burly Americans named Tyson and Crest, wanted out as well. They hated Africa, hated the people. Serving beside them meant listening to constant racist insults against a people Justice considered pawns in a game they had no hope of understanding. Or winning.

Two of the ancient silver Douglas DC-4s pulled ahead of the third. One kicked up a dust storm as the aircraft accelerated for takeoff. The four propeller-driven engines roared as the plane left the ground for the mountains in the distance. The second followed. The choking dust enveloped the Jeep. Tyson coughed as he drove, shouting another racial insult as if it helped matters. Justice covered his face. Crest didn't seem to mind, but the lenses of his glasses were quickly covered.

A small crowd hovered around the last plane, small-statured Nigerians begging a taller man in a tan pilot's uniform for permission to board. They waved paper money. They waved items of value. The pilot was not dissuaded. He waved his hands and shook his head and told everybody to try again next time, but nobody knew if *next time* would come. The plane was there now; their opportunity was now. To go back where they came from meant certain death. To try to link up with a convoy heading to another state also offered little odds of survival.

As Tyson stopped the Jeep, they heard the pilot's explanation of the plane already being full. Justice didn't listen. He and the other two, carrying their automatic rifles and heavy packs, marched to the plane. Faces with bright and desperate eyes turned their way; the mercenaries ignored them.

Bypassing the pilot for the open rear hatch, they almost reached the steps. The pilot rushed to them, pushing Crest away. Crest shoved him back. The thin pilot staggered, almost falling. The Nigerian citizens shouted protests. The mercenaries climbed aboard to find space on the metal floor in back.

The pilot jumped in and pulled the hatch shut, turning to yell at Crest some more, and Crest stuck a pistol in his belly.

"Shut up and fly, you goddamn halfwit!"

The pilot swallowed a lump in his throat and started for the cockpit. He navigated the narrow aisle. The twin rows of seats lining either side of the cabin were packed with Nigerians and their belongings. Their faces looked worn, they looked at the mercenaries blankly. Nobody had the energy to keep up the pilot's argument.

Justice sat in the corner against the fuselage and swallowed a gulp of water from his canteen.

The DC-4 began to taxi, the engines loud, hurting Justice's ear. He closed his eyes and groaned. It was going to be a long flight to wherever they were going.

The three mercenaries took the rough ride harder than the passengers. They had nothing to hold onto. Finally, the plane left the ground, the wings swaying as the pilots tried to stabilize.

The pilot appeared in the cockpit door, rushing back to the mercs.

"You are making us too heavy. We need to land. You need to wait for another plane."

Crest took out his pistol again. "We like this plane."

"No! It's too dangerous. We won't make it!"

"Do not land." Crest rose, Tyson with him. Justice let out a breath and looked bored.

"If we're too heavy, drop some of these...*things*," Crest said, gesturing with the pistol at the nearest passengers. "We've fought your war. We deserve priority."

Tyson opened the hatch, hot wind rushing inside. Startled passengers began to panic and yell. Tyson grabbed a young male from his seat, the man reacting with a scream and swinging arms. The thick-bodied Tyson ignored the ineffectual blows.

"Let's start with this one!"

He pushed the flailing man to the hatch.

Justice jumped to his feet.

Hell no.

"Stop it, Tyson!"

Justice punched Tyson as he turned his head, the blow stunning the big merc. He let go of the man, who collapsed on the floor, still yelling.

Justice stepped over the man's legs and landed another

punch on Tyson's face. He grabbed him, forcing his body toward the hatch. Tyson let out a high-pitched scream as Justice shoved. Tyson continued screaming as he fell out of the plane. They were high enough Justice knew the landing would probably kill Tyson. He was buzzard bait.

Justice let out his own startled yell as Crest crashed into him, pushing *him* toward the open hatch. Justice grabbed onto the upper edge to block the thrust.

He kicked back, missing, then stomped a foot on Crest's right boot. Crest howled. Justice struck with his left elbow, turning his body slightly to score the hit. His elbow landed solidly on Crest's left cheek, sending his dusty glasses flying. The grip loosened. Justice let go of the doorframe and pivoted, blocking a return strike, kicking Crest in the groin. Justice delivered another blow to Crest's nose, blood spilling out. He forced Crest to bend at the waist for the push out the door.

Crest didn't scream as he passed through the doorway and into the air.

Justice grabbed Tyson and Crest's packs and rifles and threw them out. He pulled the hatch closed. The plane rose higher, finally gaining required altitude. Justice wrenched the lock into place an faced the pilot.

"We light enough now?"

The pilot's stunned face and lack of words provided the only answer. The pilot helped the other man back to his seat. His family pulled him close. The young girl with them stared at Justice as he dropped into his corner again. He swallowed another mouthful of water.

Justice ignored the girl. He stared at nothing. All we wanted was out of Nigeria. As the pilot returned to the cockpit and the plane flew on, at least he'd accomplished the goal.

He vowed to never fight anywhere in Africa again.

Three days later in Istanbul, Justice awoke in a quiet hotel room in a soft bed.

He was exhausted, sore all over, and didn't plan to leave his room until he felt better. Room service delivered promptly, and the food was good. He had no reason to go elsewhere.

His phone rang.

He picked up the phone from the nightstand and looked at the caller ID. The display showed Sam Raven's name.

"How are you, bud?"

"Busy, Roger?"

"Not at the moment."

"Can you meet me at the usual spot?"

"What's going on?"

"I require your expertise for a demolition expedition."

Roger Justice laughed. The hell with Istanbul and rest. A job from Sam Raven wasn't something he was going to turn down.

"I'll be on the next plane."

CHAPTER TWENTY-FOUR

It felt good to finally be home.

Chartered flight or not, luxurious King Air or not, the flight had been taxing for both Raven and Mara.

He hoped a few days at home base might recharge their batteries prior to the next stage.

"You live on this?" Mara said.

"It's cozy, with all the comforts," Raven said.

Carrying their luggage and a sack of groceries, Raven and Mara stepped off the wobbling jetty and onto the deck of Raven's houseboat.

It wasn't the largest or most extravagant craft in the Navishamn Marina in Stockholm, but it was Raven's home. The water was calm, the marina surrounded by a cluster of green mountains. It was a tranquil spot for reflection and rest.

And it fulfilled Rule Two in a big way. No roots. Raven's domicile sat on water.

The houseboat contained two levels, rectangular in shape, the lower level Kermit green. The upper lounge, half the length of the lower deck, contained brown paneling. White window frames on either side.

An enclosed sitting area extended from the upper half, running to the length of the lower portion. Several plastic chairs and an old poker table taking up the space.

Raven unlocked a door and led Mara inside.

The interior surprised Mara. It resembled a well-appointed hotel suite.

Wood floor, couches, chairs and a wall-mounted television at one end. On the opposite side of the wall was a small bathroom and shower.

Dining table in the middle, complete with adjoining kitchen counters. Gas stove. Small refrigerator.

Windows on all sides let in plenty of light. A blooming green plant, spilling over the pot in which it lived, hung from the ceiling near one of the windows.

A set of steps across from the dining table led to the second level.

Mara examined the kitchen as she and Raven set down the grocery bags. The counter surfaces showed a patina reflecting their age.

"This is it?" Mara said. She set her suitcase near the dining table where Raven placed his.

"It's enough for one person."

"What about your friends?"

"I have cots. It will take up most of the space and we'll be tripping over each other, but it's only temporary."

Mara's skeptical expression communicated she didn't believe him.

"Come on, it's only a few days. Once we get Oscar's information, we'll be heading out."

"Where?"

Raven opened the refrigerator to start loading groceries inside. The only items inside were bottles of water, and Raven paused to hand her one. Mara twisted off the top and drank.

"Not sure yet," Raven said, his back to her as he worked.

"Is there hot water?"

"Yes, Mara, I have hot water." He proved it by showing her how the shower worked, and she stuck a hand under the spray of water to test the temperature.

Raven turned off the spigot.

"Anything else?"

She said nothing.

Raven finished with the groceries, folded the paper bags to drop them in a corner, and turned to her. He smiled. "The real prize is upstairs."

He climbed the steps. She followed. The steps led to a second bedroom, fully appointed, and a doorway to the outside deck. Raven stepped onto the deck and took a deep breath.

"Smell that fresh air."

Mara didn't comment.

"You can sit here and watch the sun come up, or set, whatever you want," he said, waving at the chairs and poker table proudly. "Sometimes I sit here from beginning to end. I don't leave my chair."

"Except to pee."

He sighed.

She looked back at the queen-sized bed in the upper deck. "Yours?"

"You can have it," he said. "I'll take the cots with the others. Actually we'll move a cot up here. You and Lia can share this room."

"She better not snore."

Raven grinned. Now he had a chance to give back some of what she'd been dishing out.

"Won't matter. You snore louder than anybody," he said.

She drank more water and looked out at the mountains. "Seems nice."

"We have quite the community here. Social hall, visitors

coming and going, you'll love it."

"I really don't want to be around people, Sam."

"Gotta start somewhere."

She frowned.

"We're free spirits here," he said. "Nobody cares about where you came from or where you're going."

"I don't know how to live that way. Not anymore."

Raven allowed some softness in his voice. "You'll get there."

She offered the half-empty water bottle. "Want the rest?"

Raven drank the remaining water down in two gulps.

Raven cooked a light lunch, and they ate on the top deck.

The meal calmed Mara considerably. She leaned back against the wall.

"I haven't been on a houseboat in forever."

"Tell me about it." He sat beside her.

"I was in high school," she said. "Every year my church did a houseboat retreat, all the high school-aged kids. Fun weekends. Got me out of the house and away from my mother. They weren't anchored like yours. Am I using the right word?"

"We'll use it," Raven said.

"We'd be out in the water, two or three houseboats, actually. The girls lounged in inner tubes and the guys would jump off the roofs to impress us." She smiled.

"Did it work?"

"Sometimes but coming home with a church boy was not something mother would have approved of. She didn't like me going."

"Why?"

"Took away her control, I guess. She wanted me to be her pet. Always in the house. She needed something to punch when the booze got to her."

"I'm sorry."

"Don't worry about it."

Raven picked at the leftover chicken on his plate but pushed it away and drank more water. The tangible pain etched on Mara's face made him hurt. Her memories seemed only filled with misery, the desire to break away from misery a common theme. There was nothing he could do to change her. She needed to fix herself. She needed to want to fix herself, find some way of proving she was her own person, free to make a happy life. Perhaps the flower shop had been her attempt, but whatever life she'd built was gone now. He hoped she would have a chance to start a new one.

Raven collected the dishes and brought them down to the kitchen, where he placed them in the sink for later. His Raiders were on the way and knew how to get to the marina. By the time they arrived, hopefully he'd have heard from Oscar Morey. Rest was fine, but what he wanted was action. A strike back against Basheer el-Dowd. And a chance to find out who was pulling the strings placing them in the crosshairs.

CHAPTER TWENTY-FIVE

If the janitor didn't get off the floor, Regan Shaw was calling off the job.

The thin Irish firecracker spoke normally. Her earbud transmitted back to the van where Tony Nestor waited.

"Anything?"

"They're almost done."

"It's been two hours."

"They're thorough janitors."

"They didn't take this long last night. Why the change?"

"I'm not a mind reader, boss. We haven't had enough time to map their movements the way we should have."

Regan cut off a curse.

"Relax," said the man beside her.

Regan turned sharply to glare at John Mercer. They waited in a car down the street from 2 Victoria Avenue, where Doctor Frank Harrison kept his office, #357.

"We don't know enough, John."

"Take a deep breath. Come on, now. We're good for it."

"I should have turned the job down."

"We need the money."

"I *know* we need the money. It's no excuse. Without proper

surveillance we're walking in blind."

"Every now and then, it doesn't hurt to wing it."

The two were polar opposites, but made a good team, along with Nestor. Regan Shaw had received a call from her "usual source" at the CIA. Their contact, via his disguised voice, instructed them to go to London and break into Harrison's office. The CIA wanted information related to a woman named Mara Cole. Regan didn't ask questions; the assignment didn't leave room for asking anything. Orders were given; orders were carried out. She'd been in the covert world long enough to know how the cogs turned. You asked too many questions, you suddenly became a liability. Get the job, do the job, hand over the data, or hand over the body, and disappear. Maybe they'd call again with another job, and the process repeated. Regan lived by the KISS principle and it had never let her down.

She was an inch shorter and much thinner than the hulking John Mercer. Mercer was a typical ex-Green Beret Army dude bro minus the ridiculous beard other dude bros wore as standard issue on their YouTube wanna-be commando videos where they taught civilians how to shoot and claimed "bro I'm the real deal and I got the medal to prove it, bro" and made Mercer laugh.

But what Regan lacked in bulk, she made up with constant training in hand-to-hand and weapons handling. She was an interrogation specialist, former Army sniper, and had seen enough of the bad stuff the world had to offer to know she didn't want to hang around in the muck any longer than she had to. If only a regular job was an option. There weren't many openings for long-distance killers and experts in chemical interrogation. Waterboarding? Only when she had to. Usually the other methods proved useful, but every now and then she dealt with a true hardcase who needed to drown a little before spilling his guts.

Mercer, the Green Beret, was the reach-out-and-kill-some-body type.

The pair had worked together during the Iraq and Afghan wars, paired up by the CIA's Special Operations Group. They traveled deep into hostile territory and got prisoners to talk, or made them dead. Plenty of close scrapes forged their bond. They weren't lovers, but they were as close as husband-and-wife. After going freelance, they added Tony Nestor, electronics and surveillance expert, to the unit. In a way, they were a small family, trying to keep the hounds at bay long enough to get the kids to college.

Nestor had tapped into the office building's security system to watch the janitors. They were the only ones in the building, and their slow progress grated on Regan's last nerve.

Doctor Frank Harrison, the target, had his office on the third floor. The plan called for waiting until the cleaning crew moved to the fourth floor, and then slip inside. They couldn't wait for the crew to leave, because the crew locked the building upon departure. The team figured it was a time saving measure for when they had to go back to their company van for more supplies.

In their defense, they often had to return to their company van for more cleaning supplies. Messing with a lock each time only created delays *they* didn't have time for. After 2 Victoria, they had more buildings to clean, much further away; at least, they'd done so the previous night. Tonight, they showed they didn't follow regular patterns.

Nestor said, "They're leaving the last office now. Heading into the elevator. Up they go to the fourth floor. Anytime you want, Regan."

"Anybody coming down for more bleach?"

"Negative. All three going up."

Regan Shaw started the car and drove the half block to the

office building. She parked on the street. With the workday done, and everybody scattered to homes, pubs, or wherever, the street was traffic-free.

Regan and Mercer didn't talk as they exited the car, crossing to 2 Victoria. Mercer reached the door first and pulled it open. Regan slipped inside, heading for the stairs. She and Mercer took the steps quietly, exiting onto the third floor.

Stopping in front of office #357, Mercer went to work on the lock with a set of picks. He popped the door open within seconds. Regan entered first. Mercer locked the door. They snapped on bright flashlights.

"We're in," she said.

"Copy," said Nestor.

The lobby held nothing of interest. They crossed to the inner office door. It was locked. Mercer took less time to get the second door open than he'd spent on the first.

Regan said, "I'm sure the classified patient files the doctor keeps are hidden, but I doubt it's anything fancy."

"Don't assume," Mercer said.

"Shut up."

"Don't doubt me."

"Get to *work*, John. The name we want—"

"Mara Cole. I *do* listen to the briefings, you know."

"Really? You're usually staring at your phone."

The goal was to search without making a mess. There should be no trace of their visit after they departed. Mercer started on the filing cabinets along one wall, picking the locks, pulling open the drawers bottom to top. Patient files. He kept pulling open drawers until he reached the "C" files, third from the top. No Mara Cole.

Regan Shaw worked the doctor's desk, checking for hidden compartments, sorting through papers.

They spent ten minutes and came up dry.

"Bookcases," Regan said.

They crossed to the bookcases and worked from either end, removing books, looking for hiding spaces, meeting in the middle. Mercer pulled out a set of books and revealed a cubby hole in the wall. It had been cut out, and a lock box placed inside.

They moved to Harrison's desk to search. It wasn't a box large enough to contain the patient file folders in the cabinets, but Regan took the box out anyway. Mercer picked the lock and lifted the lid.

Mercer laughed.

"Told you so," Regan said.

Several rolls of paper, wrapped with rubber bands, sat in the box. They had to undo the rubber bands and examine each set of papers.

"A lot of blackmail material here," Mercer said.

"We wouldn't live long enough to make use of it," Regan said.

"Here she is," Mercer said. He unrolled four sheets of paper banded together. Regan looked at the name on the top sheet. Mara Cole. Bingo.

"Let's go," she said.

Nestor in her ear.

"We got a visitor."

Regan and Mercer remained in place. Regan said, "Who?"

"A man. Late 40s. He parked next to the janitor's van. He's inspecting the van. Checking the doors. Now he's heading for the front door."

"Cleaners' boss," Mercer said.

"You think?"

"I'll bet you a steak dinner it's a quality check. He's here to make sure they're scrubbing the toilets till they shine."

"Think he'll check the offices?"

Mercer raised an eyebrow. "It's an inspection, Regan. Remember those?"

She cursed.

They were trapped.

Terry Carlsson liked to joke he started his own janitorial company so he would never have to clean another toilet.

The truth was, since starting his own company, he'd taken great pride in his ability to scrub clean any surface whatsoever.

Every month, he liked to spot-check his guys in the field. Carlsson liked keeping clients happy. If any client ever complained a night's cleaning hadn't been done properly, he handled the matter personally. He showed up with the crew at the place of business and assured the error wasn't repeated.

The two-man crew working 2 Victoria were very good, had never received any complaints. Carlsson had to be fair to his employees and check up on everybody in rotation.

He started up the stairs and called the crew. They told him they were on the fourth floor. Carlsson began his check-up on the first, starting with the bathrooms, the top area of complaint for most clients.

The first-floor toilets looked spotless. Nothing missed. He used the master key to enter a random office and checked inside. The search took a few minutes as he examined the nooks and corners, then moved on to another office.

He whistled while he walked.

Regan rasped, "Tell me something, Tony."

"It's a check-up. He's going into random offices."

"Not all of them."

"No."

"He may skip this one."

"I wouldn't count on it."

Regan said to Mercer, "What do you want to do?"

"We can hide, and hope he doesn't check, or walk out like we own the place."

"Working late?"

"Exactly."

Regan let out an exasperated sight. "What the hell."

"Told you we can wing it."

She frowned as he put the Mara Cole papers inside his jacket.

They started for the hallway door.

"Where is he, Tony?" Regan said.

"Second floor now. Checking the bathrooms. If you hurry—"

"We can miss him. Copy."

They walked briskly down the hallway, heading for the stairwell door at the end.

"Keep us advised, Tony," Regan said.

"Still on the second floor."

Regan and Mercer entered the stairwell and started down, hurrying, their steps scratching on the carpeted steps all the way to the lobby. Out the door, across the street to their rental.

"Get clear, Tony," Regan said.

"See you at the rendezvous."

"Copy."

Regan hit the unlock button the car's remote, and she and Mercer jumped inside. She started the car and drove off.

Mercer let out a whoop.

"I'd rather not repeat this experience," Regan said.

"We got what we needed. Mission accomplished."

"Yes," she said. "Now let's go get the doctor."

CHAPTER TWENTY-SIX

Doctor Frank Harrison, seated at the bar, finished his whiskey and asked for a refill. The bartender refilled the glass, stopping when Harrison waved a hand. Only half a glass for his second round. He had to drive home, after all.

He drank slowly. The activity around him, the other patrons and their voices, might as well have been zero considering his thoughts.

And they were always the same. Thoughts about his ex-wife, how their relationship ended, what he might have done to make a difference.

If his patients knew he was drowning his sorrows, doing the exact *opposite* of what he counseled, they'd call him a hypocrite and find another therapist. He'd deserve the name, and the loss of business.

But when you're hurt, you're hurt, and one must be allowed to wallow in hurt for a short time. It was the intermission before bucking up and dealing with a problem in a healthier fashion.

Harrison wasn't there yet.

He'd spent a lot of time at the pub when he was married. It might now have been the smartest thing, but it was a way to avoid their problems. Another no-no. Eventually they'd avoided problems so long, she divorced him to end the problems once and for all.

Fair enough solution. Maybe he wasn't cut out for marriage. He liked his books. He liked to sit and study. He talked so much every day he had no energy to talk at home. He spent each day talking to others about their issues. The last thing he'd wanted was to go home and continue the process.

A man deserves to rest a bit.

It didn't matter any longer.

Now he could return home to his apartment, not say a word, and spent the night with his face in a textbook or journal, learning how to do his job better.

He finished the whiskey, paid his tab, and wandered into the fresh air outside.

He never made it to his car. Arms grabbed him. Somebody plunged a needle into his left arm. He felt the jab. Turning his head, he looked into the bright eyes of a thin female, at his other arm, a hulking male. Then he passed out.

Harrison came to strapped to a gurney.

He panicked. His wrists were secured at either side, his ankles tied at the end. The gurney mattress was bare. No crinkly paper found in medical offices all over the world.

The walls around him were devoid of any decoration or identifying marks. Florescent lights shined above him, and it was very cold.

Then he noticed the IV drip attached to his right arm, the stand for the drip over his shoulder.

"He's awake," a man said.

The hulk. He spoke with an American accent.

Harrison managed to lift his head, though the effort made him woozy. "What is happening?"

"Relax, Doctor."

A woman. Harrison looked left. The woman sat on a folding chair near a collapsible table. Papers were spread out on the table. He recognized the papers. His notes! Notes regarding patients sent to him by the CIA and MI6.

"What's the meaning of this? Why do you have my papers?"

The woman left the chair and took the hulk's place in front of the gurney. The man sat at the table.

"We need to ask you a few questions, Doctor."

"Are you CIA?"

"No."

"Is this about—"

"About what?"

"The other two who visited me? The brute and the woman. They wanted to know if I sold information. I told them no. I'm telling you no as well. There's no need for this."

"You know something, Doctor."

"I know a lot of things, young lady. You'll have to be more specific."

The woman smiled and went to the IV. She grabbed the cord with the rolling switch controlling the flow of the drip. She said, "This is what we call a 'hot drip'. Are you familiar?"

"Goodness sakes, *no.*"

"When the drip starts, your body temperature rises. It's going to feel really hot in here, doctor. The more I increase the drip, the hotter you get. You can get so hot it feels like you're burning from the inside. Get it?"

"You're going to torture me?"

She smiled and used her thumb to move the switch.

Harrison sucked a mouthful of air. He felt the effects right away, a warming sensation throughout his body.

"Tell us about Mara Cole."

Harrison breathed heavily. "You have to stop!"

"Don't make me repeat myself, Doctor."

She moved the switch some more.

Harrison screamed. The heat inside him was intense, like standing in the middle of a furnace. Yet his skin still felt the room's chill.

"All right!"

The woman eased back on the drip.

Harrison lay back, catching his breath a moment. He tried to move his arms, but the ties holding down his wrists didn't budge.

"You were saying?" the woman said.

"Mara Cole is an American," the doctor said. "Former CIA. She came to me because of some PTSD related to an imprisonment in Afghanistan."

"What did she tell you?"

"She was tortured and raped and she was having nightmares."

"What else?"

"You need *more*?"

The woman's finger tapped the IV switch.

"No, no, no! There were faces in the nightmares. She wanted to see if I might help her identify the faces."

"How?"

"I don't know how. She thought I had a magic wand or something."

"Why did she want to see the faces?"

"She wanted to identify the man who raped her. She said not knowing his face wasn't helping her recover."

"Why would knowing his face change anything?"

"She'd know who to look out for. In case he came back again."

"What did you tell her?" the woman said.

"I told her I wasn't the kind of therapist who could help her. We could talk, do some exercises, work on coping techniques. There was no way for me to sharpen vague memories collected under stress."

The woman looked over at the man.

The man said, "Matches his notes."

The doctor shouted, "Of *course* it matches my notes! Now let me out of here!"

The woman nodded at the man. The man collected a hypodermic from a medical bag on the table. Harrison let out a squeal as the man approached him, his body tensing, and then the needle slammed home and the lights went out.

Harrison awoke again, face down in the carpet of his apartment. He'd drooled a puddle under his chin. Rising slowly, wiping his mouth, he looked around, determining he was alone. He went into the bathroom to vomit.

After washing his face, he decided to head to bed. He'd file a complaint with the CIA in the morning. Both arms where the needles had pierced his skin were sore. How lovely. His body still felt warm, an aftereffect of the chemical they'd used on him. He'd file a nasty complaint for sure. This was unconscionable.

He wondered, as sleep drifted to him, if he'd be in trouble for telling as much as he did. Because he had no idea if the interrogators were CIA or not. The Agency surely wouldn't admit to sending them.

But somebody had. Harrison was in no position to get on his own back in this case. He rolled onto his side and then onto his back once again. His arm hurt worse with his weight on it.

"Bloody hell," he said, rubbing both hands on his face.

He'd have to call in sick tomorrow. Ask his secretary to reschedule his appointments.

He'd have more than a drink and a half at the pub, too.

CHAPTER TWENTY-SEVEN

James Duran, once again in the parking lot of the Starbucks away from headquarters, spoke into his cell phone. He didn't hold back.

"It's what I suspected, Senator. She's trying to identify you."

"That cave only had candlelight."

"It was enough to give her a glimpse."

"This doesn't change anything. She needs to die. Raven too. And whoever is responsible for that website."

"In progress."

"How?" Welles said. "What are you people doing?"

"Raven has friends and contacts throughout Europe. He works with a lot of informants. My people are going to hit spots he's known to visit and see if they can find any of his friends and get them to talk."

"This is taking too long, James. And you say he's not talking to Wilson any longer?"

"For now, no. He will."

"You're sure?"

"Eventually. And he'll check in on Wilson's cell. I have a blank cell phone with some Bluetooth software on it. I'll connect with his phone and copy it. All I need to do is get close to him for about ten minutes. He likes to go to lunch alone. Off campus. I'll accidentally-on-purpose bump into him. Don't worry. It's being handled."

Welles said he worried quite a bit, as if he knew a piano was going to fall on his head, but he didn't know when or where.

"Let's talk about the therapist again."

"Harrison is raising hell. He's a dead end."

"No, I mean what she wants. What type of therapy can help her get a better picture of whatever's in her head?"

"Hypnosis maybe," Duran said. "There are some other techniques I'm reading about that may help her. Advanced stuff, not every therapist is qualified."

"Find the ones who are. They're somewhere in Europe; look there. It might be better than your people wasting time chasing Raven's friends who are only going to tip him off."

"Fair enough. I'll redirect them."

"We can't fail," Welles said. "We've come too far to be derailed by this."

"I'm not the one who couldn't keep his pants zipped, Senator."

"This is *my* fault?"

"If the shoe fits."

"I don't like your attitude, James."

"You have me doing the dirty work, Senator. Any time I want, I tell my people to change targets. Don't forget."

"Oh," Senator Welles said, "I won't, *Mister* Duran. Not at all."

"Sam?"

Raven left his chair on the top deck and leaned over the rail.

"Lia! Come on up!"

Lia Kenisova, carrying a tote bag and jacket, was dressed in jeans and a tight Tee-shirt, her long red hair tied back in a ponytail. She entered the houseboat and joined Raven and Mara on the top deck. Raven introduced the two, adding they'd share the upper deck bedroom.

Lia tossed her stuff on the bed.

"Knock, knock!"

Raven leaned over the rail again. "Roger! Perfect timing."

Raven and the two women went downstairs to greet Roger Justice, who put his stuff on the dining table. He and Raven shook hands and Lia received a peck on the cheek.

"You look a little tired," Raven said.

"Nigeria," Justice said.

"Say no more." He grabbed beer from the refrigerator and handed bottles to Justice and Lia; Mara refused. Raven put her bottle back and snapped the top off one for himself.

"Where's Darbo?" Lia said.

Raven gestured out the window. "Right on cue."

Zaven Darbinian entered the houseboat with a smile. More warm greetings all around, Mara off to the side watching. She shook Darbo's hand and forced a smile.

"Any beer left?" Darbo said.

Raven quickly retrieved another bottle. The crew sat around the dining table, Raven leaning on the kitchen counter. Mara sat on the steps, away from everybody.

"What's the emergency?" Roger Justice said.

"Call it black ops blowback of the worst kind," Raven said. He told them the story, beginning with meeting Victor Matson in Madrid. He ended with him and Mara escaping London.

"This el-Dowd sounds like a piece of work," Darbo said.

"What I want to know," Justice added, "is why your mission failed. Did somebody make a mistake, or were you compromised from the beginning?"

Raven considered his answer, watching the bubbles in his beer bottle. He looked at Mara. "Care to make a guess?"

She shook her head.

Raven took a long drink, then: "I think we were compromised. It's the reason I didn't want to deal with Clark Wilson any longer, though I didn't tell him so. The way our mission went bad always bothered me. Like there was a faction within the CIA who had no interest in taking el-Dowd out of play. They set us up once they learned of the raid."

Lia Kenisova said, "Who did your friend Clark replace?"

"What do you mean?"

"Whoever ordered the raid had his job at the time, right?" she said. "How long did he keep the position after the raid? Say this other faction wanted him out. Why did they pick Clark?"

"What you're asking is," Raven said, "did they hire somebody agreeable to their agenda?"

"Yup." She swallowed some beer.

"It's a good question, and a scary one. Clark and I were good friends once."

"Why past tense?" Lia said.

"Long story, and I'm afraid it's all on me. He didn't do anything wrong."

Raven glanced at Mara. She looked small, scared, her knees close to her chest as she sat on the steps.

"I've never doubted Clark before," he said, "and I have no reason to doubt him now. It's everybody else I don't trust."

Mara finally spoke. "He could have found us in London."

"Maybe," Raven said. "I never told him specifically where we were."

"You called his office," Mara said. "They log calls, remember? He could have pinged your cell to locate us."

Raven nodded.

"The only way to figure this out," Darbo said, "is to get on the road and start fighting back. Sam, what do you have in mind?"

"Quite a bit, actually," Raven said. "We need to call my buddy Oscar for the basics."

Clark Wilson stayed late at the office once again.

He had the same questions about the el-Dowd raid as Raven and wanted to make an attempt at finding answers.

Seated behind his desk eating a take-out sandwich, Wilson sorted through the el-Dowd file.

The mission to take him out had been proposed by his predecessor and signed off by the director of Special Activities. There was a note in the file from James Duran opposing the mission, describing Basheer el-Dowd as a faithful asset providing the CIA with intelligence against the Taliban. Wilson's predecessor wrote a note opposing Duran's point of view. The director sided with Wilson's predecessor and gave the mission a green light.

After the mission failed, Wilson's predecessor was part of the fallout. He was transferred to an overseas post. Shortly after, the Agency recalled Wilson from Greece and put him in his current job.

And nobody proposed going after el-Dowd a second time. Wilson certainly hadn't; his hands had been full with other anti-terrorist matters. He knew about Afghanistan's opium production, but it wasn't top-of-mind. The anti-drug section of Special Activities handled those matters.

Why had his predecessor wanted el-Dowd dead? Did the opium king have connections to jihadists?

It didn't add up for Wilson. His crap detector sensed treachery on the part of Duran. Had he compromised the mission? And for what purpose? Was el-Dowd such a valuable asset the CIA required his continued existence? Did Duran have an ulterior motive?

Wilson sat back and stared at his glowing computer screen. He no longer saw anything on the display. His mind was elsewhere.

He was thinking of the "Conspiracy Man" website.

The appearance of any anti-CIA website stirred attention within Langley. Employees had been whispering about Conspiracy Man for months. Wilson had visited the site out of curiosity, and when he discovered the pictures of Senator Aiden Welles visiting el-Dowd's compound, he did a double-take. Thinking about the picture now, he wondered if Duran had been serious. Any asset important enough for a senator to visit suggested there was more to Basheer el-Dowd than what appeared on the surface.

But Conspiracy Man didn't think so. Welles masked his trip as a fact-finding mission for a report to the Senate Intelligence Committee. He actually used the trip, the website claimed, to pledge support for a CIA-sponsored Afghanistan-US heroin pipeline. Welles, as the broker, would pocket his share of the profits. And James Duran hadn't wanted el-Dowd taken out. Was he also part of the deal?

Wilson leaned forward and cleared the screen, accessing Duran's personnel file. It didn't take long to find the notation in his resume he hoped wasn't there.

Duran, as a junior paramilitary officer, had worked security for Senator Aiden Welles on several overseas trips to the Middle East.

Wilson opened another file, this time on Welles. Anybody traveling with CIA protection had a file describing work done, why it was important, and who had been assigned to watch his back. His position on the Intelligence Committee also required a full background check before allowing him security clearance. Duran's name was in the Welles file, of course, but the amount of trips Welles had taken to Afghanistan surprised Wilson.

Five trips. Not all the visits involved el-Dowd's compound, but they were in the same region. And the dates on the Conspiracy Man web page matched the date of one of the visits. A sense of dread washed over Wilson. The date corresponded with Raven's mission to kill el-Dowd, and their capture. They'd escaped two days *after* Welles departed the area.

Wilson didn't like the thoughts forming in his head.

The next document detailed more information on the protection team assigned to Welles. Wilson scanned the list of names with growing alarm. Eight of the ten listed had been killed in action. Only Duran and a man named Martin Green remained.

Wilson cross-referenced dates. How much time elapsed between the death of the Welles security team members and the first three ex-agents on Raven's team? Two weeks.

Wilson flipped back to Martin Green's name. Was he Conspiracy Man? A check on Green's file didn't help. Green had left the agency after a bad medical review. The CIA psychologist cited growing mental strain. A follow-up search did not reveal a current address. Green had dropped off the radar.

Wilson let out a frustrated breath. Too much for one night. He needed to get home.

With his appetite gone, he trashed what remained of his sandwich, cleared his computer, and grabbed his jacket.

He probably wouldn't sleep much, but he had to try. He had a lot to think about. How to prove Welles and Duran were conspiring with Basheer el-Dowd?

And what did he tell Raven?

Raven plugged a laptop into the wall-mounted wide-screen and booted the machine. Mara and the Raiders sat on the couches and chairs, watching.

Raven's cell phone sat on the coffee table. The speaker function allowed Oscar Morey's deep voice to fill the cabin.

"Ready yet?" Morey said.

Raven typed a password into the laptop and the desktop appeared on the widescreen.

"Dial in and show us a few things, Oscar."

From his end, Oscar seized control of the laptop and began showing information on the television.

CHAPTER TWENTY-EIGHT

Oscar Morey's gravelly voice narrated visuals on the TV screen.

"You asked me to dig up information on Basheer el-Dowd. Here is his latest picture."

The image flashed on the screen. The picture showed him exiting a car near the Nice airport in France.

"He hasn't changed much," Raven said. "Don't tell me he's one of those who never looks older and never sees gray hair."

"The picture is three months old, so I'm afraid he may be one of those."

"May he die a thousand times," Raven said. "Go ahead, Oscar."

"He has quite a history," Morey continued. "Second-generation drug lord. Inherited the empire from his father. Both father and son supported the Taliban in the early years, despite the Taliban's crackdown on the drug business. They still managed to squeak out enough to stay afloat. Once the United States invaded, business boomed. They helped the CIA find Taliban forces and sympathizers, which grew their business. Some of those sympathizers were actually competitors. They moved in on the vacated territories and still supplied the CIA with information."

"Father dead?" Raven said.

"Long dead."

"Status with the CIA now?"

"Unknown. No official connection, no rumors. But he's still free. Maybe that tells you something."

"Current whereabouts?"

"Fortified compound in southern Afghanistan, next to one of his poppy fields. Protected by walls and a force of at least one-hundred men. It's probably the same compound you were supposed to destroy, Sam."

Raven showed no reaction. He stared at the picture. He didn't want to look at Mara either.

"What's next?"

"You asked for targets. I offer you these."

The picture changed to a man and a woman, mug shots from the French police.

"Brother and sister. Joel and Fabienne Granet."

Joel's shaggy hair was his main feature, while Fabienne sported close-cropped hair and a nose ring.

"The Granets are el-Dowd's connection in France. They run an import and export company in Marseille named after the family."

"Legitimate?"

"Partially. They import foreign goods to sell in France."

The picture changed again to an overhead shot of a warehouse near the Port of Marseille.

"The warehouse is near the port. Ships dock and unload large cargo containers into a container yard adjacent to the dock. Those containers are then put on trucks and taken to the warehouse for unloading."

The warehouse picture showed a line of semi-trucks and their cargo containers along one side.

"The containers," Morey continued, "are off-loaded at the warehouse. Everything usually comes in crates, and the crates with the contraband are separated from the legitimate cargo."

Darbo said, "We can torch the place."

Raven said, "Hold your ideas for the moment. Oscar, what else?"

The picture changed again. "Wonderful villa on the French Riviera. This particular villa is in Saint Raphael, near the Agay Beach. Standing at the rail overlooking the sea is a man named Rupert Andain. He's the boss of the Granets. His job is to make sure street dealers get the drugs entering Marseille."

"Current whereabouts of Mr. Andain and the Granets."

"They are in Marseille," Morey said. "I can provide home addresses for the Granets if you wish; Andain is at the villa. He's hosting a party in three days for his associates."

Roger Justice said, "Imagine all the pins we can knock down."

"Oscar, how close is the villa to other homes, and the town itself?" Raven said, looking out for Rule One. No gunfights where innocent people were at risk.

"He's isolated. The villa is surrounded by trees and well away from neighbors. It's a ten-minute drive into Saint Rafael."

"Good," Raven said. "Overhead shot?"

The picture changed again. The villa, with its pool deck facing the ocean, had three levels. An access road from the street wound through lush greenery before ending at the front door.

"Sam," Darbo said, "unless you have a stash of weapons and gear, it will almost take a day or two to get what we need."

"I hear you," Raven said. "Not much time for a proper advance recon. We'll do what we can. Oscar, forward all of this to me and we'll get to work."

"What about el-Dowd?" Morey said. "You aren't thinking

of going into Afghanistan, are you?"

"The whole point of this exercise is to get el-Dowd *out* of Afghanistan. No way can I afford to get us there, even with my reserve funds. If killing his smugglers isn't going to accomplish the goal, we need another option."

"I'm working on it," Morey said. "El-Dowd's parents are gone, but he has a sister."

"Where is she?"

"Not certain. She's not part of the family business, I can tell you that."

"Find the sister," Raven said. "She'll be our ace. We'll play her last."

"I'll be in touch."

Morey clicked off the line. The television screen returned to the view of the computer desktop.

"What gear do we need?" Darbo said.

"Full kit for all of us. Mara, you feel like suiting up for a fight?"

Mara Cole, on a couch next to Lia Kenisova, only blinked in response.

Mara wasn't sure what to think of Raven's Raiders. They seemed like good people. Her inability to open up and trust anybody prevented her from making a full investment.

She listened to the briefing quietly. The mention of el-Dowd's desert compound didn't shock her as she'd expected. She genuinely felt nothing. The compound was where everything changed for her. To go back and face those demons might have been therapeutic, but it wasn't an option. Morey's estimated number of defenders made the task impossible for a team of their size.

They'd need an army of their own. Air support. Heavy

weapons.

She knew the mercenaries could get a lot of gear at a moment's notice, but not the required gear for a major invasion. Attacking the compound meant nothing less.

Mara thought back to the roadside gun battle where she'd taken down one of the two men trying to kill them.

Shooting the bastard had felt good.

Really good.

She needed to shoot more of the bastards. Take back control. Show el-Dowd he had no power any longer, not against a determined force, albeit a small one, out to end his reign of terror.

She blinked at Raven, unsure how to answer. Then she voiced the first thought that entered her head.

"Let's go kill these sons of bitches," she said.

CHAPTER TWENTY-NINE

Raven's eyes brightened with a smile. He had expected Mara to give a different response. He had expected her to want to stay behind, out of the fight. The shootout on the road to the cottage had changed her for the good, and he hoped she'd warm to their compatriots.

"Very good," he said. "Now, let's talk details." Raven opened his email and downloaded the information Morey forwarded. He put the images on the screen.

"Two teams sound about right," Raven said, "with Darbo arranging for weapons. "Mara and me will hit the villa, starting with a day or two of surveillance, before we strike during the party. Lia and Roger, you take the warehouse. Now I want every single one of you clear on our objectives. We aren't looking for information. We are going to Marseille to kill bad guys. No prisoners. Unless you blast a guy holding a book that says 'next clue', nobody brings anything back. That's all. Any questions?"

Roger Justice said, "We don't want to be in Marseille longer than we have to."

"Certainly not," Raven agreed. "Getting arrested by the local police is not on our agenda. Let's make a shopping list for Darbo and call our usual sources and get this show on the road."

The Raiders started talking at once as Darbo hustled to write down requests. Mara slipped outside. Raven gave her a few minutes and followed.

He found her at the end of the pier staring into the water.

"Are you okay?"

"I'm fine. Really."

He put an arm around her. She remained stiff for a moment, then leaned against him.

"I thought you were going to say we were going to Afghanistan," she said.

"Mara, I'm not sure even I could go back there even if the army gave me a tank division."

"Are you sure I can do this?"

"I'm positive. If you were going to freeze up, it would have happened in London. You didn't."

She said nothing.

"What do you think of the crew?"

"They're loyal to you," she said. "Why is that? They aren't the types to come running when anybody calls, but they came running when you called."

"I'm not sure," he said, "but if I could find out why and bottle the formula, I would be a rich man."

"That's not true."

"What's the reason then?"

"They believe in you," she said. "Same as I believe you. Whatever happens in Marseille, I know you're telling me the truth."

She put her arms around him and squeezed.

"When this is done," he said, "you'll have your life back. A clean slate."

"What about you?"

"I've made my choice," he said. "There's no going back."

"Are you sure?"

"Too many reasons not to."

"Reasons or excuses?"

His face tightened, he wanted to refuse to answer, he wanted to yell at her for doubting his crusade. Then his face softened again. There was no need for an argument, and she wasn't asking anything he hadn't pondered himself in quiet moments. There was only one answer to her question. Raven expected Mara to trust him with her life; he owed her the truth. But he wasn't willing to go all the way. There was only so much truth he was prepared to admit.

"I'll let you know," he said, "if I ever figure it out."

Raven and his crew departed Stockholm on the chartered King Air. Darbo spent most of the flight on the phone arranging for a delivery of weapons and equipment.

Checking into a hotel to use as home base, Raven and Darbo collected the gear. Raven paid through a digital money transfer and brought it back for inspection. Heckler & Koch MP-7s for the hit on the villa. The submachine guns impressed Raven. An improvement over the old HK MP-5, the MP-7 fired a potent 4.6x30mm cartridge. The pistol-sized round was designed to hit with the power of a rifle cartridge. Thirty-round magazines curved from the bottom of the magwell. Raven didn't doubt the reliability and power the MP-7 provided any user when there was deadly work to be done.

The MP-7 barrels were threaded for suppressors, and the gear included those.

They checked the explosives next. Along with C-4 with remote detonators, their purchase had included thermite bombs. The intense heat of the thermite bombs would reduce anything not destroyed by the other explosives to atoms.

A shooting raid on the warehouse made no sense. If they struck at night, they'd more than likely be facing hired security rather than Andain's men. Andain would want the warehouse to appear as normal as possible, so no armed guards. The hired security might have weapons, but their appearance wouldn't be out of the ordinary. Raven had no intention of shooting working stiffs. Better to blow the warehouse from within. The goal was destroying el-Dowd's drugs. The explosives would suffice.

Raven accompanied Lia Kenisova and Roger Justice to the warehouse. They cut through a fence facing the port. There was only a single watchman to worry about, and they let him pass. He completed his rounds and returned to the guard shack at the road entrance. Justice broke off to keep an eye on the watchman while Raven and Lia entered the warehouse.

Picking the locks on a warehouse door was simple, and they locked the door behind them. They expected an alarm. Justice reported the watchman receiving the alarm notice on a panel.

"He's coming your way."

The watchman remained on foot and walked the 100 yards to the warehouse.

Raven and Lia worked fast, setting their charges. Justice stayed in touch. The watchman checked doors, windows, looking for the reported breach. He checked the door they'd entered through, finding it locked. He scanned the area with his flashlight and gave up the search as a false reading and returned to his shack.

Raven and Lia exited the warehouse after hiding until Justice radioed all-clear. They departed the way they'd arrived.

Surveillance on Rupert Andain went smoothly. Raven and Mara assumed the responsibility of mapping his movements. Andain stayed mostly at the villa, greeting associates as they came and went. A caterer showed up, Andain and the man discussing the party. Raven noted they'd have to delay their strike until the caterers had delivered and departed. When Mara asked if Andain would have servers around, Raven said no. Andain wouldn't risk talking business with civilians in close proximity.

It wasn't as thorough a surveillance as he would have liked, but they achieved the goal of learning the layout of the villa. Many windows provided a view of the interior. They knew what to expect inside. It was enough. Barely. But enough.

Perfect day for a party.

And a wonderful day on the French Riviera, as Rupert Andain observed from the pool deck. Behind him, laughter, music, splashes in the water. He stood at the deck rail over-looking the Mediterranean Sea, glancing at the clear blue sky. The touch of the gentle breeze felt good on his smooth face. He once again blessed his good fortune and thought ahead to more of the same.

He was dressed in gray slacks and blue sweater, the collar of his white shirt above the sweater's collar. Thinning hair slicked back, a ready smile, a man in charge of his world and finding little cause for worry.

He wasn't worried about killing a man later, either.

Andain turned his back to the sea and watched the party. Babes in bikinis splashed in the pool. Other women, dressed casually but still provocative in a subdued way, entertained his mid-level street managers at a table. Plenty of food and beverages. It was a "serve yourself" party, the caterers having departed.

Inside the house, he noticed several of his upper-level associates clustered in a corner near the den. They spoke intently. A few armed guards stood around, quiet, anonymous. Another pair of guards watched the grounds.

It wasn't difficult to discern what his upper-level team was talking about. They had a dirty job to do before the party ended. Andain believed in discipline. Self-control. He dealt not only with volatile connections in the Middle East, but European law enforcement and United States authorities. One needed discipline and self-control to navigate the many mine fields. Some in law enforcement were susceptible to bribes to look the other way and bury evidence. Not all were so helpful. There were plenty of cops, detectives, and drug agents not easily pushed aside.

Andain wandered into the villa. A counter served as the bar; adjoining tables contained the spread of food. He picked up a glass of champagne.

The bubbly tasted sweet. As he took a second sip, one of his lieutenants approached with a grim expression.

"Jean-Pierre has arrived."

"Good. Bring him to the den."

The lieutenant nodded and walked away. Andain went back into the house. Andain grabbed something to chew on from one of the two tables as he passed the cluster in the corner. He waved for them to follow.

The den, in one corner of the house, had tinted glass windows at a 90-degree angle instead of walls. The only wall blocked off the interior of the house, and Andain's desk sat in front of it. He perched on the edge of the desk. His associates entered. Nobody sat.

Andain's lieutenant escorted the mid-level street manager into the den.

"I'm glad you could all be here," Andain announced, raising his champagne glass in a toast. Nobody returned the gesture. No problem. They had business to attend to, and maybe after they would relax and enjoy the remainder of the party.

Jean-Pierre, a tall but slight fellow, appeared nervous as everybody's eyes landed on him.

Andain took a deep breath before speaking.

"Jean-Pierre, we have a question for you."

Jean-Pierre blinked. "Anything."

"Why are you ripping me off?"

Jean-Pierre began to sweat. His eyes remained on Andain. "Do you deny it?"

"A mistake, Mr. Andain—"

"It's not a mistake. You've siphoned off at least a million euros in the last six months. You thought you were clever to only take a little at a time, but the discrepancies weren't hard to find. Your books said one thing; the accounts said another."

Andrain drank more champagne. He waited for Jean-Pierre to refute, but all he did was stand and sweat.

"And then," Andain added, "we extracted a confession from your friend Suzi."

Jean-Pierre swallowed hard.

"Have you wondered why she stopped returning your calls, Jean-Pierre?"

The man grinned. "Bad lay?"

"Hardly. I told her to get out of France or I'd dip that lovely face of hers in acid."

"I can pay back the money, Mr. Andain. Right now."

"I'm sure you can. I'm sure it's no trouble. But remember, Jean-Pierre, I like discipline. We have to be a disciplined outfit if we are going to keep our masters happy. Yes, even I answer to somebody, as you well know, and were I to step out of line, my masters would respond swiftly."

Andain paused a moment, then: "As you can understand, I must respond in this case, or it's me on the wrong end of a gun. Can you see my dilemma, Jean-Pierre?"

Andain waited for a reply.

CHAPTER THIRTY

Sam Raven dropped to hands and knees and Mara Cole stepped on his back and reached for the top of the wall. She peeked over per his instructions. "All clear," she said. She swung up one long leg, then the other, rolling over the top to land on the dirt ground on the other side.

Raven followed, landing beside her. She had taken a knee, her suppressed Heckler & Koch MP-7 tucked into her shoulder. They might have been in a forest somewhere in the country. Trees surrounded them, solid trunks providing plenty of cover. Plenty of foot traffic had worn pathways into the dirt. The ground sloped leading to Rupert Andain's fancy villa.

The noise from the party, albeit muted, reached their ears.

"Stay close," Raven said. "Remember the plan."

"Copy," she said. They took off at a trot. Both were dressed in street clothes and wore combat harnesses. Grenades hung from the straps. Ammunition for the HKs and their pistols were secured to the thick belt around their waists. Mara's pistol, a .45-caliber Glock-21 rode on her right hip. A suppressor extended from the Glock's barrel. Raven carried his Nighthawk Custom in a similar fashion. He packed his usual lead sap for quieter dispatches.

He moved left, Mara six feet behind him. They weaved through the trees. He found a bench beside a small fountain. It was probably Andain's preferred spot for silent reflection. All drug dealers needed moments to gather their thoughts. He moved ahead, closer to the house. The white wall of the lower level beckoned.

A daylight raid was never high on his list. Neither was running an operation without proper planning. But they had an opportunity to deal a death blow to an important cog in the el-Dowd drug machine, with a time limit. As much as Raven hated rushing, the only way to get the edge on el-Dowd was to hit hard, hit fast, and get away. The one-two punch in Marseille fit the bill, and the villa was far from civilians; no collateral damage. The only people getting killed were the ones who deserved death.

Raven and Mara moved closer.

Jean-Pierre's eyes didn't leave Andain's.

"I'm waiting," Andain said.

"Do what you must, Mr. Andain."

Andain set down his glass and stood, reaching into a pocket. "Turn him around."

Jean-Pierre struggled against the hands grabbing him from behind. He kicked back and stomped a foot. As one of Andain's men yelled, Andain punched Jean-Pierre. The dealer's head snapped to one side. A follow-up blow to his stomach bent him over, and one of his men forced him to his knees.

Andain produced a garrote from a pocket and wrapped it around Jean-Pierre's neck. He pulled hard. Jean-Pierre's eyes bulged as he choked, clawing at his neck to get his fingers under the wire. Soon his strength faded. The arms dropped. Jean-Pierre's head sagged. His body went limp. Andain held the pressure a little longer, grunting with the effort, then let go. Jean-Pierre's body collapsed.

Andain folded the garrote and returned it to his pocket. The statement had been made. Discipline maintained. His men would keep the incident in mind going forward. The rest, when they noticed Jean-Pierre's replacement, would also get the message.

"Take him away."

Three of his men grabbed the body and carried it out.

Andain grabbed his champagne again and downed the glass. Only two of his people remained. He smiled at them.

"Back to the party. Enjoy yourselves!"

The men left without another word.

Andain returned to the bar for another glass of champagne. He bumped into Fabienne Granet who filled a small plate with snacks. She included a generous selection of decadent chocolate fudge.

He admired Fabienne's petite figure. She looked particularly good in the tight jeans and pink halter. His admiration ended when he caught a flash from the nose ring in her left nostril. Of all the ridiculous body adornments of the modern era, nose rings were the worst, second only to tattoos. At least she didn't have any of those.

She said, "Is the unpleasantness over?"

"Yes. You did good noticing his discrepancies."

Automatic weapons fire crackled. Andain and Fabienne, startled, looked out. His guards drew pistols. Andain started shouting orders as the party switched from festive to red alert.

Raven faced the left side of the house. The white wall reflected the sun. He dropped beside a tree as a group of men exited through the front door.

Mara knelt beside him. "What are they doing?"

"Carrying a body out to the cars."

A cluster of vehicles sat at the top of the sloped driveway. A black Mercedes was the apparent destination of the crew with the corpse.

"They play a mean game of musical chairs," Mara said.

Raven snapped the MP-7 to his shoulder as movement on the left caught his eye. Man with a gun. Automatic rifle. He spotted Raven too and let off a burst. Bark split from the tree, pelting Raven in the face. Raven responded with return fire. The suppressed MP-7 spit a salvo, and the gunner dropped.

A second gunner appeared over the top of the wall on the second-floor walkway. He aimed fired, the shots kicking up dirt and gouging chunks of the trees. Raven's view of him was partially blocked by hanging leaves. "Take him!" he shouted.

Mara moved ahead. Her first burst blasted plaster out of the wall. The second burst scored and decorated the white with red. The gunman fell out of sight.

Raven pulled a grenade and lobbed it at the startled corpse crew, who had stopped to see what was happening. The grenade blast vaporized the men and left a crater in the concrete. A thick smoke cloud drifted into the trees.

Raven ran forward. A voice was shouting, drowning out any others. Raven yelled for Mara to follow him as he changed direction, heading for the front door. The moment of surprise had vanished. Time to go for a goal before the defensive line organized a counterattack.

A gunman in a tan suit met them halfway. Raven stitched him stomach-to-chest, leaping over the body as it fell across the entry way. He stopped long enough to change magazines. Mara entered the house, her MP-7 chugging rounds.

Raven charged ahead. His quick scan picked out two gun-man, one close on his right, the other across the room on the left. He fired two shots into the chest of the gunner closest to him, pivoting to take the other, holding back as Mara shot the target with a burst of her own.

Rupert Andain ran across the room, heading for another doorway. Raven fired at him, missed, the shots breaking the glass wall on the far side of the room.

Raven ran for the deck. Drug thugs stopped short as they attempted to run inside. Some clutched pistols, one grabbing a bikini-clad blonde and hauling her in front of him. Raven shot one of the thugs through the throat, then shifted his aim to the man holding the blonde. He had shag-gy hair. Joel Granet. He was shouting something at Raven, Raven ignoring the yelling as he settled the front sight. The blonde was crying, struggling against his powerful grasp. Raven touched the trigger. A single shot burned through Joel Granet's head, splashing bits of bone and brain on the glass behind him. He pulled the blonde to the floor with him, but she scrambled away.

Mara dropped behind a coffee table to change magazines as Andrain ran across her vision. Up on a knee, she fired, another miss that tore chunks out of the doorway as he reached the den. She followed. Andain leaned out with a pistol. Mara sidestepped as his shots cracked. He tracked her with the muzzle, Mara slamming against a wall, firing again. Andain left the doorway to come at her. She tossed a grenade. The high explosive orb sailed behind Andain and through the doorway. The resulting blast did the job. The villa rocked with the blast, the wall cracking and dropping chunks onto the carpet. Andain screamed as the force of the explosion opened his back like a suitcase. He fell forward, his upper body mangled and bloody. Mara fired and took a chunk out of his head.

Raven ran onto the patio, shifting left where more of An-dain's thugs had turned over a table. Party girls screamed, running at him, screaming for him not to shoot, and Andain's men took advantage. They swung pistols over the top of the table. Raven used his left arm to shove the women aside. He pumped single shots into the three associates of Andain. As the bullets ripped into them, blood splashed on the other party girls. They scrambled away on hands and knees.

Back inside. He yelled for Mara. She joined him. He didn't have to ask about Andain; his dead body was plainly visible on the carpet.

"Look out!" Mara shouted.

A woman with short-cropped hair and a nose ring charged from behind the bar, a carving knife in one hand. Raven dropped as Mara raised her HK. The MP-7 popped twice, but Mara missed, Fabienne tackling Mara and pulling her to the floor.

Mara lost her grip on the MP-7 as Fabienne slashed with the knife, Mara attempted to block, Fabienne pulling back. The short-haired woman plunged the knife toward Mara's face. Mara blocked it with her left forearm while trying to punch back, but Fabienne put more grunt behind her push and the tip of the blade touched Mara's neck.

Raven held his fire, trying to find an opportunity to shoot. He didn't want to hit Mara. They struggled erratically, and any shot he took might miss.

"Get on top of her!" Raven shouted. If Mara pinned Fabienne Granet to the floor, he'd have a head shot.

Mara began to panic as the tip of the blade settled. She wasn't strong enough. She fought back rising panic as a solution flashed through her mind. She grabbed the Glock .45 from the holster on her hip. Mara jammed the snout of the gun into

Fabienne's side and fired twice.

Fabienne Granet's face twisted in pain as she recoiled from the shots, falling to one side, and Raven had his shot. He pinned Granet to the floor with a burst from the MP-7.

"Are you hurt?" He helped Mara to her feet.

Mara shook her head, wiping sweat from her face. She grabbed her fallen MP-7.

"Let's get out of here!" Raven shouted. He and Mara ran.

CHAPTER THIRTY-ONE

A few miles away, Raven's Raiders sat in a van across the street from the warehouse.

Darbo, in the passenger seat, consulted his watch. "They should have left the villa by now."

Roger Justice started the van's engine.

Lia, seated in the back with an electronic panel on her lap, flipped a series of switches. She looked out the window at the warehouse. They'd worked so quickly placing the charges she had a moment of doubt. Would they go off? Had they been discovered? They didn't have a back-up plan in either case. Raven wanted to be in and out of Marseille as fast as possible. They'd hidden the charges carefully, but Murphy's Law never failed.

The explosive booms shook the ground enough that they felt the vibrations under the van. Lia smiled. Perhaps Mr. Murphy had taken a vacation or was interfering with somebody's else's covert mission. Smoke blasted out windows, flame flashed through vents in the ceiling.

"How come the walls aren't falling?" she said.

Then she received her answer. One of the outer walls buck-led. part of the roof collapsed. Soon the warehouse was nothing but a flaming hulk sending black smoke into the sky.

Justice drove away. Lia set the panel on the seat next to her. "Kind of anti-climactic," she said.

"But job done," Justice said.

"Let's hope Raven and Mara made it out okay," Darbo said. "If they didn't, we have to decide what to do next."

"We finish the job," Roger Justice said. "No question."

Darbo and Lia agreed. They'd know for certain if all was well when they reached the rendezvous point.

They found Raven and Mara in a shopping center parking lot as expected, and the pair climbed into the van. Their weapons and combat rigs were stuffed into backpacks.

Raven and Mara sat on the third row of seats in the back of the van. Justice drove off again.

"We've been watching the smoke," Raven said. "Good work."

A rush of fire engines, sirens screaming, raced along the street toward the blaze. Raven looked out the rear window. "Nice work indeed," he added.

Mara sat quietly but breathing hard. She had her hands on her knees. Raven put an arm around her and squeezed.

"Too close," Mara said.

"You did great."

Lia turned to face Raven and Mara. She looked at Mara with concern but said nothing.

"You should have seen her, Lia," Raven said. "Like riding a bike."

"Sorry I missed it," Lia said.

Mara finally managed a smile.

Lia added, "I have a feeling I'll be seeing more of it later."

Raven sighed, let go of Mara, and sat back. Success, yes. But the price had almost been more than he was willing to pay.

At CIA headquarters, Clark Wilson entered the break room. He refilled his coffee mug under the spout of a corner machine, selecting French roast.

James Duran entered and crowded him.

"Whoa," Wilson said, drawing back. Duran's face was flush with anger. "Something on your mind, Jim?"

"Your pal has some explaining to do!"

"I don't know what you're talking about."

"Marseille. We got a bunch of dead drug dealers and a warehouse burned to the ground."

"I told you already," Wilson said, "he cut me off. I have no idea what Raven is doing. He's not telling me."

"But you can reach him!"

"I can try, but what am I supposed to do? He's not on the payroll any longer. We don't control him."

"He's putting lives at risk," Duran said. "If the French find out an American did this—"

"We deny responsibility. Raven knows the risks."

"I have half a mind to tell the French who to look for."

"It's your decision, Jim. I can't stop you."

Duran scoffed and stormed out.

Wilson let out a breath, poured cream into his coffee, and returned to his office. He'd expected a reaction but had to admit Duran's response went a little too far. Raven was nothing if not thorough. He wouldn't shoot up France unless he had control over where the bullets were flying.

He asked Heinrich for a rundown of what happened in Marseille, and pondered calling Raven. Should he let Sam know the Agency might tag him for the job?

He'd have to leave the building to do so. He didn't want to risk using a company phone.

Raven, Mara, and the mercenaries sat in the cabin of the King Air. The chartered plane traveled at high altitude out of French airspace. Mara took the beer Darbo offered and sat with the mercenaries. Raven excused himself to call Oscar Morey.

"Everybody is buzzing about Marseille," Morey said.

"News travels fast."

"In those circles, yes. You back in the air?"

"Heading for Stockholm. Unless you have another idea."

"I found the sister," Morey said. "She's a schoolteacher in Belfast."

"I'm listening."

Morey gave Raven a rundown on the woman's name, work location, where she lived. He'd email the information for Raven to look over.

"I think if you grab her," Morey said, "el-Dowd will have no choice but to respond in person."

"They're close?"

"She's his only living relative. I think it's a good idea."

"I'm having second thoughts about involving the sister. This isn't her fight."

"She's benefitted from the family business as much as her brother, Sam."

"How did she get to Ireland?"

"Claimed refugee status because of the war. Northern Ireland agreed to let her stay."

"Does she share any of her brother's jihadist sympathies?"

"Unknown. You looking for an excuse?"

"I certainly am."

"Time will tell. If she does, she'll put up a fight. If she doesn't, hell, maybe she'll help."

"I highly doubt that. Families stick together."

"Make up your mind, Sam. Grabbing the sister goes right to the heart of this."

"We'll have to be careful."

"It's el-Dowd you want. When he shows up, you end this, then let the woman go."

"You make it sound so simple."

"It actually is simple," Morey said. "You're making it complicated."

Raven held back a reply. He was sure Morey was right, and wrong, at the same time. Continued strikes would only wear out him, Mara, and the Raiders. He could either put el-Dowd's sister at risk or put his people at greater risk. Neither option seemed palatable.

"War is hell, Sam," Morey said.

"You're not kidding."

Both remained silent a moment. Raven glanced at Mara. Darbo was in the middle of a story and she was laughing. It felt good to see her laugh. He was fighting for her. Had it only been him on the vengeance trail, he might have changed his mind.

"What do you want to do, Sam?"

"We'll alter our course for Belfast. Send me the information."

"On the way," Morey said.

CHAPTER THIRTY-TWO

The chartered King Air made a refueling stop in Berlin before continuing to Belfast.

With his English roots, Raven had strong opinions about Northern Ireland. While he leaned toward supporting the British, it wasn't hard to understand the point of view of the Irish. But it was difficult to support a rebel group whose idea of independence was their own form of Marxism. They wanted to trade one form of "tyranny" for another. Had they succeeded the country might have found itself mired in another civil war. Raven didn't think Irish citizens, as proud as they were, would take kindly to following the orders of thugs. An IRA victory only would have brought more tragedy to a land which had seen enough already.

Landing at George Best airport, Raven felt a swell of emotion. Northern Ireland, and Belfast in particular, had improved with the end of the Troubles. The thriving city delighted him. As they boarded two taxis for their hotel, Raven felt a sense of hope. Hope there was an end to an endless war, and his own struggle might have a natural conclusion. A conclusion not brought about by a bullet in the back.

His war would only end when the ghosts in his dreams

finally rested.

Or he took a bullet in the back.

But he preferred the other version.

There was only one hotel in Belfast worth visiting. The Europa, known as "the most bombed hotel in the world". The IRA had targeted the establishment over thirty times during the Troubles. The hotel always cleaned up and carried on. The world's press flocked there during the war where they pooled information for reports.

The hotel's bars also became a gathering point for mercenaries, paramilitaries, and anybody who wanted in on the fight. The IRA had set off so many bombs in and near the hotel because of the press. Any IRA-related event in the building received coverage and brought publicity to the IRA's point of view.

Later, during the negotiations of the 1995 peace accords, the Europa hosted foreign dignitaries and VIPs to close the peace deal. Raven had no love for politicians of any stripe but appreciated the symbolism. Their stay at the Europa signaled to the world peace was now the order of the day in Northern Ireland.

Raven secured two adjoining rooms on the sixth floor. Mara and Lia would occupy one while Raven, Darbo, and Roger Justice took the other.

Raven addressed the crew after everybody had a chance to settle down, and food had been sent up. He sat at a table with his laptop screen facing Mara and the Raiders.

"Here's our target," he said. "Ameena el-Dowd."

The image on the screen showed a dark-haired female, very thin, with high-cheekbones, narrow jaw, and a thin neck.

"She's a schoolteacher at Elmgrove Primary School," Raven said. "She and her brother are close. She's his only remaining living relative, and if we grab her, we'll pull el-Dowd out of Afghanistan. He'll come and deal with the situation himself."

"You sure he won't send a bunch of guys and stay hidden?" Justice said.

"It's a risk, but what would you do, Roger?"

"I'd be here. I'm not going to let my guys accidentally kill her."

"Exactly. El-Dowd should have the same reaction."

"You aren't sure," Lia said.

"We can't be one-hundred-percent positive of anything," Raven said, "except the sun rising in the east."

"And death and taxes," Darbo pointed out to light laughter.

"We begin surveillance on Ms. El-Dowd tomorrow, me and Mara to start, then we'll tag team with Roger and Lia."

"What do I do?" Darbo said.

"We need more gear after depleting everything in Marseille. Know anybody local?"

"Plenty, but not all of them are...shall we say...reliable sources. You can't buy guns here without the current version of the IRA sticking its nose in your business."

Raven nodded. The "Real" IRA, they called themselves. The "true" IRA carrying on the fight against the British. In reality, they were a criminal organization nicknamed the "Rafia". Drugs, human trafficking, and other criminal activity received more focus than their "fight for freedom".

"We need weapons," Raven said. "We need a place to keep the woman. I need you to secure both, Darbo."

"The guns might give us trouble," Darbo said, "but a place to stay is easy. I know a guy who can get us a cottage in the country."

"With a wide field of fire? Defensible on all sides?"

"I'll throw in a garden and a creek filled with fish."

"Good."

Raven concluded the briefing, and the Raiders turned their full attention to the food. Mara asked Raven if she could speak with him privately. They went out to the hallway.

"What's on your mind?"

"What happens after this?"

"I don't know what you mean."

"Say we get el-Dowd to come here. He tries to rescue his sister and we kill him. Does it solve our problem?"

"Not in the least."

"What then?"

"I'd like to find out who those Americans were who showed up when we were in the caves."

She froze.

"I think the answer," he said, "lies in your suppressed memories."

"You think I can pick out the faces? How?"

"There are ways," Raven said. "We have to try them. I know of a doctor in Switzerland we can go to, but it's up to you."

"You're putting this on me?"

"You want me to tell you what to do? I'm asking you to dig into your memories in ways you've never done. Clarify who was there, as thin a clue as it may be. So, yes, it's up to you."

She took a deep breath. "All right. I'll do it. And then we go to the US?"

"It's where Americans tend to be." Raven smiled.

She tried to smile back, but it quickly faded. She folded her arms instead.

He pulled her close and rubbed her back. "Dig deep, Mara. We're almost there. This is almost over."

She put her arms around him, face buried in his chest.

"I trust you," she said.

Elmgrove Primary School was a set of red brick buildings surrounded by a wrought-iron white fence with brick posts.

Raven and Mara, posing as husband and wife planning to move into the nearby area, toured the school with a staff administrator. The woman showed them the playground and cafeteria, informing them of the benefits of the school, and how their two children would find their educational needs met with the "outstanding" curriculum.

Raven asked most of the questions while Mara remained silent. Her focus was on the number of teachers whose rooms they passed. She wanted to pick out Ameena el-Dowd, and when they passed an open door where a child was calling out, "Miss Amy!" she made a point of stopping to look. Raven and the school administrator stopped as well. They continued their conversation about test scores and science programs. Raven had told her he was an engineer, so a good science program was high on his list of priorities.

The administrator noticed Mara's interest in the class. She lowered her voice to describe Ameena el-Dowd as one of their best and brightest teachers.

"She's from the Middle East, speaks three languages, and her kids love her to pieces. They call her 'Miss Amy'."

Raven and Mara seemed pleased with the knowledge. They'd want their kids to have a teacher like Miss Amy.

After the tour they waited until classes let out at 2:50. The flood of traffic from parents picking up their kids clogged the street. Buses chugged out of a "buses only" crescent on one side. Raven and Mara waited in the staff parking lot watching for Ameena el-Dowd.

They finally spotted her an hour later, after the rush of parents and buses had gone. Ameena el-Dowd, carrying a purse and backpack, unlocked a Honda coupe. She waved goodbye to a passing colleague and put her bags in the back seat. Raven and Mara followed her onto the street.

Twenty minutes later, she turned into the underground parking garage of an apartment building. Raven, parked in a red zone across the street, noted the address, before pulling away and making a left turn.

Oscar Morey's information had been confirmed. Raven's hands began to sweat; he wiped them on his pants at a stoplight.

"You all right?"

"I don't like involving somebody who may not deserve the trouble," he said.

She said nothing.

"But we're going forward," Raven said. "I'm breaking my rule this one time."

The light changed and he drove on.

Ameena el-Dowd locked the door behind her and set her purse and backpack on the kitchen table.

She brewed a cup of tea and unloaded the pack. A stack of papers joined a second stack already on the table, papers she needed to grade and return to her students. Her students were 10 and 11 years old, and they created a big workload. She preferred the older students. Even more work, yes, but she found most of them took in her lessons like a sponge taking in water. They asked tough questions and offered insights she often hadn't thought of herself. And she'd been a teacher for over 15 years.

She'd started in Afghanistan and had tolerated Taliban rule. But once the United States and its allies invaded, she had to get out. A newspaper article about Northern Ireland accepting refugees had caught her attention, and she'd made arrangements to get out. Her brother, Basheer, had financed the trip. He hadn't wanted her in harm's way.

She knew all about the family business but had nothing to do with the day-to-day running. She lived off a portion of the spoils. The source of the money didn't bother her. Many of her countrymen depended on opium crops for their survival. Anything threatening such livelihood was anathema to her.

But work would wait a while. She sat with her tea with a grin. Tonight, she had a date. A blind date arranged by one of her fellow teachers, a fellow who was anything *but* a teacher. Eric Doyle worked as a city engineer. Her friend said he had a solid physique and bright blue eyes and didn't drink.

An Irishman who refused alcohol? Worked for her!

Finishing her tea, she selected an outfit from her collection, a red dress with spaghetti straps. Being out of Afghanistan allowed her to shed the Muslim rules of dress.

After a quick shower she lingered over her makeup. The dress fit perfectly. She was too tiny for her own good, but often joked a child or two would fill her out. And then she'd have an excuse to shop for new clothes.

She and Doyle had plans to meet at a pub for a light dinner, and butterflies flapped in her stomach. Dates didn't always go well for her, and she wanted this one to work out. She departed the apartment and drove away.

Darbo grumbled.

Roger Justice said, "You don't sound happy."

"Raven, Mara, and Lia get the good stuff while we're freezing in the middle of nowhere dealing with a gang I'd rather not have to hand money to."

"It's not nowhere, per se," Justice said. "It's a nice industrial area. Nobody around. Empty parking lot. What could go wrong?"

"A lot."

"If these guys are so bad, why—"

"They're the worst of a lot of bad options."

"As long as they provide what we need."

Darbo grunted again. He sat behind the wheel of their rented Nissan SUV, Justice in the passenger seat. Roger Justice had his nine-millimeter Beretta autoloader in his lap. He might not admit it, Darbo decided, but his actions expressed the doubt his verbal answers didn't betray.

A van approached, headlamps bright. Darbo flashed his lights. The van turned toward them.

Darbo removed a pistol from his shoulder holster and checked to see a cartridge seated in the chamber.

"Here we go," he said.

He opened the door to exit. Roger Justice followed.

CHAPTER THIRTY-THREE

Ameena el-Dowd stood at the bar of O'Malley's Pub and nursed a pint of beer.

Her fetching outfit and exotic looks attracted male attention. She more than once had to explain she was waiting for somebody. The lads seemed to have bets going on who could get a conversation started, but she kept shooting them down.

She wasn't the only lone female at the bar. Ameena noticed another woman, a redhead, drinking straight vodka. She looked around as if she were a shark hunting for plankton. Her resting bitch face kept men away, poor retch. Maybe Ameena could adopt the look on demand.

The pub wasn't full yet, there were still booths open, and tables should they want one. Ameena was impressed with the old-world décor. Even the signs for brands of beer behind the bar were subtle; nothing gaudy or flashy.

Eric Doyle finally showed up, two minutes late, but when she saw him, she forgot about time and anything else.

My goodness! He was the exact hunk her friend had described. Tall, blond, broad-chested with a chiseled jaw and a smile showing a small gap between his two front teeth. He quickly covered the gap by pressing his lips together. She was immediately mesmerized by the gap; it defined him, in a good way. He looked much sharper than the other lads in the bar in his slacks, button-down shirt and sport coat. The other male patrons still wore their dirty work clothes or casuals. They weren't trying. Eric Doyle had an impression to make, and he made one on Ameena el-Dowd.

He ordered a pint as well and they found a booth.

"You look lovely," Doyle said. "Certainly not any teacher I ever had."

She laughed. "You're not the only one to say so."

"I didn't mean to sound gross."

"It's fine, I appreciate the compliment. Sandy says you're an engineer?"

Doyle swallowed a mouthful of beer. "Been working for the city for ten years now, yeah."

"Enjoy it?"

"It's a step."

"To what?"

"Something better as soon as I find it. Meanwhile it's a solid job and pays my mortgage."

She brightened. "I'm still living in an apartment."

Doyle smiled, but kept his lips together. He didn't want to show the gap in his teeth. *So he's shy too.* She fell for him some more.

They ordered food and talked more, the conversation more animated as time passed.

Neither noticed they were being watched.

"Pub grub," Raven said, "is the *best* grub."

He sat across a small table from Mara Cole and sank his fork into a plate of bangers and mash with a side of baked beans. His own pint of beer accompanied the meal. Mara ate large forkfuls of cottage pie.

"This is better than London," she said.

"Don't let the Brits hear you."

Mara grinned.

They had a clear view of the booth where Ameena and her beau sat, Raven with the full view, Mara a partial one. At the bar, Lia Kenisova covered another angle.

"This is like those quiet dinners we used to have," Mara said. "The café near HQ? Remember?"

"I do."

"I always thought you took me there because it was cheap."

"I did," Raven said. "Had to stretch the dollar, you know?"

She smiled. "It's a nice memory."

"I'm glad."

Lia chimed in over the earbud com links each wore in their right ears.

"I can hear you two," the Russian said.

"Oh, dear," Raven said. "We've upset mother."

Mara laughed again. Raven smiled. Finally, she'd cracked the ice she'd encased herself with. The recent action had done her a world of good.

Lia Kenisova chugged another mouthful of vodka and waved for a refill, her fourth. The bartender didn't bat an eye. She made the gesture; out came the bottle; the bottle filled her glass with liquid elixir; she drank.

She was stuck, alone at the bar, watching two couples get lovey-dovey and it made her want to vomit. She never had trouble meeting men when she turned on the charm. She most certainly did not have the charm running tonight. She was dressed plainly, with a leather jacket, her hair down her shoulders, and looked mean. The lads gave her glances, but she offered no encouragement.

She was working, after all. But as she scanned some of the well-built men around her, she decided, after the job, it might be fun to return and see how much Irish she could get in her.

"It's a shame," Mara said in her ear, "we have to re-connect this way."

Oh, gawd...

"Are you changing your mind?" Raven said. "You don't want me out of your life when this is over?"

"You're going to leave anyway."

"Well—"

"Don't ruin this by lying to me, Sam."

Lia drank some vodka. At this rate, it was going to be a long night.

She said bowed her head and muttered, "You're not paying me enough for this, *Sam.*"

Raven's chuckle sent a red flush up her neck.

Roger Justice, gun in hand, moved the hand behind his right leg.

The van containing the gun dealers stopped halfway. The driver made a 180-degree turn, then backing toward the Nissan. The van stopped. The side door opened, and two men stepped out, both showing empty hands.

"We better not have a problem," Justice said. "Without this gear, we'll be throwing rocks at el-Dowd's men when they show up."

"Stand by, Roger."

"Copy."

"Good evening," said one of the gun runners. He was shorter than his companion, with flat black hair sitting on his head like a wet towel. "No need for the guns, mates. We're here for business."

"So are we," Darbo said. "Let's get this done and we can all be on our way."

"Of course," said the short man. His taller companion opened the rear doors. The interior contained four stacked trunks. The short man gestured for Darbo and Justice to come closer. Justice stayed beside the car but took two steps to the right to keep an angle on the interior. Darbo approached the van.

The short man stepped away while his taller companion opened two trunks, lifting the lids. Justice couldn't see inside, but he did watch Darbo lift out a Galil short-barreled automatic rifle. Darbo examined the gun, nodding, and examined more from the second trunk. He hefted an old US M-249 Squad Automatic Weapon, a light machine gun firing 5.56mm ammunition via standard magazine or linked ammunition through an attached cloth pouch.

A cursory check of the other trunks satisfied Darbo as well. Inside, Claymore mines, a trio of LAW rocket launchers, and assorted ammunition. Darbo held the heavy ordnance up for Roger to see.

The short man stepped forward. "And the money?"

Darbo reached into the back pocket of his jeans. Justice had no idea how Raven had as much money to throw around as he did, buying weapons, chartering fancy jets. Obviously, he knew where to find cash, and Justice was eager for a tip. Darbo handed two stacks of wrapped bills to the short man.

The Irish gun runner thumbed through both stands, nodding. "All right. Need help loading?"

Darbo used the Nissan's remote to pop the trunk and gestured for Justice. Roger opened both rear doors of the sedan before going to the van. He put his gun away.

Darbo and Justice transferred the trunks to the Nissan. They put the bigger trunk with the heavy machine gun in the back seat. The Irish gun runner said, "A pleasure, mates," and his companion shut the rear doors. They climbed back into the van. The van drove off.

Darbo and Justice returned to their SUV and Darbo hit the starter button. He drove off in the opposite direction of the van.

They both let out a breath.

"Guess we were wrong," Darbo said.

"Didn't hurt to be careful."

Justice turned in his seat to look out the back window. Darbo drove normally. After a few turns and lane changes, Justice turned around again and said, "I think we're clear."

"Let's get this out to the cottage," Darbo said. "I don't think Sam would appreciate us bringing it back to the hotel."

Justice laughed. "I think they'd be used to having guns around the place."

Darbo had secured the cottage earlier in the day, renting from a friend. He promised his pal he'd need to do a lot of cleanup by the time he and his crew departed.

"You expect trouble?" his friend asked.

"We're advertising for it," Darbo told him. "We're going to shoot this place up quite nicely."

His friend didn't react. "You'll want the extra insurance then."

Darbo agreed and spent more of Sam Raven's money.

"How far to the cottage?" Justice asked.

"Not long. Want some music?" Darbo turned on the radio.

Roger Justice said music was a good idea.

Ameena and her date left the pub after dinner, Raven and Mara leaving at the same time. The man walked Ameena to her car, where he kissed her goodnight, and they promised to see each other again soon.

Raven and Mara climbed into a rented BMW and followed the schoolteacher.

"You with us, Lia?" Raven said.

"Two cars back."

"Do we take her now?"

"For heaven's sake, let her get out of the dress," Lia said.

"Back to the hotel then," Raven said, making the next left while Ameena continued on. "We'll grab her in the morning before work."

Lia agreed and signed off. Raven and Mara plucked the earbuds out and set them in the cup holders.

"Like the old days," Mara said.

"It's all coming back to you?"

"I'm focusing on the good things."

"Like what?"

He felt her hand touch his legs. "You."

He squeezed her hand, and wished they weren't sleeping in separate rooms. At the same time, he reminded himself to remain focused. He was here to do a job, not fall in love. When the job was done, he'd move on. Like always.

But this time, leaving would be different. He'd leave behind nothing but pain. For him and Mara.

He let go of her hand. She withdrew. Raven drove on.

They picked up Ameena's trail from the apartment the next morning.

Raven and Mara in the BMW; Darbo, Justice, and Lia in the Nissan.

Heavy traffic slowed them down, but they managed to keep Ameena's Honda in view. There was a straight stretch of roadway halfway to the school where they planned to make their move.

Raven didn't speak; neither did Mara or the Raiders in the other car. All were focused on the task. Get Ameena, throw her into the back of the Nissan, cover her with a blanket, and proceed to the cottage.

Raven had his leather sap with him to smack her into cooperating if need be. He hated to do it, but they had no other way to subdue the schoolteacher. And they needed her subdued to avoid her trying to flag down help.

Presently the three cars reached the straight road. Traffic thinned a little. Raven drove alongside Ameena while Lia put the Nissan in back-up position.

Raven wrenched the wheel, using the BMW's left fender to nudge the Honda. Ameena overcorrected, smacking into the BMW. Raven bumped her car again, forcing it off the road and onto the grassy shoulder. He stopped in front of her car, diagonally. It would look like an accident to anybody driving by.

Raven and Mara hopped out of the car as Lia stopped the Nissan behind the Honda, Justice and Darbo jumping out.

Ameena climbed out of the car, her face red despite her darker skin tone. She didn't look behind her.

"What are you doing—"

Darbo grabbed her in a bear hug, lifting her off the ground. She screamed. Raven swung the sap, a light tap on her head. She went limp in Darbo's grip, unconscious. Mara opened the back door of the Nissan. Darbo and Raven shoved Ameena inside. Mara straddled the other woman to tie her wrists and ankles, jam a washcloth in her mouth, and throw a yellow blanket over her.

Darbo grabbed Ameena's purse and backpack from the rear of the Honda. The team jumped back into their cars and blended with traffic once again.

Raven's pulse raced as he drove, the lump under the blanket in the back seat centered in his rearview mirror.

"Take the lead, Darbo," he said.

"Copy."

Lia drove ahead of the BMW. Raven fell behind. Darbo directed them out of the city to the country, and the cottage he had secured for this phase of the mission.

Not much longer now, and Basheer el-Dowd would be in Sam Raven's gun sights.

CHAPTER THIRTY-FOUR

The cottage outside Belfast, isolated in the country, suited Raven's needs perfectly. Darbo couldn't have selected a better home base.

Raven stopped the BMW in front of the cottage. Lia parked the Nissan SUV around the side. Ameena remained unconscious beneath the blanket.

The cottage had a stone exterior, thatched roof, and stone chimney. The cottage sat in a green field with a stream running east to west about 20 yards from the front door. The rolling green hills complemented the location, and the blue sky was welcome.

Raven considered the cottage very defensible. Terrific fields of fire for a force lying in wait. Sniper on a hill; heavy machine gunner beside one of the trees. Plenty of natural covers. Hills, cutouts, trees, fallen trunks hollowed out and surrounded by overgrowth. The high grass would prove an advantage, as well as rocks and boulder clusters.

He wasn't sure what to do with the stream. He'd have preferred it not be there, but a line of trees with intertwined trunks on the opposite side had a certain appeal. Great place for a sniper.

The cottage's stone construction provided solid protection from small arms fire. He didn't assume the walls would survive a grenade or a shoulder-fired missile strike.

They exited the cars. Raven and Darbo carried the still-unconscious Ameena el-Dowd into the well-furnished cottage. There was actually too much furniture and it made the interior feel small. The kitchen was small as well, big enough for two, if they didn't mind bumping into each other. Darbo had stocked the kitchen with canned goods and a bag of potatoes. Meat, chicken and vegetables were in the refrigerator.

They put Ameena el-Dowd in one of the bedrooms, on the bed, and Raven pulled the gag from her mouth. Ameena lay with her mouth agape, her body slack.

"Now what?" Mara said.

Raven looked grim. "Let's find her cell phone."

Darbo, with Ameena's purse, dumped the contents on the polished dining table. Lia emptied the backpack of papers and other miscellaneous items.

"I guess her students," Lia said, examining the papers, "will have to wait a little longer for their grades."

Raven grabbed her cell phone. He swiped the screen. It wasn't locked and didn't require a password or thumb print.

He was conscious of his team staring at him as he scrolled through her contact list. He told Mara to wait in the room with Ameena for when she woke up. Mara departed.

Raven found what he wanted. Her brother was listed simply as "Bash". He put the phone in a pocket.

"Not ready to call?" Justice said.

"Let's get the weapons ready, and I want to walk around the cottage and get ideas for a defensive line," Raven said. "I want el-Dowd's people walking into a crossfire."

The Raiders nodded. Darbo and Justice hauled the trunks from another room. The four set about oiling and loading the weapons and setting them aside.

Raven was familiar with the US M-249 from his 82nd Airborne days. He inspected the weapon with a sense of nostalgia.

The automatic rifles purchased by Darbo were also top-notch. The Galil ACE 5.56mm was a recent favorite of Raven's for its ease of handling and reliability.

What really caught his attention was a pristine example of the latest special operations sniper rifle, the Barrett-manufactured Mk21. With its long barrel, bolt action, and three caliber option, it was a good choice. Raven had yet to fire the weapon but had heard nothing but praise for its capabilities. He noticed their particular example was chambered for 7.62x51.

Darbo volunteered to be the group's sniper.

They inspected the rest of the house. A hallway led to the remaining bedrooms and single bathroom, but no back door. Which meant they had one way in, and one way out, and no option for retreat.

"Who wants to retreat?" Justice said after Raven pointed out the observation.

"You never let me down, Roger," Raven said. "We'd be better served staking our positions outside. Let them assume we're in the house until we show them otherwise."

They walked around the cottage to pick out where they'd set the Claymore mines, deciding to spread the mines to cover any potential attack point. The rear shed behind the cottage contained landscaping equipment. It was open only on one side and Raven didn't consider it tactically sound.

Raven and Darbo then wandered the terrain, looking for positions to set up a crossfire converging at the front of the house.

Mara called them from the doorway.

"She's awake," Mara said as Raven brushed past her.

Ameena el-Dowd did not look happy as she lay on the

bed with her wrists and ankles secured, her hair a mess, eyes wide with fury.

"What are you *doing*?"

"Relax," Raven said, leaning in the doorway with his arms folded. "We aren't going to hurt you."

"You already *did* hurt me! You *hit* me!"

"Minor headache. I promise it won't happen again."

"Where am I?"

"Outside Belfast. Let me explain what's going on. I want to have a conversation with your brother, Basheer. You're going to assure he shows up."

"I haven't talked to my brother in months!"

"He'll be glad to hear from you, I'm sure."

"What am I supposed to say to him?"

"You might start by telling him you've been kidnapped."

She scoffed. "You aren't going to get away with this!"

"You watch too much television, Amy."

She almost lurched off the bed. "*Don't* call me that."

"Get comfortable," Raven said. "We'll talk again shortly." He pulled the door shut. She started yelling.

"Should have put the gag back in," Lia Kenisova said.

Darbo and Justice laughed.

Raven took Ameena's cell phone from his pocket and crossed to a couch put up against the front window. The polished coffee table matched the dining table, bracketed by love seats on the other three sides. Mara and his Raiders sat around the table with him.

Raven tapped Basheer's name and put the phone to his ear. Three rings.

Then: "Ameena?"

"No," Raven said.

Basheer el-Dowd's tone turned grim. "Who is this?"

"Sam Raven."

A pause. Then: "Why do you have my sister's telephone?"

"Because I have your sister tied up in a bedroom."

"Why?"

"You and I require a rematch, Basheer."

"Do I have you to thank for the disaster in Marseille?"

"Write my name in bold, Bash."

"You have no idea what beast you've unleashed."

Raven laughed. "I might say the same thing. We were no threat to you, yet suddenly my team and I are moving targets. Why?"

"You have no idea."

"Did we see something we shouldn't have? Perhaps the Americans who visited?"

"Make your best guess."

"Why did you keep us alive, Bash? There was no reason for that."

"My jihadist friends were going to pay good money for five CIA agents." El-Dowd chuckled. "Your exposure would have caused a wonderful scandal."

"Sorry we interrupted your plans by doing something as silly as escaping. But back to our current state. I have your sister. One assumes you'll want her back."

"If you want a rematch, Mr. Raven, I'm eagerly anticipating such an event."

"Good. We're outside Belfast." He gave the mailing address of the cottage. "You'll love the place. Little cottage in the country."

"You expect me to meet you there?"

"Of course."

"You're insane."

"You'll be here, Bash. You don't have a choice. I have your only living relative, and you have seventy-two hours to get here before I mail her back in small pieces. You can reassemble her body when you get them all." Raven laughed.

"You've made a terrible mistake."

"No, *you* made the mistake. You made a *bigger* mistake when you murdered three of my friends."

"See you soon, Mr. Raven. I'm bringing an army."

"I'll put the kettle on." Raven ended the call.

He looked up at the faces of his team.

Lia Kenisova spoke first. "Did I hear him say he's bringing an army?"

"You did." Raven set the phone on the cushion beside him.

"Are we able to fight off an army?"

"Lia, this isn't the time for doubts. We have him right where we want him."

"Well, *darling*, you better hope I don't break a fingernail."

Raven smiled. "Anybody else afraid of breaking a nail?"

Darbo said, "I don't want to chip a tooth."

"I broke all my nails already," Justice said.

The two men laughed.

Lia scowled. She folded her arms. "You're *quickly* getting on my bad side, gentlemen."

Mara sat quietly, her eyes darting back and forth between the Raiders.

"All is as it should be," Raven said. "All we have to do now is—"

"What?" Lia said.

"Why don't we do some cooking and enjoy the country? A nice Irish stew sounds great."

Mara chimed in. She thought getting food going was a great idea.

Lia, her arms still folded, stated she was not cooking at all.

CHAPTER THIRTY-FIVE

James Duran needed answers. If Sam Raven thought he could cut off Clark Wilson, the former agent was mistaken.

Duran needed to catch Wilson off campus to make any attempt at duplicating Wilson's cell phone. The opportunity finally arose at lunch. Wilson left the complex for a down-town sandwich place, and Duran "just happened" to visit the same spot.

The burner phone in Duran's pocket contained only neces-sary operating software to perform basic functions. No apps, no internet. It was blank other than special software working off Bluetooth. What looked like a normal phone hid something beneath the façade making it anything but normal.

The phone contained a Bluetooth-based hacking tool devel-oped by the CIA. Duran knew there were several similar tools available to the public if one knew where to look. The CIA's gear was much better.

Every cell phone contained exploitable vulnerabilities the average user didn't know about. No tech security is foolproof no matter what any manufacturer claims. The CIA tool found those weaknesses like somebody cutting through a security fence.

The program, using Bluetooth, wormed into the target phone's system and transferred the data to the burner phone. Cell phones are small computers, but nobody treats them that way.

It was one of the primary reasons why cell phones weren't allowed on military bases or at CIA HQ.

Duran was counting on the program's effectiveness as he joined his employee at an outdoor table. Traffic on the street, and the buzz of other diners' conversations, covered their chat.

All he had to do was keep Wilson talking long enough for the phone's software to do its work.

"You've been working late, Clark. Any reason why?"

"Are you kidding?" Wilson ate a potato chip. His lunch was a hot turkey and bacon sandwich. "I've trying to sort the el-Dowd issue."

"I want you and Heinrich off of that," Duran said. "We have other matters requiring our attention."

"We've lost a lot of people over this, Jim."

"I'm assigning somebody else, somebody not as close to the situation. As long as you had contact with Raven, it made sense to keep you there. Since that's no longer the case, I want you on other things."

"Who's taking my place?"

"Doesn't matter." Duran ate some of his roast beef sandwich. He washed it down with a sip of bottled water.

"Raven may reach out again."

Duran shook his head. "When he does, let me know."

Wilson retreated within as he ate some more, keeping his eyes away.

Duran watched him. He was trying to think of another reason not to be taken off the el-Dowd case. Duran let him chase his thoughts. When he felt the burner phone vibrate in his pocket, he knew the duplication had completed.

Wilson finally shrugged and looked up. "Fine. I'll move on."

"Thanks for making it easy, Clark."

In more ways than one.

Duran wrapped the remaining portion of his sandwich and headed back to the office. He left Wilson sitting alone.

All James Duran required were the current whereabouts of Sam Raven. El-Dowd had reported his sister's kidnapping and demanded help. Duran had already confirmed the cottage address. Belfast news reports mentioned a car accident where witnesses described a woman carried off against her will. The Belfast police had little to go on. The roadway where the "accident" had taken place wasn't covered by CCTV cameras.

Duran expected the information on Wilson's phone to provide actionable data. If Raven had called, or his cell number was listed in the contacts, Duran could pin the location. Narrow the search. Solving the "Raven Problem" might be as simple as directing a drone strike to take out the cottage.

And to hell with el-Dowd's sister. If murdering a bunch of people to protect their drug operation was the solution Welles and el-Dowd deemed appropriate, there was no reason not to include Ameena el-Dowd among the targets.

He left the restaurant and drove a few miles to a mall parking lot, where he stopped his car under the shade of a tree. Examining the copied phone, Duran scanned Wilson's contacts. He found no number listed with Sam Raven's name attached. He peeked through Wilson's photo gallery, mostly family and pets. He checked out Wilson's high score on Angry Birds. No phone messages to listen to; the text messages were between him and his wife and two teenagers.

As a first shot across the bow, the phone didn't yield anything useful. Raven had cut Wilson off because he was beginning to have doubts the CIA had ever had his team's best interest in mind. He suspected a traitor had compromised the mission and didn't want Wilson tipping off whoever engineered the treachery.

But Raven surely trusted his old friend. Eventually he'd make contact.

Duran put the copied phone away and found his own cell.

He had to deliver some bad news to a man who'd apparently had his fill of bad news for a while. He kept the windows rolled up so nobody passing by heard his conversation. He had a feeling the chat might become a heated exchange indeed.

"Did you copy the phone?" el-Dowd said after a brief greeting.

"You sound awful," Duran said.

"I'm not sleeping. The man has my *sister.*"

"I copied the phone, but there's nothing on it we can use yet."

"Did you check out the address Raven gave me?"

"It's a cottage, like he said. Middle of the country. You could set off a nuke there and I don't think anybody would notice."

"I'm preparing my people now."

"It's a trap," Duran said.

"I *know* it's a trap. I cannot leave Ameena in danger. I may not be a nice man, but I'm not going to sacrifice her to you American savages."

"Is she tied to the business in any way?"

"None."

"You can bet Raven knows. He's bluffing. He's not going to hurt her. She's a non-combatant. He goes out of his way to not hurt civilians. If you wait the three days and don't do anything, he'll let her go."

"I can't take the chance. His action in Marseille has cost us millions of dollars. Product is delayed. We'll be rebuilding for months before we can ship out of there again."

"We have other options, Basheer."

"Those options, as you put it, are serving other areas of the world. I can't simply redirect our people in Greece to ship product to the US."

"Our new friends won't be happy. Demand is going to go up and they may rethink our arrangements."

"Placate them, Duran. I'm busy."

"I'm telling you he's bluffing. Use your head!"

"I do not require your permission. If you and your senator pal have a problem, you better find a way to stop me."

"Must we?"

"If you think not having drugs to sell will be an issue, wait until I'm no longer around. So, please, do your worst."

Duran opened his mouth to reply when the call ended with a beep. He scowled at the phone.

Pounding the driver's door in frustration, Duran took a few deep breaths to consider his next move. He had to update Welles. Who did they have in Afghanistan who could intercept el-Dowd? The opium king had now become a liability. Raven was luring him into a trap. He might not kill el-Dowd, but instead extract information.

Suddenly an idiot with a website wasn't such a big problem.

Duran called Welles. His assistant, Lucy Hunt, told him Welles was in a meeting. Duran demanded she get him out of the meeting and on the phone. Lucy complied. A few moments later, Welles spoke.

"What's the meaning of this, James?"

"We have a problem." Duran updated the senator, adding: "El-Dowd is out of control. He's not thinking straight."

"There's a reason going after a man's family is an effective way of gaining cooperation, James."

"I'm aware."

"Basheer is no different than anybody else."

"I expected more."

"Everyone has a weakness."

"We need a solution," Duran said.

"You have people in the area?"

"Yes."

"I suggest you call them and put them to work. El-Dowd cannot leave Afghanistan."

"What about—"

"There's a line of ten guys waiting to take his place and reap the benefits of the relationship we've established. The network will carry on without Basheer el-Dowd."

"And our Italian friends?"

"You let me worry about them. They'll listen to reason."

Duran laughed.

"It's not a joke," Welles said. "All I have to do is remind them of how much money is coming their way, and they'll calm down."

"Pissed off gangsters could ruin us, too. Permanently."

"I will *handle* them, James. It will be okay. Get on the phone and take care of el-Dowd. The next time we talk, I expect you to tell me he's tits up."

The call ended and Duran sat for a moment with a fist clenched tight and trying not to scream. It was a hell of a job. In the end, he hoped the money made it worthwhile.

CHAPTER THIRTY-SIX

Raven wandered up a hill, holding a steam mug of tea. He wasn't armed for a change, and it felt good not having his regular iron dragging down his left side.

The green hills stretched forever, meeting the blue sky in the distance. Birds chirped. It was a wonderful place. He hated to bring violence to it.

"Sam?"

He turned. Lia Kenisova stopped beside him.

"What's going on?"

She handed him his cell phone. He'd purposefully left it inside and let out a low groan.

"Who is it?"

"Clark Wilson."

Raven took the phone. Lia excused herself.

"Hello, Clark. What time is it there?"

"Late enough," the CIA man said. "But we need to talk."

"Sounds urgent."

"I've been going over a few things, and I wanted to bounce a few ideas off you."

"Let's hear it."

"Have you ever wondered why your el-Dowd mission failed?"

"We've talked about it," Raven said. "Why?"

"Because I wondered too. I looked through the files—" and Wilson explained his theory, that James Duran, or somebody else, compromised the mission to serve another agenda, an agenda that remained a mystery. He talked about the Conspiracy Man website, and the posted photos showing Senator Aiden Welles chummy with Basheer el-Dowd.

"Interesting," Raven said.

"That's all you have to say?"

"I'd like further proof before I kill a man, Clark. Or several, since you think Senator Welles is also involved."

"That's the hard part. But the pictures don't lie, and the trip is noted in the files. He was *there* during the time you and your team were held captive. I'm not sure—"

"You can't go around asking without stirring the pot."

"I'm not you," Wilson said.

"That's a good thing, Clark. Be grateful."

Wilson continued talking, describing how Duran wanted him to stop looking into Raven's case.

"Isn't it curious," Wilson said, "he did so knowing you had decided to cut me out of things? Like suddenly I was of no more use?"

Raven said nothing.

"Are you still there?"

"I'm thinking."

"I've been doing too *much* thinking. We're talking about the deputy director of Special Activities conspiring with a senator to aid an enemy of the United States."

"When el-Dowd shows up, I'll ask him."

"He won't be in a mood to talk, Sam."

"I'll ask the sister."

"Think she'll tell you?"

"Only one way to find out. Thanks for the call, Clark. Get

some rest."

"Don't get killed, Sam."

"I'll try not to."

Raven ended the call and went into the house. Mara and the Raiders sat around the living room with the TV on, watching a game show. Raven reflected, after a brief look, that the Irish presented their game shows same as the US.

He crossed to the bedroom where they had Ameena el-Dowd tied up. They'd allowed her to use the bathroom and eat, but only when supervised by either Mara or Lia. She remained on the bed, laying on her side, her face drawn.

Raven leaned in the doorway.

"If you answer some questions," he said, "I'll see about adjusting your accommodations."

"Piss off."

"It's your brother I want, not you."

"I'm not going to help you kill him."

"What if I told you all I wanted was information."

Ameena blinked.

"Who are the Americans working with your brother?"

"Beats me."

"The CIA, and a senator. They've visited your bother many times. Give me names, and I'll untie your hands."

"I'm perfectly comfortable, thank you."

Raven laughed. "My compliments. You aren't the weeping willow I expected. Your family trained you well."

"Go away."

"Your arms must be numb. Surely, you'd prefer a better arrangement. I only want names."

Ameena el-Dowd shut her eyes tight. Raven looked at her thoughtfully. She had to know she risked not getting out of the cottage in one piece. If she was counting on her brother to defeat Raven and his crew, she was placing her eggs in a very small basket.

She opened her eyes. "Promise you won't hurt me?"

"Have we done so already? I think you've been treated very well, in spite of how we brought you here."

"I don't know names," she said. "I only know what my brother talked about."

"Tell me."

"There is a senator, somebody on the Senate Intelligence Committee. Basheer thought it was a major score to get him. He called the man 'Cowboy' because he's from Arizona."

"Uh-huh."

"And the CIA *is* protecting him, but I don't know who, and I don't know how. It's a deal he made before the American invasion."

Raven sighed. "How unfortunate."

"Is this where you tell me you were lying to me?"

"No." He called for Darbo and asked the big merc to cut the ties on Ameena's wrists. Darbo produced a folding knife from a pocket and complied. Ameena rolled onto her back, her arms flopping at her sides, and winced as the pins-and-needles effect began.

"That's all, Darbo."

Darbo grunted and went out.

"Are you sure you don't know specific names?"

"No. I'm not supposed to be involved."

"Why did your brother tell you then?"

"He was *bragging*, okay?" She started rubbing her hands against her hips.

Raven had no further questions. He pulled the door shut behind him and called Clark Wilson again, stepping outside. He'd left his tea on the porch. He took a sip, but it was cold. He put the mug down again.

"Sam?"

"Hope I didn't wake you."

"Who can sleep?"

"Ameena el-Dowd confirmed a CIA connection, and a senator on the Intelligence Committee. From Arizona."

Wilson cursed. "It's Welles." He cursed again.

"Tell me about him."

"Defense hawk. Plays up the patriot angle. Never saw a missile he didn't want fired at somebody for whatever reason the president dreamed up."

"And you said Duran was one of his bodyguards—"

"Is it making sense yet?"

"It's foggy but getting clearer. What is the address for the website you mentioned?"

Wilson told him.

"I'd like a look at those pictures myself."

"I'll do what I can on my end in the meantime."

"*Quietly*, Clark. Don't do anything stupid. Think of your family."

"I'll be in touch."

This time, Wilson ended the call.

Raven pocketed his phone and went back inside to warm up his tea. He felt calm. His reaction surprised him. He'd have expected to feel rage at being sold out from within. It had been easier thinking his crew had run into bad luck. Instead, the agency they had worked so hard for in order to serve their country had set them up to die.

He re-heated his tea and stood in the kitchen looking at Mara as she watched the television.

He wasn't sure what to tell her.

Raven went back outside and used his phone to access the internet. Time to look at the mysterious pictures. Perhaps the appearance of the photos answered the *why*. Welles and Company were willing to let sleeping dogs lie until the photos surfaced, but then they had to act.

Raven grimaced as he examined the pictures and the supposed dates on which they were taken. Wilson's theory seemed confirmed.

Accounts would be settled.

Soon.

CHAPTER THIRTY-SEVEN

Basheer el-Dowd's home was a mountaintop oasis.

Spread out over the top of a flat hill, the L-shaped single-level sat among palm trees. Rocks decorated the open front patio, with an adjacent helicopter pad.

From the turret-style room sprouting from the center of the house, tinted glass offered a 360-degree view of rich poppy fields in various stages of growth and maturity.

Armed soldiers in Toyota trucks patrolled the perimeter. Others were stationed at the house. They were men on loan from various jihadist factions to gain experience before being deployed to the field.

El-Dowd stood in the turret, a king overlooking his kingdom. His second-in-command, Mohammed al-Bari, reviewed a list of items for el-Dowd's trip to Ireland.

"The chopper will take you to our airfield," al-Bari said, "where the plane is waiting for you. You'll fly into Northern Ireland," al-Bari continued, consulting a clipboard, "where our contacts will collect you."

"Where am I landing?"

"A strip controlled by the IRA."

El-Dowd laughed. "You mean the group currently *calling*

itself the IRA."

"They're prepared to help."

"They better. We've paid them enough."

"They're working with our brothers already there who entered as refugees. There will be no conflict with them."

"From the airfield—"

"You'll be provided with weapons and taken to the cottage."

"How many men?"

"Twenty."

"Is that all they can spare?"

"It's everyone available. Our brothers are risking—"

"I don't care what they're risking, Mohammed. I care that they can do the job. We have no idea how many soldiers Raven has."

"It might be only him and the woman."

"I don't trust my fate to such fantasies, Mohammed."

Al-Bari said nothing.

"They will have to do," el-Dowd said.

Al-Bari continued. "You'll be provided with all-terrain vehicles to travel to the cottage. They have a route planned."

Al-Bari kept talking, but el-Dowd only half-listened. His thoughts wandered to his sister, and what hardships she was facing.

He hadn't slept since Raven's call. When he tried to sleep, he heard her crying softly.

Ameena had never been cut out for the family business. She was always a nurturer, not a hunter. Her personality pleased their father, who didn't want her in the drug business. He'd planned, always, to turn the empire over to his son. He didn't want his son and daughter at odds with each other. Ameena benefited only with her portion of the money generated by the opium sales. She had more tied up in a trust she'd receive when she married.

El-Dowd let out a sigh. If he died rescuing her, so be it. As long as she survived. Nothing else mattered to him. His father had made him promise to look after her, and he'd been against her move to Ireland. But at the same time, getting her out of Afghanistan protected her. Now he realized he had made a mistake. She'd have been safer staying close to home, teaching Afghan children. She'd insisted upon going, and el-Dowd knew she'd leave with, or without, his help. It had been easier to help her.

Al-Bari stopped talking.

"Is that all?" el-Dowd said.

"Unless you have any questions."

"I do not."

"In that case—"

"Yes, time to go."

El-Dowd turned from the tinted glass and followed a spiral staircase to the living room. Al-Bari walked behind him. Collecting his single leather suitcase from a couch, he exited the house. On the helicopter pad, his transportation awaited.

The chopper was a blue Bell 505 Jet Ranger X equipped with the latest GPS navigation, roomy cabin, and leather seats. He'd had his people rig a rocket pod on the starboard side, as well as anti-missile countermeasures. They were in Afghanistan, after all, and shooting down the chopper while he rode within was a reality he had to face. So far, so good. The rockets had never been fired in the five years he'd owned the chopper. The only drawback was the lack of insulation in the cabin, and the engine and rotor noise became quite loud. He solved the problem with earplugs.

El-Dowd climbed into the chopper. The pilot started the engine and the rotors picked up speed. El-Dowd offered only a wave in farewell to al-Bari, who stood watching. The chopper lifted off, rising above the roofline, then tipped forward and turned left.

El-Dowd watched the poppy fields flash by below. He looked ahead at the mountains in the distance. He hoped it wasn't his last look at home. He wanted to return in one piece, with his sister, and be able to tell Welles and Duran he had rid the world of Sam Raven.

The two-man CIA team watched from a cluster of rocks.

"Chopper incoming."

Greg Macedo, paramilitary officer, nodded as Mitch Storey confirmed what he saw through his binoculars. Their camouflage uniforms matched the terrain. A pair of Igla shoulder-fired rocket launchers lay at their feet. The Russian weapons, minus any US markings, were perfect for the job.

The 9K38 Igla fired an infrared homing surface-to-air missile. After a batch of the weapons had been stolen from a government stockpile in Libya, the CIA, by proxy, acquired the launchers on the black market.

Their orders were simple. Shoot down the helicopter. The orders had come from the top, and Macedo, veteran of two Middle Eastern deployments, had never failed to complete a mission.

He didn't know the identity of the target, but Duran, in his direct communique, had made it clear a major sponsor of jihadist activity would be aboard. An easy kill. They had two launchers to make sure at least one rocket scored a hit. Macedo had no intention of missing.

Storey put down his binoculars and reached for his Igla as Macedo grabbed his. They leaned against boulders, the launchers resting on their shoulders. Macedo sighted through the electronic scope. A little closer...

"Fire!"

Macedo let his rocket go first. The high-explosive projectile left the tube in a flash of flame and smoke, spitting skyward at speed. Storey's rocket followed, and the smoke trails zeroed in on the blue Jet Ranger X.

El-Dowd yelled, "Rockets!" He pointed. The pilot was al-ready taking evasive action, the sharp turn throwing el-Dowd against the side of the door.

Duran!

He had no doubt. The CIA was trying to kill him. They didn't want him traveling to Ireland. He held tight, powerless to do anything more.

The pilot hit a switch on his console, activating the counter-measures at the rear of the chopper. Flares flashed from the chopper, followed by a burst of chaff. Another sharp turn in the opposite direction, and el-Dowd looked out the port side window. The missiles flew wide, fooled by the chaff, and the pilot steered the chopper for the launch location.

A cluster of rocks. The fading contrails pointed directly to the spot.

The pilot didn't need further orders. He put the chopper into a dive, arming the rocket pod. He pressed a red button on his control stick. The chopper shuddered as the rockets left the pod, streaming their own trail to the rock cluster. A flash of explosions followed their smashing impact. The chopper sped overhead, el-Dowd twisting in his seat to see the damage. Smoke covered the site. No bodies evident. He sat back with satisfaction anyway. The rockets had to have done their work. Duran's attempt on his life had failed. El-Dowd inhaled deeply, exhaled slowly. The pilot regained altitude and continued with the flight plan.

He'd get Ameena back, kill Sam Raven and the woman, Mara Cole, and personally deal with Duran and Welles. He'd destroy their entire arrangement for this outrage. It wouldn't be hard to form another alliance with their replacements or work directly with the Italians Duran and Welles were so proud of. If the Americans thought they could treat him like one of their peons, they were dead wrong.

CHAPTER THIRTY-EIGHT

Mara Cole said, "I don't like that you untied what's-her-name."

"Ameena."

"I *know* that. Don't humanize her."

They sat on the rocks near the front of the cottage, Mara with her coffee, Raven with his tea. The Raiders remained in the cottage, Lia taking the primary responsibility for Ameena for the time being. Raven didn't want the men having much to do with her, because he didn't want Ameena alarmed in ways she shouldn't be. He trusted Darbo and Roger not to do anything untoward. It wasn't a question of whether they might, but Ameena didn't know that.

"I forgot," she said, "we often have to do terrible things. It's hard not to think about being back in the cave with what we're doing to her."

"Bad example."

"Why?"

"She's being treated far better than we were. We've done much worse. I have done much worse."

"That bothers me too. It's one of those things you think about after the fact, know what I mean?"

"No."

"You still behave the way you were trained. They taught us to do whatever it took to beat the enemy, whoever the government *said* was the enemy. I'm having doubts about what they told us. But when you're out of that life, back in the civilian world, it's easy to start wondering if you made the right decisions."

"I can't say I've wondered."

"We did everything right," she said, "*every* time?"

"You can't avoid mistakes. What you need to avoid are mistakes resulting in the deaths of your own people. How many of the enemy died doesn't bother me."

"So you don't care about the enemy, yet you refer to el-Dowd's sister by her first name."

"I don't think it's a big deal."

"You *brought* her into this."

"Reluctantly."

"She's bait for her brother."

"Yes."

"You'll kill him when he gets here."

"Hopefully."

"What happens to her?"

Raven sighed.

"You're making my point, Sam. You're doing something terrible because you think it's right, but is it?"

"You told me a second ago not to humanize her."

"I've been out of it too long," she said. "The only way to tolerate this is to make her a *thing* instead of a person."

"Where was this doubt in London? When those killers were shooting at us, and you tagged one?"

"Heat of the moment. Self-defense."

"You said that shooting felt good."

"It did."

"Then what's your problem, Mara?"

"What we're doing with this woman is premeditated, and she might not have anything to do with her brother."

"She's not innocent at all."

"How do you know?"

"What I know for *certain*," Raven said, "is that she's a member of the family running drug operations in Afghanistan. She has benefited, financially, from the business. She might not have picked any poppies or killed anybody, but she sure knew the answers to the questions I asked about American involvement. She's up to her neck in this same as her brother, so what happens to her truly doesn't concern me in the least."

"Wait. You asked her what?"

Raven cursed. This wasn't how he wanted to bring up the subject.

He took out his cell phone. He'd saved the pictures from the Conspiracy Man website and showed her one of them. The picture showed Senator Welles and el-Dowd standing together, talking. They stood with the assurance of two men with no fear of anything disturbing their conversation.

"Does that face look familiar?"

She examined the picture. Her face remained blank.

"Who is he?"

"That's el-Dowd."

"Right."

"The other man is Senator Aiden Welles from Arizona. He sits on the Senate Intelligence Committee. Allegedly, he was in Afghanistan to see how best to deploy CIA assets in future missions."

"So?"

Raven put the phone away. "That picture was taken when we were being held at el-Dowd's compound."

Realization spread across her face. Her mouth fell open.

"Are you suggesting—"

"They were the Americans we heard. Ameena confirmed her brother has an arrangement with the CIA and this senator."

"For what?"

"Who knows. Protection in return for payoffs used to fund covert operations off-the-books; line pockets; whatever. Maybe they want to corner the heroin market in America and make more money. It's always money with these people."

"And one of them raped me."

"Yes."

"Let me see the picture again."

He showed her. She stared at the faces a long time, then shook her head.

"I can't be sure. It was dark except for the candle they left, and whoever attacked me blew it out. I was too groggy to see him clearly. It could have been any of them."

"Only Welles and Duran are still alive." He explained further his conversation with Wilson.

"They meant for us to die on that mission," she said. "Didn't they?"

"Yes. We were a side project. El-Dowd wanted to share with his jihad buddies." Raven put the phone away a second time. He drank some tea. The peace of the country was now disturbed. Raven felt a heavy weight on his shoulders. He said, "Now do you understand, Mara? There's no room for doubt. We're about to do terrible things to terrible people, and I'm not pausing to second-guess myself."

She nodded. "You're right."

"You need to be sure you can do this, otherwise find someplace to sit out the fight."

"No," she said. "I'm staying with you. Forget what I said."

"For what it's worth, I owe you an apology. I was unable to protect you when you needed it most."

The story of my life...

She scooted closer and touched his leg. "There was nothing any of you could have done."

"I don't see it that way. We heard you screaming."

She choked back a sob and leaned on his shoulder. He put an arm around her.

"Does...revenge make you feel better?" she said.

"What do you mean?"

"You're looking for revenge, right?"

"I had mine. Now I try to make sure nobody else faces what I went through."

"Does it help?"

"Sometimes. It hasn't brought anybody back. But there is solace in knowing I've done something nobody else can do. Another reason I don't have trouble sleeping at night."

"I've been out too long," she said. "Too much thinking."

"Thinking is good. Regret is good. It's what separates us from the enemy."

She was quiet a moment. She drank some coffee. Then: "Something Dr. Harrison said to me once. I'm afraid to move on because the man who attacked me is still out there, and since I didn't see his face, he could be anybody I pass on the street."

"Sounds about right," Raven said.

"How do you keep doing this, Sam?"

"It's the life I chose."

"I don't understand."

"You would," Raven said, "if what happened to me had happened to you." He sipped his tea. "And in a way, it did."

"But when this is over—"

"I know. You'll rebuild."

"And you go on to the next fight."

"I could use a rest. Maybe—"

"Do you think you can? Stay with me awhile?"

"For a while."

"I think it would be nice if you did."

They stopped talking. Raven held her close. She felt warm against him, yet fragile at the same time. No matter what happened, he'd see she returned to the civilian world, help her pick up the pieces, and live again.

For him, only an everlasting war remained.

CHAPTER THIRTY-NINE

A chill raced down Senator Aiden Welles' back.

"What do you mean they *missed*, Jim?"

"How else can I describe it? My team failed. El-Dowd made it to the airstrip and is now on his way to Northern Ireland."

Welles drummed fingers on his cluttered desk blotter as a hot flush crept up his neck.

"He's going to come after us."

"Worse, he might tell Raven the whole story."

"No," Welles said. He stopped drumming his fingers and sat back in his chair. He was alone in his office, his assistants busy beyond his closed door. When Lucy Hunt announced Duran's call, he'd ordered he not be disturbed.

Welles continued: "He's not the type to turn. He'll want revenge himself, not use a proxy. He'll keep his mouth shut and get his sister back and rid us of Raven, but what will it matter? We're next. He'll reach out to his jihad buddies who will call their sleepers here and you and I are worm food."

"Sounds like we're rooting for Raven now," Duran said.

"At least with Raven, we stand a chance."

"They're about equal, Senator."

"I'll bring the Italians up to date. They can help."

"You haven't talked to them yet?"

"Been busy, Jim."

"For real, or busy banging Lucy?"

"None of your *business*, Jim."

"We need to get you some security," Duran said.

"I want you here."

"I'm not available."

"I *need* you here, Jim. It's been you and me all this time. I won't trust anybody else; I don't care who you say they are."

"I'll make it happen."

"We go down together, or survive together, get it?"

"I don't plan on dying this week."

"Neither do I."

Duran said, "I do have some good news."

"I'd love to hear it."

"I cloned Wilson's cell, and Raven called."

"Did you monitor the call?"

"No, but the cloned phone did record Raven's number. I have somebody on it now. We'll be able to track his phone."

"Good."

"Assuming he survives—"

"Yeah, yeah, I get it, we have an edge. Let's not squander it."

"I gotta run."

"See you in church," Welles said, and ended the call.

He set the phone on his desk, eased back in his chair, and let out a tired sigh.

Was the money worth having a target on his back?

He shook his head. He wasn't going to wallow in negative thoughts. If el-Dowd won in Belfast, he'd get the Italians to help. They'd love a chance to whack a few rag heads. If Raven won, they'd track his phone, and know ahead of time when he was heading their way.

The way Welles saw it, they couldn't lose.

With that, his spirits lifted, he called Lucy Hunt into his office. He told her he needed some stress relief. Now? Yes, now, dammit, get over here and bend over the desk.

With a smirk, she did what she was told.

Basheer el-Dowd entered Northern Ireland airspace in the dark. The plane touched down at an airstrip where the landing lights didn't activate until the last second.

But his plane touched down without incident. As he took the steps to the ground, carrying his one piece of luggage, a Land Rover parked nearby rumbled to life. The headlamps flashed on him. He raised an arm to block the glare.

Two men stepped out of the shadows near the nose of the plane. They held weapons. El-Dowd identified himself. One of the men spoke into a walkie-talkie, received an answer from somebody in the Land Rover confirming his identity, and the men lowered their weapons. They were Irish, and el-Dowd asked about his own people. He met them in the Land Rover, where one sat behind the wheel, another in the passenger seat, and the IRA men sat in the back with him.

The Land Rover drove over the rough ground, el-Dowd unable to see anything other than what the headlamps provided. They were in an open field surrounded by forest, and the Rover rocked slightly as they traveled. When the tires finally touched the tarmac, the ride smoothed. El-Dowd finally relaxed.

"What's our status?" he said to nobody in particular.

The man in the passenger seat turned to face him. El-Dowd didn't know his name, but there was no mistaking his Arab complexion.

"We've been watching the cottage from a distance. There's only five of them."

"Five? Against our twenty?"

The passenger smiled. "God is on our side."

"I'd say so."

"We'll take you to our command site, and tomorrow you can have a look at the cottage yourself."

"Any sign of my sister?"

"She's been inside. We've not seen her."

"How is the other side fixed for weapons?"

"They've tested small arms and a sniper rifle," the passenger said. "Our spotters have watched them pick out locations to fight from. The cottage is made of stone with small windows, and the only way in or out is the front door. I don't think they'll fight from inside."

"They'll be outside."

"Yes."

"Easy to overrun."

"We have more firepower, yes. And vehicles. One of our trucks has a .50-caliber US machine gun mounted on the back."

El-Dowd laughed. "They don't stand a chance. And that stone cottage may provide ample protection for my sister. Things are looking bright."

"God has approved our actions."

El-Dowd nodded, and the passenger faced forward. No more talking. El-Dowd let his thoughts run. Mister Sam Raven, for all his alleged smarts, had no idea of his mistake. He had no clue about the defeat he was about to face, and el-Dowd decided he'd do what he should have done a long time ago.

Kill him.

It was not a mistake el-Dowd was going to make again.

After killing Raven and his people, he'd see Ameena returned home.

And then he'd go to the US and deal with Welles and Duran. He could call for more help there, but it was better to let the brothers in the sleeper cells remain hidden. No, he didn't want help for the second part of his vengeance mission. He knew Welles and Duran; knew their strengths and weaknesses. Duran might find help, but not before el-Dowd showed up and punched his ticket. Then Welles.

Yes, the situation was looking brighter by the moment.

CHAPTER FORTY

Day three.

Deadline.

Raven lay in a patch of high grass, scanning the area behind the cottage. He, Mara, and the Raiders were dressed for war, fully armed, connected via wireless com units. Ready for el-Dowd's arrival.

They'd made appropriate plans, setting the Claymores, moving their vehicles out of the vicinity, setting up firing positions for maximum effect.

Raven's only question was how many troops the opium king had managed to muster. The answer came quickly. Darbo's voice crackled in Raven's ear.

"Got incoming," the big merc said. "Approaching from the east."

They had broken the cottage into zones, using the directions of a map to break the areas down. The rear of the cottage was north, either side east and west, and the front faced south with the stream a dividing line. Darbo, on the opposite side of the stream hidden within the cluster of intertwined trees, had the Mk21 sniper rifle as his primary weapon, and a clear field of fire in the southern zone.

"You're on, Lia," Raven said.

"Copy."

Raven glanced at Mara, who lay beside him. She nodded in reply to his silent question. Yes, she was ready. No, she didn't doubt what they had to do.

Lia Kenisova, covering the eastern zone, peered through a gap between two rocks. She said, "Two pick-up trucks. One has a machine gun in the back."

"Looks like five gunners per truck," Darbo added.

"Rest of force on ATVs," Lia said.

Lia set her Galil rifle down and grabbed the Claymore detonator from her combat vest. The enemy dipped into a small valley, then began to rise over the next hill. As they traveled down the slope, Lia readied the detonator. The force approached a set of trees where the Raiders had placed a trio of Claymore mines.

The enemy vehicles moved at a steady pace.

Darbo radioed, "I see mostly small arms, looks like AKMs and FN FALs. One of the trucks has a US .50-cal., air-cooled."

Raven, listening, took a deep breath and wiped his sweaty right hand on his fatigue pants. He regripped the Galil. From the western side, he had no visual contact with the enemy, but not for long.

Lia said, "They're approaching the kill zone."

"Let 'em have it," Raven told her.

Lia Kenisova smashed the detonator trigger three times in rapid succession, and then the ground shook.

The three Claymores blasted at the enemy, the fiery explosions creating a brief screen between the two trees. The ATVs in front of the trucks took the brunt of the blast, tires shredding, riders ripped to pieces. As bodies tumbled and ATVs rolled over, the remaining force took evasive action.

The ATVs broke off left and right, but the pick-ups continued forward, through the smokey haze, breaking through the kill zone.

Lia reported the maneuvers and picked up her Galil. She placed the muzzle between the gap. The pick-ups, now in the lead, neared. Her index finger touched the trigger, and she tucked the stock firmly against her shoulder.

A little closer...now!

The Galil ACE crackled on full auto, ejected casings smacking against the boulders. But the stream of fire scored, rounds sparking against one of the trucks, crashing through the front grill and walking up the hood. The windshield broke into spider-cracks. She adjusted her aim and fired another burst. The section of windshield covering the driver's face caved, the driver's head snapping back. The pick-up began to drift to the driver's left, the crew in the bed of the truck leaping out. The truck crashed into a boulder and stopped.

The troops started running, using the second pick-up for cover. The second pick-up, with its mounted machine gun, returned fire. Flame spat from the long barrel of the .50, and the rounds split the air over Lia's head and smacked into the ground around her.

Her next burst missed as the pick-up swerved right. With the narrow gap, she couldn't track the vehicle and adjust her aim. No matter. It left the five troopers exposed. She fired at one, missed, triggered her final burst, and cut down one as he rose from cover.

Hurriedly reloading, she pitched a grenade overhead and waited for the blast. When it came, she bolted from the rocks and ran for the cottage. "Coming your way, Sam!" she shouted.

"Copy."

Raven and Mara watched as a group of ATV riders converged on the north zone. They opened fire, single shots, aiming for the tires of the small vehicles. Return fire came their way,

Mara flinching as the rounds came close. Raven maintained concentration on his sight alignment as he continued to fire. One trooper fell from his ATV, another dodging his fallen body to speed into some trees.

Raven shifted his aim to a running figure heading their way. He held his fire. Lia dropped beside him as another salvo of enemy fire raked the ground.

"Getting hot!" the Russian said. She started shooting, single shots now, taking careful aim.

The pick-up with the .50-cal came around the front of the cottage. Roger Justice, in another part of the eastern zone, fired one of the M-72 LAW rockets. The projectile flashed from the tube with a trail of smoke, striking the truck as it neared the cottage. Justice had aimed for the rear, where the gas tank was, and the resulting blast lifted the front of the truck into the air and flipped it over. The trooper behind the .50 cal., crushed as the truck landed, didn't move.

But somebody had escaped the passenger side at the last second and took cover behind the cottage.

"We got one bogey at the cottage," he said.

Raven copied.

Darbo, watching the second group of ATV riders approach the cottage, put the Mk21 sniper rifle to use. His first shot lifted one off his vehicle, a second shot missing the man behind him. The second man swerved, overturning his own vehicle to use it for cover. The trooper fired in Darbo's direction, the rounds going wide. Darbo fired another shot through the ATV's body. The trooper ran for the cottage. Darbo fired again and missed, then swung to another target, fired, hit. The trooper dropped.

"Two at the cottage," he said.

Raven didn't reply. The Galil spat flame as he continued shooting at the onrushing troops, now numbering three. The attackers fired over the handrails of their ATVs. The swarm of bullets came uncomfortably close.

"Fall back!" Raven shouted to Lia and Mara, changing mags, switching to full auto. He covered the retreating women with several bursts, taking down one of the ATVs. Lia shouted, "Grenade," and Raven put his face in the ground. The blasts detonated, showering his position with chunks of dirt. When he looked up, the last two ATV riders were down, one of the vehicles rolling in circles on its own.

Raven slammed another magazine into the Galil and joined Lia and Mara. They'd moved to a large rock planted deep in the ground, and Raven leaped over the top to land between them.

Darbo said, "We got most of them. Maybe five left and they're near the cottage."

Raven said, "Me and Mara and Lia will take them. Roger, Darbo, keep us covered."

Both men copied.

Lia reloaded, Mara slapping in a new magazine as well. She looked at him with wide eyes.

"Stay on my six," Raven said, "and we'll go in low."

The women nodded.

Raven charged over the top of the rock and onto the soft ground, following the low slope to the waiting cottage.

Basheer el-Dowd tumbled out of the pickup as the LAW rocket struck.

He scrambled to his feet as the heat of the blast erupted, the force of the explosion shoving him violently to the ground. Breath left him and he scrambled forward on his belly, ignoring flaming debris and the risk of shrapnel as he bolted to his feet and ran to the cottage's stone wall. Around the back to the shed. He stopped there, leaning against the wall, finally catching his breath. The heat from the burning truck, and the

252 | BRIAN DRAKE

sick smell of burning flesh, filled the air. He moved forward to check the shed.

He carried an AKM, a weapon well-known to him, charged with a 30-round magazine, finger on the trigger. He shouted Ameena's name as he reached each window, but drawn drapes prevented him from seeing inside. He started to panic upon discovering no rear entry. The only way in was from the front.

Movement behind him, feet stomping. He pivoted with the AKM at his shoulder, holding fire as he recognized one of his own.

"We need to get inside!"

The trooper swung his FN FAL around and smashed a window with the buttstock, hammering at the leftover glass. He reached in to rip the drape down. He gestured for el-Dowd to come closer as he dropped to hands and knees.

El-Dowd slung his rifle and stepped onto the trooper's back. He grasped the windowsill and hauled head and shoulders through first, then the rest of his body to land on the wood floor inside. On his feet, he grabbed his rifle again, back against the wall to cover the room as the trooper climbed inside.

"Ameena!" el-Dowd shouted.

A head popped up from behind a chair. El-Dowd swung his rifle to the target and applied pressure to the trigger.

The shooting jolted Ameena el-Dowd to full alert.

She sat up on the bed, swinging her legs to the floor. Her ankles were still bound tied with a plastic tie. There'd been no way to loosen it. She hopped across the room to the doorway, bracing there a moment. The living room was empty. Raven and the others had taken positions outside to await her brother's arrival. She was alone.

Ameena hopped like a bunny. She reached the dining

table, paused, her mind racing. The kitchen! There were knives there. She hopped toward a wall, using it for support as she continued to jump, finally grabbing onto a corner of the kitchen counter. Opening drawers, she found the forks and knives on the third try. Grabbing a sharp knife, she dropped to the kitchen floor and sliced at the plastic tie. Once, twice. Third time, the tie snapped.

A window shattered, glass falling onto the floor, somebody outside ripping away the curtain.

Knife in hand, she ran for the couches near the television, hiding behind a chair.

A man crawled through the window, then another.

"Ameena!"

Her brother's voice!

She raised her head. Basheer swung his rifle toward her. She shouted, "No!" and he lowered the weapon.

Brother and sister rushed to each other, meeting in the center of the room in a quick embrace. El-Dowd hustled his sister back to cover and knelt beside her. The other trooper remained standing, his rifle at the ready.

"Did they hurt you?"

She shook her head, brushing hair from her face. She wiped her hands on her jeans. El-Dowd pulled a pistol from his hip holster and handed it to her. She glanced at the handgun a moment, then gripped it as he'd taught her. She nodded.

The shooting outside continued with a flurry of single shots close by.

El-Dowd ordered the trooper to climb back through the window and cover their exit. He did so, signaling he was out, and el-Dowd helped Ameena through. Then he exited, dropping next to his sister, bringing the AKM to his shoulder.

The trooper shouted, "Down!" as he lifted his rifle with one hand and tried to push el-Dowd to the ground with the other.

Raven steadied his aim as three of the five troopers mentioned by Darbo fired from the corner of the cottage.

Raven fired a burst, then another, yelling for Lia and Mara to continue as he fired a third. His shots whined off the stone wall, smacking one gunner in the face, the other two spreading out. A sniper round from Darbo split one's head open and Raven fired a single shot to kill the third.

He ran after the women, who had stopped, dropping flat, ten yards from the cottage. The back wall of the shed was directly in front of them. Raven ran by, gesturing for them to follow. More gunfire crackled. Roger Justice radioed that he nailed the last two stray troopers. Raven copied.

They stopped. He gestured for Mara and Lia to take cover while he side-stepped the corner carefully so as not to expose too much of himself at once.

A trooper stood by the window, rifle in hand. Ameena el-Dowd dropped from the broken window, followed by her brother.

Raven raised his rifle.

The trooper shouted for el-Dowd to get down, trying to force him to the ground and fire one-handed. Raven snapped off a shot. The sizzling slug split the trooper's nose in half, plowing out the back of his head to whine off the stone wall behind.

Raven shifted his aim to el-Dowd.

Ameena, with a pistol, screamed and aimed at Raven.

Two shots cracked.

The round punched through Ameena's upper body, her face registering shock and pain as she fell back, her head striking the cottage wall. She lay still.

Mara, the muzzle of her Galil trickling smoke, stopped next to Raven.

El-Dowd moved like a tiger, leaping forward, Raven firing, the shot splitting the air over el-Dowd's head. The opium king collided with Raven's chest, both men tumbling to the ground. They kicked and punched and become a tangle of arms and legs as they struggled against each other.

Lia pulled Mara back.

Raven winced as el-Dowd pummeled him with fury, a fury he understood all too well. But he wasn't going to grant the opium king a moment's sympathy. He blocked a punch, grabbed an ear and pulled. El-Dowd screamed, Raven getting a knee between them to push. El-Dowd rolled away, springing to his feet, scooping up a rock.

He moved in swinging, Raven ducking back as the rock passed less than an inch from his face. He kicked low, turned his body, and struck with an elbow, a solid blow to el-Dowd's mouth. El-Dowd swung as he recoiled, Raven raising an arm to block, the rock striking his upper arm. Raven let out a startled howl.

Raven grabbed el-Dowd's wrist, pulling his arm toward him and twisting hard, forcing el-Dowd to turn with the twist, arching his back. The rock fell from the opium king's hand. With his left hand, Raven grabbed for the combat knife on his left hip and plunged the knife into el-Dowd's neck. He let go, still holding the knife as gravity took over, and el-Dowd fell. He grabbed for his bleeding neck and made a harsh choking sound. Struggling for breath, he twitched, his legs kicking out in defiance, and finally died.

Raven, panting, bent to wipe the bloody blade on el-Dowd's shirt.

Lia said, "All clear?"

"No more hostiles," Roger Justice said.

"Confirm," Darbo said.

Raven rose and put away his knife. "Mission accomplished,"

he said. "We need to pack up and get out of here."

The team acknowledged.

Raven looked at Mara. She nodded. They had revenge against el-Dowd, but the true enemy lay across the ocean in the United States.

CHAPTER FORTY-ONE

Raven, Mara, and the Raiders loaded the vehicles and drove away from the cottage. They left behind a landscape torn by explosions, dead bodies, a smoldering truck, and a load of ATVs in various stages of destruction.

"Glad I paid for the extra insurance," Darbo said.

"Hey, Lia," Justice said, "did you break a nail?"

"You're not funny, Roger."

The crew drove back to the Europa where Darbo said he would take care of disposing of the weapons and leftover ammunition. Raven gave everybody time to get cleaned up and changed. They'd put on street clothes before leaving the countryside, but still looked frightful, cut, sweaty. Raven asked Mara to come see him after she showered.

Twenty minutes later, she knocked on the door, and they went out to the hall.

"We need to decide something," Raven said.

"What?"

"Do we go straight to the US, or do you require an extra measure of proof before we confront Welles and Duran?"

She folded her arms. "How do we go about that?"

"I know a doctor in Switzerland."

"You told me."

"She specializes in a technique that can help you recall memories. Do you want to go see her?"

She nodded. "I think we'd better. I know you're right, and what's-her-name confirmed, but it's all circumstantial."

Raven grinned. "You watch too many true crime shows."

"I'm serious. If I can put one last puzzle piece together, you won't get any argument from me, no matter what terrible things we do next."

"Do you really think you can recall Welles' face?"

"I doubt I'll remember his face. But he talked to me. If I can hear his voice again—"

"All right. Let's tell the others."

"Are they coming with us?"

"I hope so," Raven said, "but I can't speak for them."

The Raiders listened as Raven laid out his plan.

"Our next target is in the United States, a senator and a CIA officer." He showed them the pictures of Welles and el-Dowd and outlined their involvement as he saw it. "I can't command you to come with us," Raven concluded, "but I'd like to have you along."

The Raiders didn't hesitate. Lia, Roger, and Darbo all agreed to help Raven and Mara finish the fight.

"Tell us what you want, boss," Darbo said.

"Mara and I are taking a detour to Switzerland," he said. "I'd like the three of you to head to the US and wait for us. We'll meet in Washington, DC."

Lia Kenisova said, "Welles will know you're coming by now. He might not stay there."

"What do you suggest?"

"What's his home state?"

Raven nodded. "Arizona. You're right, he might go there seeking the protection of home. In that case, go to DC, and

TERMINAL MEMORY | 259

stand by for further instructions. Be ready to jump on another plane at a moments' notice."

Raven arranged for their flights out of the country, and then told his King Air pilots to prepare for a flight to Zurich, Switzerland.

The news from Belfast broke slowly. By the time James Duran knew of the details of the battle at the cottage, he knew Raven and Mara Cole were long gone.

He confirmed their movement by checking the location of Raven's cell. The signal was heading southeast. For France? Possibly. But a little more time gave away their true destination. Zurich, Switzerland.

He went through the routine of contacting Regan Shaw and her kill team. They were close, monitoring potential therapists Raven might seek out. Duran promised more details as soon as he had a sure fix on Raven's position.

Later, when Duran broke the news to Welles, the senator only said, "I need a drink."

Duran decided that wasn't a bad idea. Welles poured two glasses.

Duran, seated in front of Welles' desk in his home office, said, "We can't stay here."

"Where do we go?"

"You have a walled estate in Arizona, correct?"

"With top-notch security."

"We go there. Let's talk with Morelli and see if he can loan us some shooters. We're tracking Raven's movements through his phone. We'll know when he's coming."

He had no doubt Raven was coming, and soon, unless Regan Shaw and her team stopped him first.

Raven and Mara checked in at Motel One Zurich where Raven booked a single room. It was a nice hotel, and a stone's throw from the office of Doctor Caitlan Oberly off Seinaustrasse.

"I don't know which way is up anymore," Mara said, setting her luggage on the bed, "with all this traveling."

"It's tough on the chassis, for sure," Raven agreed.

Raven called Caitlan to make an appointment, and they scheduled for the following morning.

"How do you know this woman?" Mara asked, after dinner. They sat in the bar, on a plush leather couch, inches between them. She drank wine while Raven enjoyed a martini made to his specifications of one shot each of vodka and gin, dash of vermouth, splash of water after the pour.

"Caitlan helped me out a few times," he said. Quiet music played over speakers in the ceiling, with only a few other patrons spread out.

"How?"

"She specializes in trauma," Raven said. "Can we leave it at that?"

"I think so."

"She's very good."

"I hope she can sort me out."

The next morning, they showed up at Caitlan Oberly's office, on time, having left Motel One early. Raven used the extra time to drive in circles, checking for tails. He was well aware Duran and Welles, especially after learning the results of Belfast, would try and intercept him. They might have learned of his previous visits to Caitlan years ago.

The precautions were in vain. The kill team closing in didn't need to follow him. All they needed was a call from Duran.

Doctor Caitlan Oberly received them in her office with a

smile and sat both on a couch while she took a chair. She was tall, blonde, and caught up with Raven before turning her attention to Mara. Raven explained part of the reason they were there and left the rest of Mara. She told Caitlan the whole story, and her hope that she might be able to remember more of her rapist's face, or his voice.

"What did he say to you?"

"'Aren't you pretty.'"

Raven flinched. But Mara told her story without hesitation.

"What I'm going to do for you, Mara, is what we call EMDR, do you know what that is?"

"Tell me."

"It stands for Eye Movement Desensitization and Reprocessing," the doctor explained. "Basically, I'm going to hold up two fingers, and you're going to follow them as I move rapidly back and forth. I want you to look forward, but move your eyes up as if you're rolling them after your mother says something embarrassing, get it?" She smiled.

Mara smiled too.

"It's an effective way of treating PTSD, deep trauma, that sort of thing," Caitlan explained. "I'm going to ask you questions that take you back to the cave, and you're going to watch the incident play out as if you were an observer. Do you understand?"

"Sure." Mara nodded hesitantly.

"It's going to be rough," the doctor said. "It will feel vivid, like it's happening again. I want you to be aware of that."

"I understand."

The doctor turned to Raven. "You'll need to step out."

"Of course."

Raven rose from the couch as Caitlan pulled closed the blinds in front of her office window and used a dimmer to lower the lights.

Raven sat in the lobby, reading old magazines and chatting with the receptionist. He sat and stared at the carpet, wondering what was happening behind Caitlan's closed door. He wondered how Mara would face her demons again.

Three hours later he had his answer.

Mara Cole looked like she'd been hit by a train.

Her eyes were red from crying, her face blank, and she clutched a wad of tissues. Caitlan led her out of the office, both hands on her shoulders. She told Raven to get her back to the hotel for some rest, and not to talk to her until she was ready.

Raven helped her into their rental car and started the engine. Mara sobbed quietly as they drove.

Back in the hotel room, she crawled onto the bed and fell asleep.

Raven sat in the room and watched her.

When she woke up, she asked for a glass of water, which he provided. She set the cup on the nightstand and went to the bathroom to wash her face. She sat on the bed again. Raven sat in the chair near the bed, leaning forward to rest his elbows on his knees. He didn't say anything.

"She wasn't kidding," Mara said.

"But did it work?"

She nodded sharply. "I didn't see his face. He blew out the candle too fast. But I heard his voice clearly."

Raven used his phone to look up any speech Welles had given and found a recent interview on a television talk program. He played the video. Welles hadn't uttered more than two words when she snapped, "That's enough!" Raven turned off the video.

She sighed, her shoulders sinking, as if all the air had been let out of her. She hugged herself tightly.

"It was him," she said.

"All right. Next stop, USA."

"I want to kill him myself."

"You'll have him."

"Promise me, Sam. This kill is mine; do you understand?"

She fixed her eyes on him without blinking. There was no doubting her intent. She was ready to do terrible things.

Raven nodded. "More than you know."

She barely touched her dinner that evening, and they went to bed early. She curled close to him and Raven held her to his chest. She fell into a deep sleep; Raven did not. His restless state allowed him to hear the scraping noise on the wall outside.

And the knock at the door.

He rose quickly, Mara waking groggily. He told her to get on the floor. He grabbed the Nighthawk Custom, with its attached suppressor, from the nightstand.

He pressed his back to the wall beside the door, shirtless, wearing only pajama pants. He checked the peephole but saw only black. The peep hole had been covered.

"Who's there?"

"Hotel security," a woman said. "We're checking on a disturbance on this floor."

"We're fine here." Raven slipped his finger onto the trigger of the gun.

"We need to check each room, sir," the woman said.

And then somebody crashed through the window.

Raven pivoted as the figure in black disengaged from a rope, brushing away the curtain, and raised a submachine gun. Mara screamed.

The Nighthawk spit, Raven firing rapidly. The big men fell back against the wall, sliding down, leaving a trail of blood behind him.

Two shotgun blasts disintegrated the hinges on the door,

a third shattered the lock. Raven dodged back, shifting to the bathroom doorway as two other figures entered. A man and a woman. Raven shot the woman through the head. She crashed into her partner as she fell, the other man's gun discharging into the dresser. Raven fired twice more. The man fell on top of the woman.

Now there was a disturbance on the floor.

Mara was already on her feet, pulling on clothes, Raven quickly dressed and stowed the .45 in his suitcase. They moved fast, not talking, both knowing what they had to do to get out of there before more people arrived.

Duran had found them, and Raven had an idea how.

When he finally met with Clark Wilson in the US, he'd put his theory to the test.

CHAPTER FORTY-TWO

Senator Aiden Welles wanted to explode at the well-dressed smug punk sitting in front of his desk.

But he held back. The well-dressed smug punk had a man standing behind him who could shoot Welles and go get a snack should his boss issue the order.

Best to remain polite for now. Welles was, after all, asking the well-dressed smug punk to lend him a few killers like the guy standing behind him.

"I'm not happy," the man said. "Really not happy, Senator."

The senator waved a hand. "I get it, Vitto. It's understandable. But it happened. We have to adjust our expectations."

Vittorio Morelli examined a manicured fingernail and made a clicking noise with his tongue. "Seems to me you plain blew it." He raised an eyebrow at Welles. "Big time. Our connection is dead, you got this Raven guy coming for you next, and you want me to bail you out?"

"Your syndicate has already made an investment," Welles said. "All I'm asking is for a little protection of that investment. A few guys. Ten, fifteen guys, max. No more."

"You think I have ten, fifteen guys laying around, Senator?"

"I only have one."

The boss of the DC-region syndicate let out a hearty laugh. "If that's the case, have *all* my guys, Senator. They're all yours!" He laughed some more.

Welles didn't laugh and stifled his rising anger. He and Duran were due to leave for Arizona in two hours. He wanted Morelli's commitment before their departure. It didn't appear he was going to reach an agreement. Duran's hands were tied. After the deaths of Regan Shaw and her team in Zurich, he couldn't allocate agency resources to their cause without going through channels not as secure as his former connection with Shaw.

Morelli said, "I thought we had a good thing here, Senator. You come to me, couple years ago, and say you got a great connection in the sand box for opium and heroin, good stuff, no doubt, it's been good stuff for sure. We've put down some of the competition with this sand box stuff. You tell us we can sell it and share in the profits. It was a great plan. *We've* done well, *you've* done well, your sand box buddy has done well, everybody's been happy. Suddenly we have problems, and it seems to me you brought these problems on yourself by trying to whack a bunch of guys because of this website and now one of them is gunning for you because your guys aren't as good as this guy. Do I understand things or am I missing something?"

Welles cleared his throat. "You have it all."

"Now you want to run home to your big house out in the desert, I don't know how you handle the heat, and I'm supposed to give you a bunch of guys because we got an arrangement?"

"I'm asking for your help, Vitto."

"All right, all right. I see you're in a spot. Enough of this nonsense. I wish you'd come to me sooner."

"International efforts aren't your thing."

"No, but I like knowing ahead of time the expertise of my people might be required. I'll give you ten guys. No nobodies either, they're good shooters. You want the gloves taken off, they're great shooters. And I'm not doing this because I like you, Senator. I'm doing this because yeah, it protects our investment, and keeping you alive is in my best interest, get it?"

"I get it. I'm glad we could reach a satisfactory conclusion."

"We ain't reached nothing yet," Morelli said. "We'll reach a satisfactory conclusion when this Raven guy is worm food."

Welles nodded.

Morelli rose from the chair and Welles stood as well. He escorted Morelli and his bodyguard to the front door. The syndicate boss climbed into the Town Car waiting at the front steps and drove off.

Welles shut the door.

Behind him, Duran said, "Well?"

Welles turned. Duran, listening from another room, leaned in a doorway.

"You heard him," Welles said. "Only ten. How many did Raven have in Belfast?"

Duran shrugged. "How do I know?"

"No way he took down el-Dowd alone."

Duran checked his watch. "We should get going."

Welles agreed. He'd told his office he was taking an emergency trip home and told Lucy Hunt to hold the fort. He hated leaving her behind, but a war zone was no place for a lady.

Raven and Mara crossed the grass to a bench where Clark Wilson sat looking at his phone. The park was quiet but for two joggers running in tandem on the dirt track on the outer edge of the grass. One of the joggers had a big white dog on a leash. The dog had no trouble keeping up with the runners.

Wilson glanced up as Raven approached. He stood.

"Sam."

"Clark."

They shook hands.

"It's good to see you," Wilson said.

"It's been too long. And that's my fault."

"I know it's been tough."

Wilson turned to Mara and they greeted each other with a short embrace. Wilson sat down. Raven and Mara joined him on the bench, Raven sitting between the CIA man and Mara.

"Welles and Duran have left for Arizona," Wilson said.

"That was fast."

"They departed last night. His office says it was an emergency trip home."

Raven laughed. "And he brings his CIA buddy?"

Wilson shrugged. "Duran told our office he was taking a few days off."

"Did Duran clone your phone?"

"What do you mean?"

"They found us in Zurich. The only explanation is they tracked me via my cell because they cloned yours."

"Cell phones aren't allowed in the building," Wilson said.

"But was there any point where you and Duran were away from headquarters and he might have pulled off a copy?"

Wilson cursed. "Yes. He found me at lunch one day. The day he told me to lay off el-Dowd. I had my phone on me because I'd called my wife."

"That's where he did it, then."

"Sam—"

"It's all right. I could use an upgrade anyway, so my old phone is about to meet with an accident." He smiled.

"I have learned a few things since Duran's order," Wilson said.

"Go."

"My analyst and I, his name is Heinrich, have been checking into Welles' accounts. He's receiving regular payments to an offshore account. Heinrich traced the origin of the payments to the same origin as the money Fatima Najjar took at the beginning of this mess."

"We don't require any further evidence, Clark."

"I figured, but I also thought you'd like to know. The worst thing is—"

"This won't be the end of the CIA conspiring with overseas drug dealers. Is that what you were going to say?"

Wilson nodded. "It goes deep. We're only talking two cogs of the wheel. They'll be replaced."

"Unless we find evidence pointing to the others, maybe?"

"You think Welles has anything?"

"Worth a look. But that isn't top of mind right now."

"What is?"

"What are we going to do with this website guy?"

"You looked at the site?"

"I did, and the little man in the black outfit with a big C on his chest was funny. Silly enough to throw off the normies, but not the hard-core conspiracy-minded folks."

"I think I know his name. Martin Green."

Raven raised an eyebrow. "I know Martin."

"Really?"

"He was on my team, early on. Tough kid. Had some problems later on."

"Right," Wilson said. "Burned out. Mental issues. Nobody can find him. I've tried contacting him through the site, but he won't respond."

"Of course not."

"Think you can get hold of him?"

"We don't need him," Raven said, "although I'm not sure if I should tell him thank you for exposing this or shoot him for sparking a chain reaction resulting in the deaths of far too many people."

Wilson nodded.

"Let's leave him alone," Raven said. "I'll send him a note after, tell him the details, and he can post till his heart's content."

"I guess then," Wilson said, "this will be a short visit for you two?"

"We couldn't continue on without a thank you, Clark. And we do appreciate everything you've done."

Mara only smiled.

"I wish I could have done more. I wish this hadn't happened."

"That's the problem with people like Welles and Duran," Raven said. "Their agendas never take into account the lives of others. They'll learn the lesson the hard way shortly, I promise."

"There is one more thing."

Raven waited.

"It's a rumor, but the FBI watches the local syndicate, right? The guy in charge, Morelli, dispatched a bunch of gunners a few hours after Welles left."

"Is Welles working with Morelli?"

"I haven't found anything," Wilson said. "It makes sense, though. He'd need somebody stateside to handle el-Dowd's drug shipments."

Raven nodded. "Add it to the list of things we need to find when we speak with Mr. Welles. I'll bring back what I can." Raven stood, Mara following, and Wilson rose last.

Wilson looked sad.

Raven said, "Don't worry, old buddy. Old Solid hasn't changed one bit."

"I wasn't thinking about that."

Raven nodded, extending a hand. He and Wilson shook again. "I appreciate the thought. It's time we left."

Raven and Mara started across the grass once again.

"Another plane ride," Mara said.

"The last one for a while."

Raven didn't look back at Clark.

CHAPTER FORTY-THREE

Raven told the Raiders: "This one is like the last one, except we're attacking, not defending."

Aiden Welles' walled estate sat in the middle of the desert between Tombstone and Tucson. *An appropriate place,* Raven thought. The one-story sprawling mansion sat on top of a hill, with a foundation wall at its base. A few inches back from the first wall was the wall surrounding the house. The second wall was eight feet high, topped with discreet razor wire.

The gated driveway led to the highway, which didn't see a lot of traffic.

The desert terrain appeared unforgiving in its overall roughness, with cactus, prickly bushes, shrubs, and flora prominently surrounding the property.

The Raiders had been busy since their arrival in the United States. Darbo once again secured weapons and equipment. Raven remarked he was going to need to find a source of income to replenish his accounts soon. But he appreciated the effort. The weapons were once again top notch, as were the explosive accessories.

Raven's orders were clear. "Nobody in the house gets out alive. If anybody surrenders, shoot them. The prizes are Welles and Duran. Are we clear?"

Nobody argued.

Roger Justice steered the truck off the 80 highway and the tires gouged a path across the desert ground.

Raven rode in the passenger seat with Darbo, Lia, and Mara in the back seat, everybody jammed together with their weapons and combat gear. The ride was rough and unpleasant especially with the lights off. Roger steered via the night vision goggles, and the butterflies in Raven's gut from not being able to see anything but pitch black did his pre-assault nerves no good.

At least he knew where they were going. For two days, the crew, in shifts, had observed the Welles estate from various points, noting the layout, and the routine of the ten shooters. At night, four of the gun crew climbed into a truck for a drive around the property. The mobile patrols happened twice an hour, at :15 and :45 minutes, and took ten minutes. Their patrol circle extended only two miles from the estate.

The clock on the dash read 2:34. The patrol truck would be heading back. Justice stopped the truck, and Lia and Mara jumped out. They'd rush to their positions south of the estate. Roger drove on. Each member of the team would strike from a different position to confuse the defense force, then converge at a main point. Roger dropped Raven off, and presently he and Darbo left the truck parked next to a trio of tall cactus.

Mara and Lia, dressed in black, faces streaked with black cosmetics, ran hard and fast, each clutching a Heckler & Koch HK416 carbine chambered in 5.56mm. Beretta 92FS auto loading handguns complemented the rifles. Standard kit for all but Raven, who used his own pistol.

The women had divided the southern zone of the estate into two areas to create a crossfire. Lia Kenisova stopped at her position, taking cover behind a dry bush. Mara ran on, her spot another 100 yards ahead.

She breathed heavy, but her mind was clear. She had one goal: revenge. For too long, she'd suffered the trauma of the cave. Tonight marked the end of the horror. From here on, should she survive, her life changed for the better. A fresh start. And even if she didn't survive, the goal would be reached.

Maybe she could salvage the flower shop. Or maybe it didn't matter anymore. She'd be free to try something else. She relished the thought of putting Aiden Welles' face in the sights of her rifle and letting him get a look at her as she pulled the trigger.

She reached her position and dropped onto her belly, breathing hard, trying not to suck in any desert sand. The ground felt rough beneath her, rocks poking through her combat suit. She ignored the discomfort.

Lights lit the estate, not only inside but out. The wall marked her only obstacle, and the razor wire on the top edge of the second wall wasn't a concern. A grenade would blast through the concrete and she'd slip through the gap.

An engine rumbled. Headlamps bounced, flashing two beams of light across the desert ground. The truck rounded the back of the estate.

Mara checked her watch. 2:36 a.m. Why had the patrol ignored the regular schedule? Had the enemy seen Roger's truck?

As the patrol unit made a turn, the bright beams of the headlamps swept over her position. Mara kept her head down. The beams continued their sweep, then swung back as the patrol truck steered for her. She let out a curse and flicked off the safety on the HK416. Speaking out loud, she updated the team.

"Patrol is still out," she said. "They found me."

"Do what you have to, Mara," Raven radioed back.

Lia said, "Coming to you!"

Mara opened fire, the HK416 popping loudly in the quiet

night. The patrol truck surged ahead, the passenger leaning out to return fire, the muzzle flash of his weapon like a beacon. As Mara aimed for the shooter, the headlamps grew larger, the beam blinding. She fired twice. No effect. Return fire zipped overhead, smacked the dirt. Mara stayed low.

The truck stopped, skidding a little as the tires bit into the ground, kicking up a cloud of dust. Gunners jumped out, four, charging at her.

Mara rose to run, triggering two more shots. Somebody screamed. The headlamps distorted the figures of the men running at her, the brightness still affecting her eyes, and she turned to run. Heavy arms grabbed her around the legs, a rifle butt bashed into the side of her head, and she toppled over, stunned, losing her grip on the HK. The gun crew hauled her back to the truck and tossed her onto the truck bed. She was on her belly, somebody put a boot on her neck. The truck spun around and bounced its way back to the estate.

Lia Kenisova, closing the distance as fast as she could, stopped approximately 50 yards from the truck. The HK bucked against her shoulder, but the rounds did no good as the patrol truck continued on its way.

"I lost her," Lia reported.

"Where is she?" Raven said in her ear.

"On the truck. They're taking her inside."

"Roger, Darbo, get back to our truck. Crash the gate on my command."

"What about me?" Lia said, standing still, panting.

"Your new position is wherever you are," Raven said. "When the shooting starts, do what we talked about."

"Copy," Lia said. She found cover and dropped to one knee, cursing a storm in her head.

Their plan had gone straight to hell.

CHAPTER FORTY-FOUR

"They found one."

Aiden Welles perked up at James Duran's announcement. He stopped pacing the circular living room, finely-furnished, decorated with African art.

"Where?"

"Outside the two-mile perimeter, south side."

"Who?"

"Not sure. But it's a woman."

Welles raised an eyebrow. "Mara?"

"Could be."

"The second sweep was a good idea, Jim." Welles smiled. "Very good."

Duran didn't smile. A hunch had told him the extra sweep would be worth the effort, but only because it had been two days. Raven and Mara had to strike quickly. They wouldn't wait a month.

"Where do you want her?"

"I have an unused room at the end of the hall. There's no furniture or anything she can use as a weapon. Put her there."

Duran nodded and left to give the orders.

Mara felt hands on her body as the truck finally slowed.
Her combat harness, containing grenades and her fighting
knife, was ripped away. Somebody grabbed her pistol. The
rough hands roamed up and down her body, looking for more
weapons. The blow from the rifle butt left her head sore, and
she was still dizzy from the blow. There was nothing she
could do to resist.

They carried her off the truck bed and into the house,
and sense began to return. They were carrying her down a
hallway. When they finally dropped her onto soft carpet in a
dark room, she pushed herself into a sitting position with her
arms behind her. The two goons stepped out. The light in the
hallway highlighted the man who took their place. He stood
large in the doorway, white haired, thick-bodied, and chills
raced down Mara's neck.

Aiden Welles laughed. "Ain't you pretty," he said.

Mara scooted back. The horror returned. *The chill of the
cave engulfed her, the flickering candlelight casting frightening
shadows on the rock walls, cold shackles bit into her wrists; she
was powerless. Again.*

"Don't," she said. "Don't—"

"Don't what?" Welles stepped into the room and snapped
on an overhead light.

Mara looked around. Bare walls. No windows. Nothing in
the room.

"Only you and Raven?"

"You wish," she said. She moved back until a wall
stopped her.

"How many?"

"Enough."

Welles laughed. "We'll deal with them, Mara. When Raven and his friends are dead, I'll come back and rape you

again, how does that sound? Maybe I'll give you a rest and then do it again." He stepped closer, his face twisted, his eyes filled with menace. "Like last time, you'll be all alone, and this time, I'll put you in a hole in the desert where nobody will ever find you."

She screamed, jumping up to lunge. He recoiled, blocking her strikes, but she managed to get her hands around his neck. She squeezed. His eyes bulged. He struck back, a hard blow to her midsection, and she fell away gasping.

Welles, sucking air sharply, composed himself, and went to the door. He said, "Don't doze off on me, Mara."

A loud crash. Both Mara and Welles jumped at the sound of a vehicle crashing through a gate. Shooting followed, single shots cracking, a full auto blast. Shouting. More shooting.

Mara watched Welles. He gave her another look, winked, and pulled the door shut. A lock clicked. She lunged for the door, turning the knob, but it wouldn't budge. She pounded hard on the door and finally fell against it, her face against the painted wood, and screamed from the depths of her soul.

She stopped, pushing back from the door, dropping into a corner. She drew her knees close, wrapping her arms around them, and stared blankly at the door soon to open. Spasms shook her body. Mara shut her eyes tightly.

Raven's here, Raven's here, Raven's here...

"Now, Roger!"

Roger Justice floored the pedal, and the truck surged through the steel gate blocking off the driveway. The front end plowed into the steel barrier, snapping either side off its hinges. He stopped the truck.

Justice and Darbo launched from either side, HK rifles cracking as they engaged targets. Gunners appeared on either side of the house, muzzles of their own guns flashing in reply. Justice and Darbo moved forward, shooting, dropping, rolling, rising to shoot more. Bodies fell.

Lia Kenisova tossed a grenade which landed on the ledge of the foundation wall on the south end. The grenade exploded. The bright blast ripped through the concrete and tore a gap wide enough to slip through. She pivoted right, HK tracking targets. Two gunners. She fired a string of rounds. One dropped. The other returned fire, the slug zipping past, and she fired again. Second gunner down.

Raven, approaching from the east side, ignored the sharp barbs ripping through his hands as he vaulted the second wall. He landed on his feet, brought up the HK, and scanned left and right for targets. None. He followed the exterior wall of the house until he came to a window. He fired through the glass and pitched a grenade through the hole. The blast shook the house, blowing out the remaining glass, and he dove through, coming up on one knee.

Dining room. He rose, spotting a doorway on the opposite side. Somebody appeared in the doorway and raised a pistol. Raven knew the face. James Duran. He fired. Duran fired. Both shots missed, Raven's gouging into the wall near Duran's head. The CIA man ducked back.

Raven approached the doorway, staying to the side. Duran's footsteps shuffled on the floor. Raven ran through into the kitchen. Duran fired again, Raven shooting back. Neither scored. Raven followed him into another room, Duran diving behind a couch. Raven switched to full auto and loosed a salvo of rounds, tearing up the cushions. Duran appeared on the other side to fire back as Raven dropped and rolled. Raven shed the HK to grab the Nighthawk Custom from his hip.

He fired twice as Duran ran for another chair. Raven's shots hammered a wall. Reaching for a second grenade, Raven fired once to keep Duran down, and pulled the pin. Duran swung around the chair and Raven tossed the grenade. He dropped flat as Duran let out a yell, and the explosion filled the room, shaking the walls. Raven, his ears ringing, peeked up. Parts of Duran now decorated the floor and portions of the wall behind him.

Raven put away the .45, found his HK, and jammed a fresh magazine into the magwell. He raked the charging handle.

One down.

One to go.

CHAPTER FORTY-FIVE

Sporadic shooting continued outside.

Raven stepped around the mangled hulk of James Duran on the carpet and into a hallway. "Sitrep," he said.

"Clear south end," Lia reported.

"Mopping up in front," Darbo said. Justice acknowledged.

"I'm going for Mara," Raven said.

He advanced down the hallway, checking open doorways, stepping into each room, his senses alert. His hearing rang from the grenade blast. He ignored the discomfort and the throbbing in his head.

He had to find Mara.

He had to find Welles.

Raven tested a closed door; the knob wouldn't turn. Stepping back, he kicked the door open and charged into an empty bedroom. He checked the closet, under the bed. Clear. Back into the hallway. A few more steps. Another empty bedroom. Further down the hall. Close to the end. He dropped low before the entryway of a circular living room. Movement on the left.

Aiden Welles fired a revolver from behind a couch. The shots smacked into the wall as Raven rolled forward. He brought up the HK416, lining up Welles' face in the front and rear sights, put pressure on the trigger, but held his fire. Mara wanted the kill. He wasn't going to deny her the one act she thought would free her from the past.

Welles fired twice more as he stood to run, and Raven took the shot. The HK bucked once. The shot tore into the carpet. Welles ran for a doorway and Raven pursued, aiming low, firing again. Welles' left ankle popped like a balloon. The white-haired senator fell forward, crying out as he landed.

Raven tossed aside the HK and took out the .45 again. Welles wailed on the hardwood floor, and Raven stepped on his head. He bent down and pressed the muzzle of the Nighthawk Custom Talon to Welles' temple.

"Where is she?"

Welles' face, contorted in pain, turned red under the pressure of Raven's foot.

"Where is Mara?"

Welles opened his mouth, but only a strangled gasp escaped his lips.

Raven smacked him with the .45's barrel. "Tell me where she is!"

Welles pointed. Raven looked. Another doorway along the hall. He hauled Welles upright, the senator almost falling as he tried to stand on both feet. Raven kept him upright.

"Hop."

He moved awkwardly with the senator down the length of the hall. Welles paused to rest every few feet, Raven jabbing him with the .45 to make him move again. The senator whimpered but complied. When they reached the doorway Welles had indicated, Raven let him drop. The senator's big body landed with a thud, but this time he bit back his cry of pain. Raven bent and jammed the .45 into Welles' neck.

"She better be in there."

"She is," Welles said. "I haven't touched her."

"You're still a dead man, Senator."

Raven kicked the door open.

Mara screamed. She curled up in the corner, turning her face away. Raven ran her to her. "It's me!" He tried to pull her arms away from her face, but she held tight. "Mara! Look at me!"

She snapped her eyes to him. Her body relaxed. She jumped into his arms, and he held her tight. But only for a moment. He pushed her away and handed her the Nighthawk pistol.

"He's in the hall."

Mara grimly took hold of the .45, her face stoic as she marched to the door. Raven watched.

Welles, flat on the floor, looked up. His face was wet with sweat, eyes wide.

"Well," she said, raising the gun, "ain't you pretty."

"Don't!" Welles shouted. He raised a hand to her, as if to block the coming gunfire. "Don't!"

Mara's finger tightened on the trigger. "Don't *what?*"

Raven said, "Not the face."

Mara fired once. She fired again and again, the hollow-point slugs punching into Welles' back, blood spurting from each hole. When the slide locked back over the empty magazine, Mara lowered the gun.

Raven took the pistol from her grip.

"It's over," he said.

Mara's face changed. From rage to peace. A weight had left her. She and Raven looked at the dead senator on the floor, and neither said another word.

Raven reloaded the Nighthawk, closed the slide, and returned the pistol to his holster. Mara stood still, her eyes on the dead senator, as he took his phone from a back pocket. He snapped a picture of the prostrate form, then stepped closer, grabbed a handful of white hair. He lifted Welles' head. Another picture. He let the head fall with a thud and put the phone away.

Mara blinked at him. "What are the pics for?"

Raven grinned. "For a certain website," he said. "Parting gift."

Darbo's voice in Raven's ear said, "We're clear, boss."

"Everybody inside," Raven ordered. "Time to find some intelligence to bring back to my pal at the CIA."

He held out a hand for Mara.

She took it.

Roger Justice turned the key, and the truck rumbled to life.

He made a U-turn in the driveway and drove through the gap, following the paved path back to the highway.

Darbo sat in the passenger seat, with Raven, Mara, and Lia in the back.

Raven clutched Mara's hand.

A search of Welles' office turned up a safe, which Darbo cracked, and the crew examined the contents. They noted information about the DC mafia connection, other members of the CIA involved in the Afghanistan drug connection, and plenty of other juicy details for Clark Wilson and his analyst crew to enjoy.

Heads were going to roll. Many CIA and other government officials would be resigning in droves once confronted with the details of their corruption, their treason. Raven hoped some resisted. He relished the thought of dolling out .45-caliber vengeance.

But as the truck rolled on and the crew sat quietly, there was only him and Mara.

He clutched her hand. She held tight. They looked at each other, and the dark didn't keep them from staring into each other's eyes.

Neither had any idea what the future held, but they could find a solution when the sun rose again.

Raven knew any moments with Mara were on borrowed time. His was a war without end, and soon the ghosts of his nightmares would urge him back into the fight. But when he left, he also knew Mara would be in a better place than when he found her. She was safe now, free from her nightmares. Someday, maybe Raven would be free of his.

Until then, the war continued.

A LOOK AT: WICKED CITY
(A SAM RAVEN THRILLER)

SAM RAVEN IS BACK!

Sam Raven is a man with a mysterious past and an unknown future. Drawn to help people in jeopardy because of his own personal tragedy, he collides with San Francisco Police Inspector Kayla Blaine after saving her from mob killers.

Kayla never expected to end up on the mob's hit list – now she's on the run. Even her closest colleagues are a threat.

Sam Raven is Kayla's only chance to stay alive. Raven uses every skill in his arsenal to outwit her enemies, but the longer they run, the closer the enemy gets. Raven and Kayla are forced into a desperate fight where only one side will survive.

From the author of the Scott Stiletto series comes an exciting new hero! Sam Raven is grittier, deadlier, and you better not stand in his way.

AVAILABLE APRIL 2021

ABOUT THE AUTHOR

A twenty-five year veteran of radio and television broad-casting, Brian Drake has spent his career in San Francisco where he's filled writing, producing, and reporting duties with stations such as KPIX-TV, KCBS, KQED, among many others. Currently carrying out sports and traffic reporting duties for Bloomberg 960, Brian Drake spends time between reports and carefully guarded morning and evening hours cranking out action/adventure tales. A love of reading when he was younger inspired him to create his own stories, and he sold his first short story, "The Desperate Minutes," to an obscure webzine when he was 25 (more years ago than he cares to remember, so don't ask).

Drake lives in California with his wife and two cats, and when he's not writing he is usually blasting along the back roads in his Corvette with his wife telling him not to drive so fast, but the engine is so loud he usually can't hear her.

Printed in Great Britain
by Amazon

37220542R00169